The Long Walk Home

When The Power Dies

Michael Ritterhouse

Table of Contents

Copyright

Dedication

For my Mom and Dad – who believed and knew.

Day One

Tommy finally boarded the plane after a long summer. He knew the summer was full of good experiences. As in previous summers, Tommy learned a lot; he deepened his outdoor knowledge and skills, rekindled old friendships, built new ones, and stumbled upon a new nemesis... and finally moved to the senior boys' cabin at Camp Wallace Creek this summer. He always enjoyed his summers in the Texas Hill Country, but moving to the senior boys' cabin was something he had looked forward to since his first summer at camp.

The older boys received special privileges, such as increased privacy and the opportunity for more fantastic adventures. Tommy didn't realize that such privileges came with responsibilities the younger campers were unaware of. Now, they were expected to keep their cabin clean instead of having others do it for them. The campers were responsible for keeping their cots and foot lockers neat, but that was it. The older boys were also expected to clean the cafeteria after meals by wiping down the tables and sweeping the floors, among other duties.

Tommy was interrupted in his thoughts by an older man who sat down beside him on the plane. "Looks like you're heading home from camp," the older man said.

"Yeah, how can you tell?"

"You're tan, look happy, and you're wearing a camp t-shirt."

Tommy looked down and sheepishly realized he had put on his camp shirt out of habit. If any of the other boys, especially those older than him or, even worse, Charley, saw him, he would be in for relentless heckling. Covering the front of his mustard-colored shirt with his day pack, Tommy answered, "I am. It was a pretty good summer, and I'm heading home now."

"I'm Richard," the older man said, offering his hand for a handshake.

"I'm Tommy," he replied as he shook Richard's hand.

"If that shirt says 'Camp Wallace Creek,' I went there when I was a boy," said Richard.

Tommy, warming up to Richard and the prospect of not needing to hide in his book or phone for the two-hour flight, asked, "When were you there? What was it like?"

"Slow down now. Gosh, it was a long time ago... I guess it was much less fancy back then, as things usually were. The camp had simple bunkhouses—eight boys with four bunk beds and a counselor in their own room. The bunkhouse was just a roofed structure with siding and bug screens that had hinged shutters for really rainy nights. Some nights were very hot and humid. The boys, at some point every summer, got into trouble. There was a trading post with important things like craft kits and ice cream. We also had a pool back then. Did I mention the latrines?"

Tommy laughed, "The bunkhouses are a lot nicer now. We have real windows and air conditioning. What do you mean, latrines? Our bunkhouses have bathrooms with showers."

"We had pit toilet latrines, some people call them outhouses, and the only showers were by the swimming pool. The counselors had their own shower house. They made sure we were all showered and clean for Parents' Day."

The flight attendant cut in on the intercom, interrupting their conversation, "Ladies and gentlemen, all cellular telephones and other portable electronic devices, such as tablets and laptop computers, must be turned off and stowed for departure. Thank you."

With the announcement, Tommy and Richard started to prepare for their flight. Tommy placed his carry-on-sized backpack beneath the seat in front of him. The pack was a birthday gift from his little brother; he knew their parents had actually bought the gift, but he still appreciated that his brother likely picked the color—orange, his favorite. He and his brother still fought, but the usual sibling rivalry was beginning to thaw, if only a little. He also put his large camp pack, similar to the one each camper received every year with the year and logo color changing, in the overhead compartment above him. He kept his book, *Watership Down*, by Richard Adams, in his camp pack along with a light sweatshirt, some snacks, and other distractions to keep close so he didn't have to disturb Richard or the other person sitting in the aisle seat to get his carry-on from the overhead storage.

Tommy saw Richard busying himself with similar, more adult tasks to prepare for his flight. Richard had a nice-looking backpack-briefcase hybrid into which he loaded the notebook he must have been working on before boarding the plane. Richard quickly stowed his bag below the seat directly in front of him, just like Tommy did.

Thinking about his summer again, Tommy was amazed by how much he had changed from the beginning to the end. This was another summer where it seemed he could not escape some guy who wanted to bully him. It wasn't that he was scrawny or anti-social. While he wasn't one of the popular kids at school, he had friends and got along easily. He was involved in sports and even experienced some success on the debate team.

Charley walked into the dining hall as the other campers gathered for their first meal: a turkey hoagie lunch with sliced fresh jalapeños for the older boys, potato chips, fresh fruit salad, and milk or grape-flavored drink. Tommy had never seen him at Camp Wallace Creek, and he guessed Charley must have wanted to make a big impression since he was going straight into the older boys' group. He looked for someone to impress the other boys with how cool he was and saw Tommy just sitting down with his tray of food at an empty table, getting ready to save a spot for his friends from previous summers, when Charley came up to him and threatened, "Get out of my spot."

"This isn't anybody's spot," replied Tommy.

Charley moved closer and repeated his statement, "Get out of my spot," raising his voice. Other, younger boys around them began to notice the interaction. The rest of the older boys were just getting out of the serving line.

Tommy responded, this time lowering his voice, "This isn't anybody's spot, and I'm waiting for my friends."

"They aren't your friends anymore, twerp!" Charley shouted, now almost at the top of his lungs.

Tommy's friends from previous summers were almost at the table, and escalation was averted when one of the senior camp counselors looked over at the commotion and yelled, "Hey, new kid, yeah you, go get in the food line and calm down!"

After the plane landed, Richard said to Tommy, "By the way, I'm not sitting by you by accident…. Your father, whom I mentored early in his career, found out I was heading home to Glenwood Springs through Denver around the same time as you and asked me to hand-deliver a note." Richard handed Tommy one of his father's larger business envelopes with "Tommy" written in his father's neat print. "You'll find something from me in there too. Your father wanted you to read it during your layover. Good luck this year!" Richard shook Tommy's hand and disembarked the plane.

Tommy looked at the overstuffed envelope again before putting it in his orange backpack and disembarking from the plane. After he exited the jetway, Tommy searched for Richard but could not find him. His mother had sent him some money so he could pick up something to eat while he waited for his next flight, which was scheduled to take him home. The wait was supposed to be about three hours, giving him plenty of time to explore the shops in the airport, too.

This was Tommy's first time alone in the Denver airport, but he had been there several times with his parents and brother. He always enjoyed eating at Milo's Grill, where he could order a Denver burger. His parents had encouraged him to try it the first time they traveled through Denver. The burger came with crumbled tortilla chips, cheddar cheese, green chiles, and a fried egg on top. He'd never eaten anything like it back home or anywhere else he traveled with his family and considered it a special treat. When he got his lunch, he ate it over the homemade fries, allowing them to absorb the juices that dripped from his medium-rare burger. He dipped those juicy fries in the special spicy ketchup that Milo's served and enjoyed the unique zing. Since his parents weren't there to tell him "No," he also ordered a Boysenberry shake. He didn't know what a Boysenberry was, but he loved the sweet-tart flavor and purplish-bluish color. After finishing his burger and fries, he wiped as much of the mess off his hands and forearms as he could with napkins and took his large to-go shake with him.

Most shops in the airport allowed people to bring drinks in while they shopped, so Tommy wandered around while he waited for his next flight. The first shop he visited was a high-end men's store that he quickly grew tired of. Even though he loved the smell of leather, he looked around for better options. Tommy's eye wandered toward the gadget shop, filled with high-end futuristic contraptions. When he entered the shop, he was immediately distracted by the various electronic objects. His father dismissively told him that shops like this lasted about twenty years before failing, only for another one to pop up around the same time. At the time, Tommy thought that fact was funny, and the items they sold seemed to constantly evolve and belong in a lovely home. After sitting in a super-technological massage chair, he spent an hour in the gadget shop; when he looked at his watch, he realized he had forgotten about the forty-five minutes he had spent eating lunch. He thought he'd better find the gate for his next flight home and use the walk to discover other shops he might browse after he got himself oriented.

On his way to where the information boards told him his next flight was, he spotted Charley walking listlessly and obviously bored. Tommy quickly ducked into the nearest Chesapeake Bookstore and Newsstand to avoid yet another confrontation. He went to the back of the store where the magazines and candy were displayed and grabbed a magazine to hide behind while Charley walked past. As Tommy looked over the magazine, he saw Charley approaching the shop, and the bottom dropped out of his gut. Tommy noticed out of the corner of his eye that the clerk was laughing in his direction, which worried him. Tommy took his eyes off the clerk and looked back to where he thought Charley might be, but he didn't see him. He panicked and quickly moved to another spot to try to find Charley. After scanning the giant hallway of the airport concourse, he spotted him heading toward a line for fast food. Tommy heaved a sigh of relief and went to replace the magazine. When he looked down, he saw he had picked up *Sensitivity Magazine* with the article title boldly advertising "20 Ways to Tell He's Into You" *and* was holding it upside-down, realizing what the clerk must have been laughing at. He sheepishly put the magazine back where it belonged and grabbed some random chocolate and an outdoorsy-looking magazine, mumbled something about grabbing the wrong magazine, paid too much, and slunk back to his goal of finding his next flight's gate.

He quickly shook off the near miss and embarrassment as he saw his gate number and walked over to get a lay of the land.

Tommy made his way to the gate, and even though he thought he didn't need to follow his mother's directions, he went to the gate desk to check in with one of the airline employees.

The gate agent looked up as Tommy approached and said, "Hi! My name is Hank. How may I help you today?"

Tommy awkwardly mentioned to the agent that he was fourteen and that his mother had asked him to check in with a gate employee.

Hank replied, "Unlike some airlines, ours doesn't require fourteen-year-olds to check in or do anything special, but I appreciate you following your mother's advice. The flight from Kansas City is on schedule, so you should be able to board your flight to Sacramento soon."

Tommy picked up his belongings and slowly walked over to a seat with empty seats on either side; he didn't feel like socializing with strangers. After he sat down, he took out *Watership Down* and started reading to appear as unapproachable as possible. Try as he might, he could not focus, so he set the book down on his chest and leaned further back in his chair. It felt good to stretch his legs out from the chair, even though he curled them back under whenever someone walked by. He thought he had parked himself in a low-traffic area, but upon looking around, he realized there was no such thing. As he looked around more, he recognized the customized sameness that every boarding gate seemed to have: the same low carpet, the colors *à la Mode* matching the airline's livery, but not too much—just enough natural materials to help travelers feel like this was still the high-end experience of early commercial flight without too much money coming from the company's bank accounts.

Tommy noticed a pretty girl about his age sitting with what he presumed were her parents. She wore a look of disdain that didn't seem to match how well she got along with her adult travel companions. Tommy decided the gentleman must be her father since he appeared to be doing everything he could to embarrass or amuse her. The girl finally succumbed and laughed at some weird chicken dance her slightly overweight but well-dressed father was doing. Then her mother and father started laughing, too.

Tommy's dad was always very busy, yet Tommy felt his father's presence throughout his life. Sure, he heard him come in late from work almost every night. Now that he was older, he was usually awake and doing homework when his dad arrived. He could always tell if his dad had a good or bad day by whether he came into his or his brother's bedroom to chat for a minute or two, always asking how their day went. If it was a really good day, his dad shared a story he understood, no matter how old he was. Bad days invariably meant their dad headed straight for the kitchen to get the meal their mother always put in the microwave— even if it was something from a restaurant in a to-go bag. After eating, he went to his sons' rooms and told them goodnight. Tommy never told his little brother or even his mom, but on really late nights, he would lie in bed and watch his father go to the doorway of his brother's room and stand quietly. He knew, because he saw his dad through his own slit eyes as he pretended to sleep, what his father was silently saying—"Good night, don't let the bedbugs bite, I love you." The same thing he said, and his mother replied, every night during their nightly rituals.

Tommy shook his head to clear his reverie and tried to gather the nerves to talk to the girl when suddenly everything stopped. Everything.

~~~

The entire airport was quiet, and there were no lights. Tommy knew what had happened, and everyone did. The power had gone out. He expected the generators to kick in like they did at shopping centers, his school, and some friends' houses. He heard the usual baby crying and the low rustle of a crowd, realizing the power was out. But something strange was happening all around him, too.

Business travelers were dismayed all around Tommy. Some were working on their laptops, while others were on their phones when all their devices powered off. He could quickly tell they were business travelers because of their attire and brusque attitudes. They, too, could identify each other, looking around at one another with mouths agape or talking to their electronics, sometimes cursing, sometimes coaxing. All of their activity prompted Tommy to pull out his phone and try to use it.

The phone didn't power up. As he saw this, he panicked a little because his mother had asked him to call home right after his flight landed in Denver, but he hadn't yet. He took a deep breath and thought it would be fine; everything would turn on in a little bit. In the past, he'd experienced hiccups like this, and sometimes the Wi-Fi would go down too, but everything always came back up quickly. The worst he'd ever experienced was waiting a couple of days after a severe storm knocked out power and internet at his home. Anyway, he reassured himself that he was just returning from summer camp where he hadn't used technology for several weeks. He heard a toddler nearby crying that his video had stopped, and he saw several teenagers looking around, confused without their almost constant social connections. Tommy started to calm down and noticed a commotion at the gate agents' desk.

"I don't know what's going on either, ma'am. No, my phone doesn't work; I know it's a landline, but it doesn't work. See, there's nothing on the phone, as I told you. I'm sorry, sir; I'm doing the best I can. I am sure your trip to Sacramento is very important, but we don't have any current information. Yes, the other agent isn't here; she's gone to the office to find out what's happening. No, she isn't back yet. It's only been a few minutes, and the office is on the other side of the airport…" Soon, Tommy tuned out because the beleaguered agent just kept repeating himself, and he didn't want to hear the same thing over and over.

Looking around again, Tommy saw quite a few others like him who seemed slightly disoriented or had decided to endure this momentary inconvenience by dozing off or re-immersing themselves in their books. He thought those folks had the right idea, so he picked his book up off his chest and started reading again. He had been reading for about ten minutes when he heard a female voice loudly announcing, "Attention! May I have your attention, please!" He realized it must be the other gate agent since she was wearing a very similar outfit to Hank, the gate agent he had talked to earlier. Her face was flushed as though she had just been running, which Tommy figured she was doing based on what Hank had told the upset travelers just a few minutes ago.

"I've just gotten back from our offices, and I don't have many answers at this time. There is no power anywhere in the airport, and no one has computers or phone service right now. None of the generators seem to be working either. The airport is trying to get some sort of air circulation going so it doesn't become too hot. Tommy hadn't noticed the lack of air circulation before but was now acutely aware of how still it was. He also saw travelers from other gates and airlines beginning to gather around to get any news. "Our offices are in close contact with the airport management, and we will update you as soon as we have more information," concluded the gate agent. Many in the earlier crowd started shouting confused and angry questions at the agent, who boldly dodged them and quickly retreated behind the counter with Hank.

Tommy sat back down in the seat where he had been standing. The crowd continued to gather around the counter with their questions, but almost everyone else seemed to settle back into their seats or lean against the walls. The situation started to hit home for him. It appeared that electricity of any kind was not working in the airport. He wondered if it was a power and communication line issue but realized it must be more than that because devices with batteries would still be operational.

During school lunches, Tommy heard his more scientifically interested friends arguing about something called EMPs, lightning, and CMEs and their applications in warfare. He tried to remember what those acronyms meant and asked his friend Boyd. He kept wracking his brain, visualizing the conversation. He saw Boyd sitting at their long lunch table with its little round, uncomfortable seats, wearing one of his beloved eighties movie t-shirts. Then it hit him! EMP stands for electromagnetic pulse. He relaxed and started to think back again, and pretty soon, he remembered CME stands for coronal mass ejection and comes from the sun. As he continued reflecting on the conversation with Boyd, he recalled that EMPs can disrupt or even destroy things, especially electronics. Boyd told him that military forces worldwide were working on weapons that used EMPs to disrupt their enemies' defenses. Tommy asked him if other military forces were conducting the research and if they knew others were using EMP weapons. Why couldn't they prepare their own equipment for those same threats? Boyd replied that was true and that technology was also sold to people for installation on their cars or for companies to use in their equipment. Tommy also remembered Boyd explaining that CMEs and lightning caused EMPs, which was sometimes why there were disruptions in TV and wireless communications. He added that most businesses working in those areas had plans to deal with that sort of thing.

Tommy didn't remember any lightning and suspected he could not tell if a CME occurred. He believed airports and airlines must have made plans to deal with an EMP-caused emergency. He looked out the window as he kept thinking about EMPs and his friends' arguments and counterarguments when he realized all the vehicles outside weren't moving either, and then it suddenly hit him—the airplanes! What is happening with the airplanes? He looked around, panicked, and saw nothing but the airport tarmac unusually calm. He hurried over to the gate counter, interrupted Hank, and asked if he knew what was going on with any planes in flight. "I don't know, kid, let me ask Angela; she's our senior gate agent." Hank walked over to Angela, who was still dealing with some upset travelers, and shook his head, turning ashen after he looked at his watch. Hank came back over, visibly rattled, and said, "Angela says the airport doesn't have any communication with the planes, and if they lost power like we have at the airport, then they have about a twenty-minute glide time, and it's been over twenty minutes."

'Oh no!" exclaimed Tommy. "Can we see anything?"

Tommy and Hank ran to a nearby window and looked at the sky. Both were straining, and neither was able to see anything at first. Then they saw one plane descending. The rate of descent looked unfamiliar to Hank, but Tommy saw no difference. They then heard a giant boom followed by a muted, immense screeching. But the noises could not have come from the plane they were watching since it was still in the air. They looked around and heard the beginnings of screams from the other side of the aisle. Hank and Tommy spun around and saw a plane skidding out of control at an angle that didn't match the runway. Both turned back, and others noticed what they were doing and joined them. Tommy heard murmurs of disbelief and concern. As the plane approached, Hank mentioned to Tommy that the plane's control surfaces weren't moving. Under his breath, he said, "It makes sense if they have no electrical power; they fly by wire."

The plane they were watching hit the runway with massive force, and Tommy heard the same sounds as just a moment ago. With more awareness, he saw sparks and parts of the plane careening off across the runway. He heard other people's cries of worry and horror. Tommy couldn't see anyone because of the distance and speed. Still, he imagined the pilots were struggling to regain control and that the passengers were all in the crash position everyone joked about during the in-flight safety briefing. He said a brief prayer for the safety of everyone aboard each flight around the world.

He turned around to see what was happening with the other plane. Tommy saw people running toward it from under the terminal. The first responders wore regular airline and airport uniforms; he didn't see any emergency personnel. The closest people were still far from the plane when he could barely make out someone on the aircraft who was managing to open one of the hatches. Tommy was astounded that there were survivors. As he looked more carefully, he saw what must have been a flight attendant starting to deploy one of those brightly colored slides Tommy had seen in videos of airplane rescues. The responders slowed to a jog, and Tommy guessed their urgency must have decreased after seeing what he had just witnessed.

Feeling like he was in a giant fishbowl of video screens, Tommy sat down, his mind reeling from what he had just seen. The airplanes virtually falling out of the sky were yet another shock to him, and, at least for a little while, a new reality was sinking in. The sounds and scenes of panic were all around: parents yelling for their children, business travelers talking to each other in shock, and couples holding onto one another in disbelief. Tommy took a deep breath and decided to go over to Hank and Angela to learn more about the situation.

Tommy looked at the pair of gate clerks and noticed tension and early signs of fatigue. He wasn't enthusiastic about burdening them with more questions, but he wanted to understand his near future better. He approached the clerks and asked, "Do you know what has happened to the other planes? I mean, there have only been these two, and I have trouble believing those were the only ones getting ready to land."

Angela looked at Hank, and Hank nodded. She said, "I don't know for sure; we haven't heard anything from the airline either. I'm working on getting my pilot's license, so I'll take a guess."

Tommy said, "I think I'm able to handle it. Go on."

Angela continued, "If they don't have any power, the results might be terrible. These planes all use 'fly-by-wire' technology, which means they use electricity to activate solenoids that control the surfaces and mechanisms throughout the plane, such as climb, dive, pitch, and yaw, fuel delivery, and even the environmental systems. Without electricity, the planes have no control. These two planes crashing must have already been on a course heading toward the airport, and the pilots did whatever they could to get them onto the runways. I can't imagine how they did it; they must be extraordinary pilots. My best guess is there have been plane crashes all over the world. One of my flying instructors told me there are usually around 7,500 to 10,000 commercial planes flying, with about the same number again in cargo, military, and private planes in the air, totaling what I'd estimate to be 15,000 to 20,000 right now. If we assume each commercial plane has an average of 200 people and each of the other types of planes has an average of ten, my best guess is that one and a half million to a little over two million people were in the air when the power went off, if this is spread around the world. All we know right now is that it is happening here. I have no idea what's going on beyond this room and outside these windows. I hope all that guessing is just the worst-case scenario."

Tears came to Hank's eyes, and Tommy just stared, dumbstruck.

"I'm sorry, I just kind of went into rational calculator mode and let my mouth keep running," said Angela. "Sometimes, when dealing with facts and data, I get like that. Those are pretty rough numbers, both in my estimates and in what those estimates might mean for all those people and their families. Again, I apologize; I know you're a kid, but you're curious, and I need someone to listen while I process out loud."

It took Tommy a few moments to collect his thoughts, and then he asked them, "So we don't know entirely what has happened, but we do know the power is out here at the airport, and I'm guessing at least in the area based on the plane crashes. It doesn't explain what's going on with generators or battery-powered devices. Have either of you heard anything else?"

"When we've had major weather disruptions, we sometimes have cots available for travelers, and there are areas for employees to rest. There's a hotel attached to the airport and several others within walking distance," Angela began. "Maybe the airport management, working with the airlines and other contractors, will implement some sort of intermediate 'wait and see' model to make everyone as comfortable as possible until they figure out what's going on?"

"Okay," said Tommy.

"I'm sorry I don't have any more information," said Angela.

"Thanks," said Tommy, and he walked back to his seat. He hoped it wasn't going to become his home, he thought grimly.

Tommy did have a lot to think about, though. That's a lot of people to lose in a short amount of time, he thought to himself. He also wondered, if this were happening at the airport, what was happening outside? Even if it was just in the Denver area, how many hospitals were nearby where people's lives depended on functioning electricity and computers? Looking out the window, his thoughts turned to the poor people who weren't even in hospitals and who relied on oxygen like his grandfather. So many things ran on electricity and depended on computers to work effectively.

Tommy was fortunate to have some leadership training when one of his teachers nominated him for a program run by a national youth leadership group. The program taught attendees to stop and evaluate situations carefully when everything was chaotic. One of the instructors said, "The hurrier you go, the behinder you get." Tommy decided to go through his backpack to clear his mind and do something productive at the same time. He started with the daypack since it was smaller. He knew what he would find, but he thought the ritual of going through it might calm him. The pack was a 40-liter size, large enough for a big, day-long hike but not so big that it was cumbersome. It had a hydration bladder, a plastic bag with a hose, and a valve for sipping; the bladder was empty, so he wouldn't have any problems while traveling. He'd kept the bladder with the pack even though he didn't like using them, thinking he might use it someday. His mother's pack had one, and she preferred hiking that way; he figured it wasn't a burden to carry a little extra weight on Camp Wallace Creek's senior boy day hikes. In one side pouch, he kept some pre-packaged snacks, while the other held an empty water bottle. In the front part of the pack, he crammed his book along with his charging cable and charger, a notepad, a pen, and a pencil. He had a small keychain flashlight hanging from the key strap. There was also the envelope Richard handed him and a small card with his information and his parents' contact information. He felt a little silly with this card, like a kindergartner with a note pinned to his shirt, but his mother insisted. His headphones were in this bag, too. Tommy packed a light sweatshirt in the larger middle pouch in case the plane got too cold. After a wilderness survival class at Camp Wallace Creek, he decided he needed a survival kit in his daypack, but he needed to modify it to get through security. In the zippered plastic bag, he included a black trash bag, a whistle, his headlamp, a Mylar survival blanket, some parachute cord, a small first aid kit, a small pair of pliers he sneaked out of his cabin's toolbox, a cheap screwdriver with a flip-flop piece that allowed it to be used as either a flathead or Phillips head screwdriver, and a camping towel. One of his friends always said he needed a towel, which was as much as he was willing to carry. He also kept a pack of playing cards with a picture of a bird in his pack just in case he got really bored and wanted to play a game of solitaire with real cards, as his grandfather taught him. The hydration bladder was in the last part of the bag closest to him when he wore it. He looked up and noticed a pretty girl looking at him curiously.

"I was bored," Tommy said defensively. The moment he said it, he realized he had lost any chance of appearing cool to the girl.

"I like to go camping with my friends and all of our parents when I'm home," the girl offered.

Tommy tried to redeem himself. "I'm on my way home from summer camp in the Hill Country of Texas. Do you know where that is?"

"Not really. I've never been to Texas; it's a big state," the girl replied.

"It's kinda in the center of the state, maybe a little south. It's really beautiful, rugged, and covered in oak and juniper trees. The heat doesn't feel quite as intense since it is drier there. Do you know what I mean?" Tommy said, hoping he didn't sound like a know-it-all.

"Yeah. My name is Bethany," the girl said, sticking out her hand.

Tommy was taken aback. He had never had a peer offer to shake hands. He was far more accustomed to casual settings. After a moment, he shook her hand. Shaking hands was always awkward for Tommy; he didn't know how much or how little to squeeze. He knew he didn't want to give Bethany a dead fish, though. He tried to find that sweet spot that was neither too firm nor too soft. "I'm Tommy."

"My parents and I are headed home from Italy," Bethany said.

"Wow!" said Tommy. "Are you guys from Sacramento too?"

"Not really, we live in Loomis."

"What did you do in Italy?" asked Tommy.

Bethany tried to describe her family's trip to Italy. She mentioned that her mother was a professor of Italian Renaissance fashion and listed all the different museums they visited in Florence, Milan, Ferrara, Mantua, Venice, and Rome. She didn't like Rome because it "was too much!" But she was unable to decide if she liked Ferrara or Mantua better. She liked Ferrara because it felt so open; even in the older parts of the town, it felt more comfortable. She blushingly admitted she liked Mantua because the food was so delicious. She went on about *Risotto con i saltaréi*, a regional rice dish with river shrimp and Parmesan cheese.

"Wow! That's a lot of information," exclaimed Tommy. "I don't know how you keep track of all of it."

Bethany blushed again. "I guess I liked the trip more than I wanted to admit. Mother and Father always make us go places to 'expand my horizons.' Sometimes, I'd rather just go camping like you."

Tommy went on trips where his parents tried to give him new experiences, but never outside of America—unless you count going to Mexico or Canada—so he'd never left North America. He was jealous, though he wouldn't admit it to his new friend. The stories he heard from Bethany and some friends at camp and home had intrigued him. His cultural trips always involved flying on a cheap flight or driving for what felt like forever to visit places like Glacier National Park or the Alamo, never to the palaces of Europe or the avenues along the Mediterranean. He'd heard from his history teacher about the gondoliers of Venice picking olives from the trees and then spitting the seeds overboard. He asked Bethany if it was true.

Bethany said, "I never saw it, and I didn't see any olive trees where they might pick them. And that's really gross anyway."

Bethany sat down across from Tommy, who was absentmindedly playing with the lanyard for his whistle. The two of them chatted about random things and laughed together, forgetting for a little while about the weirdness around them.

~~~

Suddenly, Tommy heard a loud, piercing whistle. Everyone around him started looking for the source of the noise, and Tommy saw Hank pulling his fingers away from his mouth. Angela was standing on a chair beside him, and a younger airline staffer was next to them, both breathing heavily.

Angela spoke loudly so everyone in the area could hear, "I need everyone's attention! We've just received word from the airline and the airport. Each airline is working together with the airport and its contractors to respond effectively to this unusual event. For those who haven't heard, while it is clear that the power is out at the airport, including any power supplied by batteries or generators, we are now learning that power is also out in the greater Denver area. Details are just now reaching us since the only way to travel is by foot, horseback, bicycle, or other non-electrical means. Fortunately, Denver has many active residents, and many are using bikes to get around. The cities of Denver and Aurora are utilizing their law enforcement bike patrol personnel to serve as a communication delivery system. We have a handful of staff members who had their bikes on car racks for recreation and fitness, so we're starting to improve communication. The cities have asked the airport to accommodate any travelers who are on connecting flights on-site while also assisting those travelers with Denver as their destination in getting into the city to eventually reach their final destination." Tommy heard loud groans and questioning shouts. Angela continued, "Details are being finalized; we're told the airport is preparing cots and other bedding in addition to arranging food and sorting out the water situation. Without electricity," Angela referred to her notes, "no pumps are working, so we don't have water pressure or pressure for natural gas lines. With these considerations, the airport is trying to provide food that doesn't require cooking, refrigeration, and minimal preparation. The airport and its contractors are working to preserve any residual cooling in refrigeration units, hoping power will be restored soon. The local governments and the airport do not yet have any answers about the cause of the total power outage. The airport will open any windows or doors, including boarding ramps, to improve air circulation."

"The local governments and the airport are asking for high-priority volunteers in the following fields: medicine, physics, all sub-fields of engineering, transportation management, and logistics. The airport is also seeking other volunteers to assist with meal preparation, bedding delivery, and to help with communication. Please see me or Hank after these announcements. While I am happy to entertain any questions, I ask that we first sort out the high-priority volunteer situation," concluded Angela.

Shouted questions, some angry and others seemingly desperate, continued to rain down on Angela as she, Hank, and the runner retreated once again behind their desk. Several adults began to approach the gate desk with a more purposeful stride, while others pushed their way through with distressed or angry expressions. The more purposeful individuals were directed to the side to speak with Angela, who was carrying a clipboard, while Hank attempted to calm the others down.

Soon, Angela called over the younger staffer, who had regained his breath. She gestured toward the individuals who must have been the requested high-priority volunteers. The staffer gathered them and said a few words. The volunteers collected their belongings and followed him down the corridor.

Angela rejoined Hank and started working with the more challenging adults who gathered around the desk.

Tommy looked at Bethany and her parents and asked if she or they wanted to join him in volunteering.

"No, we'll watch your stuff, though. It sounds like they need the help. By the way, my name is Jason Brown, and this is my wife, Amy," said Bethany's father.

"Thanks!"

"Thanks, Dad!"

Tommy and Bethany approached Angela and Hank to see how they could help.

Angela said she was sure she needed a lot of help and thanked them but sent the two off to the Main Terminal, saying, "I bet they need help even more than we do here. I was told to send extra volunteers to the Tourist Information Office; that's where they're figuring out where they need the most assistance."

They asked for directions and quickly understood why the runner was so out of breath and why communication seemed to take forever. They were in Terminal C, and the Automated Gateway Transit System, or the Train to the Gates, wasn't functioning like anything else that relied on electricity. Walking to the Main Terminal via the emergency walkway was just over a mile. They went downstairs to the train tunnels and started walking toward the Main Terminal. As they continued down, the light grew dimmer, and they didn't have flashlights, not that they would have worked.

"I wonder what happened," said Bethany.

"I don't know. Back home, during lunches, some of my friends talked about electromagnetic pulses coming from the sun or even being used as a weapon in war. They said they might cause damage that sounds a lot like this. I sure hope it isn't war. I haven't heard anything about it. Have you?" asked Tommy.

"No, my dad would have talked to me about it. He always tells me to pay attention to national and world events. I try to, but I want to do really well in school, so I spend most of my time studying, working out for different sports, or volunteering. I hope you're right about it not being war. If it is an electromagnetic pulse from the sun, do you think it will last much longer?"

"My friends said the electromagnetic pulse is caused by a coronal mass ejection when part of the sun explodes. The pictures I've seen are beautiful. I just listened to my friends. I don't know how long this will last if it's that."

The two young teenagers approached the first emergency exit. They felt the hot air coming down from the open door. They appreciated the fresh air and the light but preferred the coolness of the underground tunnel. They could barely make out where the next open door was. Angela told them there were emergency exits every four hundred yards, just enough for light to travel from one to the next.

Bethany suggested they jog to get through the tunnel faster. The darkness of the tunnel unnerved her. Tommy agreed it was creepy. They quickly reached the next light and thought they might see other volunteers at the next emergency exit.

As they drew closer, Tommy realized it was a group of three guys their age and maybe a little older. He thought it would be great to volunteer with peers, imagining they'd all be runners or doing meal prep, socializing, and having fun while helping during a time of need.

"Hey guys! How's it going?" shouted Tommy, waving perhaps a little too enthusiastically.

They turned around, and Tommy recognized one of them. It was Charley. Tommy's heart sank, and suddenly, he felt a horrible chill. He slightly turned to Bethany and whispered out of the side of his mouth, "Watch out!"

The biggest boy, who had to be a junior or senior in high school, smiled and said, "Things just got better!"

Feigning a happiness he had just lost, Tommy said, "Great! Are you all going to the volunteer station?"

"Yeah, we are!" said the older boy, nudging the third boy, a scrawny, wild-eyed younger teen wearing a tank top under a tan plaid pearl snap western-style shirt. He looked up at the older boy and nodded vigorously.

"Hey Tommy, nice shirt," sneered Charley.

Tommy looked down and groaned inwardly.

The older boy, who was the leader, said, "You know this guy, Charley?"

"Yeah, but I don't know the girl. What's her name, Tommy?"

Bethany answered, with defiance in her voice, "Bethany."

"Did you forget how to talk, Tommy?" asked the ringleader.

"I don't think we've met," said Tommy, extending his hand.

Reaching out and firmly grabbing his hand, the older boy was stronger than he looked. "I don't think you want to know my name."

The older boy pulled Tommy close and punched downward at Tommy's face, hitting him on the side of his right eye. The boy wearing the pearl snap shirt grabbed Tommy, while Charley went after Bethany, who was doing her best to keep him away by kicking at him and yelling. Tommy felt a trickle of blood starting where he had been hit.

Feeling indignation and anger rising in him, Tommy suddenly began to violently jerk his body around, trying to free himself from the grip of the larger boy and Pearl Snap. In one of his wild motions, his free hand, balled into a fist, unintentionally struck Pearl Snap hard in the throat. Pearl Snap quickly began coughing and struggling to breathe, letting go of Tommy to lean on his knees. The older boy holding Tommy's hand tried to use his other hand to subdue Tommy, attempting to catch the flailing fist.

Bethany was snared by the wrist, and Charley kept trying to back her into a corner in the emergency exit stairwell. She slapped Charley's head with her free hand, causing him to weave and duck. Occasionally, she kicked wildly, trying to make contact with any part of Charley's body, only rarely landing a glancing blow on one leg or another. When she hit his shin with a kick or landed a solid hit on his face, he exclaimed, "Ow, you stupid…" She kept at it, but Charley wasn't able to gain control.

Tommy's wild flailing was starting to pay off in another way. He felt the grip of the older boy beginning to lessen; his sweaty hand was becoming looser with each violent motion. Pearl Snap was still trying to catch his breath; Tommy thought he must have really walloped him. All of a sudden, he felt his right hand go free! He jerked back and regained his balance. He lowered his shoulder and charged the older boy, who was caught off guard, and an "Oof" escaped his mouth when Tommy's shoulder collided with his gut. Tommy pushed him against the wall and bolted over to where Bethany was fending off Charley.

Tommy pushed Charley from behind, throwing him off balance. He reached out, grabbed Bethany's hand, and pulled her away. She used the opportunity to lurch forward and started running with Tommy down the walkway toward the Main Terminal.

Neither of them noticed when they ran by the final emergency exit as they continued. They had just made it out of the stairwell, exiting to the Main Terminal when they slowed to a jog and finally started walking. Out of breath, they both turned around to see if the boys followed them. They didn't see anyone. Tommy and Bethany looked at each other and started laughing, breaking the tension.

"So, one of those boys is your friend?" asked Bethany sarcastically.

Going along with the tone and a sense of relief, Tommy said, "Yeah, we're best friends."

Walking again, still hand in hand, Bethany exclaimed, "Wow! How'd we get out of that? Whatever happened, I'm glad it's over. What do you think they were after?"

"I don't know," said Tommy. "Looking for a thrill, stealing something, I have no idea."

"Oh, you got hurt!" said Bethany, noticing Tommy's cut eyebrow.

Tommy reached up, letting go of Bethany's hand, and felt the blood, now beginning to crust, at the side of his eye. He looked at the blood on his fingers and said, "I guess I did. I didn't even feel it happening in the heat of the moment. I'd better clean up before we volunteer so they don't think they're recruiting any thugs."

"You mean like those boys?" Bethany said, looking down at her shorts and red and white Mantova 1911 t-shirt covered in dirt from her struggles. "I'd better clean up too."

They walked up the stairs, still slightly out of breath from their ordeal. Bethany tried to shake the dust from her clothes, and Tommy kept gingerly touching his cut as they emerged from the stairwell. They saw the restroom signs in the dim light. They walked over to them and went in, only then realizing there was no power, and each was suddenly in the dark. In the men's room, Tommy shrugged and groped his way to the sinks. He turned on the faucets, but only a little water dribbled out. He cursed his luck and grabbed some paper towels to try to clean up in the main terminal building's hall.

Exiting the restroom, he saw Bethany still trying to brush off the dust. She looked cleaner but not as clean as she had been before the altercation. She smiled when she saw Tommy walking toward her. "You forgot, too," she declared.

Tommy laughed and said, "Yeah, I did my best," holding up the paper towels. "I forgot the water pumps aren't working either. It smells pretty grim in there. I didn't even think about how the restrooms would be without power."

"Gross. I didn't make it through the door, so I barely smelled it."

"I thought girls were all sunshine and roses and didn't emit any odors," joked Tommy.

Still smiling, Bethany said, "Well, it's true for me, but not for other women."

They both laughed. Tommy said, "Let's go over and sign up."

~~~

A frazzled-looking woman wearing glasses and an airport uniform wrote down a traveler's information at the Tourist Information Center desk. Several people were in line behind the traveler. Tommy and Bethany guessed it was the line for volunteers and joined it.

"One person at a time," said the frazzled woman.

"Oh, sorry," Bethany and Tommy said in unison.

"You go ahead," Tommy said to Bethany.

"Are you sure? Okay," said Bethany, stepping up to the desk.

Tommy heard the woman ask for her name, phone number, and address. She then gave Bethany a list of volunteer jobs. Bethany said something and then added, "Thanks! I'll be over there," pointing to an empty spot on the wall nearby.

"Next!"

Tommy stepped up to the table. The woman took his information down on the top sheet of a small, messy pile of similarly filled-out sheets. "Okay, we still need help in almost every job we've got. We've got runners, food preparation, first aid helpers, water delivery, bedding delivery, pet care.... I know I'm leaving something out, but it's a good start. What do you want to do?" said the frazzled lady.

"Pet care?" said Tommy quizzically. "I'm sorry, I don't want to do that; I just hadn't even thought about it. I want to be a runner."

"Yeah, we've got quite a few pets that didn't get transferred to the planes for their owners, and someone needs to take care of them while airport personnel care for humans. Okay, I'll mark you down as a runner. See the walkway over there? Yeah, that one. Go over there and tell them you checked in at the volunteering station and that you're a runner. Thanks, we need all the help we can get."

Tommy turned around and walked over to Bethany. "What did you volunteer for?" he asked.

"I decided I wanted to help at first aid. How about you?"

"I'm going to be a runner. It sounds like something I'd enjoy. I play soccer for the school team, and I'm curious to hear and see what's happening around the airport."

"Soccer? Me too! Oh, anyway, my grandfather is a doctor, and I like doing first aid, so I thought it was a good fit for me. Do you think we'll see much of each other?"

"I don't know; I bet we will. I think I'll be all over. Where will you be?"

"They're sending me to the main first aid station in the center of Terminal B. It sounds like there are smaller ones in each building, but they need the most help there. Did the lady ask you if you wanted to help dig latrines?" said Bethany incredulously.

"She didn't even give that as an option. She seems pretty overwhelmed. But after my experience in the men's room, I'm glad they're doing something."

The two young teens started walking back the way they came.

"This is where I'm supposed to go. I hope I get to see you later," said Tommy.

"That lady said I needed to wait near here anyway," said Bethany. "She mentioned there are reports of gangs roaming the tunnels and that they're sending groups of volunteers with security. Imagine my shock."

"Yeah, weird," said Tommy sarcastically.

"I hope you come by the first aid station in Terminal B. After I get the hang of things, I bet I'll get bored, and it will be nice to talk to someone."

~~~

As Tommy got closer to the incident command center meeting room, he saw more people, and in their eyes, he noticed stress and determination. He approached the security officer in front of the ICC and asked if this was where he was supposed to report. The officer simply pointed to what looked like some cubicles converted to counters. Around the counters, several athletic-looking people of different ages dropped off and grabbed sheets of paper as they approached. He walked over, and a young, balding man looked at him and said, "Where's your name tag? Never mind. Here, take this note to InterWorld Airlines' main desk. You don't know where it is? Look at the map over there! Here, take a vest."

Dazed by the balding man's brusqueness, Tommy walked over to a map where a couple of other runners were staring. He looked down at the vest Clarence had handed him, one of the high-visibility vests many airport personnel wore. He put it on. One of the other runners looked at Tommy and said, "Clarence is a bit intense. You'll get used to it. Some full-time assistants have told us he means well but gets worked up easily. He is amazing. I've only been here a couple of hours, and he keeps all the information flowing in his mind. He may not remember your name, but ask him about any of the information we're sending out there, and he can almost quote it perfectly. My name is Greg." Greg extended his hand.

"Thanks, I was starting to worry about what I'd gotten myself into. I'm Tommy," he said while shaking Greg's hand.

"I have to go! There's so much going on," said Greg, jogging off through the double doors to the skyway.

Tommy looked at the map and found where he needed to go. The next several hours were a blur of jogging, sometimes running, back and forth. He began to grasp the workflow, even though Clarence's mood changed depending on his perceived urgency. Tommy learned that Clarence was good at indicating which messages were of greater importance. Only once did one of the stations to which he ran inform him that the information he was given was highly important. Tommy sprinted all the way back, and when Clarence opened the message, his eyes went wide, and he ran the message into the ICC himself. Tommy didn't see him again for several trips.

As Tommy continued with the message delivery, he started to see the effects of the situation on the staff and travelers. Many staff members tried their best to remain upbeat and attentive, but the strain began to show. He asked an airline office manager if any of them would be able to go home, and she responded that she didn't know. She had already been working for more than twelve hours and wasn't sure how she would get home if the next shift office manager might make it in or even if her family were safe. Tommy noticed cots beginning to appear in offices around the airport. The staff and volunteers did have access to extra snacks and drinks. Fortunately, the airport had prepared for winter emergencies, and additional supplies were available. Tommy didn't know how much, but he saw evidence of some and heard executives discussing the use of their supplies of emergency ready-to-eat food; one of the other executives told him they needed to use up the fresh food they had first. Still, Tommy worried that the stress and lack of information about friends and family would take such a toll on the staff that they'd start abandoning the airport and walking home.

~~~

The situation for travelers was just as stressful but very different. Many were on connecting flights like Tommy, but most were business travelers. There were undoubtedly more vacation travelers since it was toward the end of the busy summer travel season. The business travelers either resigned themselves to the current situation and were napping, reading, or doing whatever work they could manage without access to electricity, or they were beside themselves with anxiety due to their inability to reach their destination and complete the work they usually did to fill their time between flights. There was less stress for recreational travelers, but it was still present since they were neither enjoying their vacation nor at home. The individuals' personalities certainly influenced these reactions for both professionals and vacationers, but the overall mood was one of stress, fatigue, and unhappiness.

The volunteers seemed to have the best situation, as they had something to do and could walk away at any moment. They appreciated having tasks to perform, especially since it made the situation more bearable and supported those trying to solve problems more efficiently.

People whose final destination was Denver mostly gave up on getting home by car, truck, bus, or train and started to walk. Fortunately, most who decided to walk home were focused on their goal, and while there was some crime, it was minimal. Many who were in the airport for their flights to destinations all over the country and the world, whose flights had not yet departed, gave up and joined them in walking home. Those headed somewhere in the southern Rockies were unevenly split; most stayed at the airport with the other semi-trapped travelers, while others joined the native Denverites in the long line of people dragging their luggage down the eleven-mile-long Peña Boulevard.

Though dry from the Denver climate, the airport's air was heavy and hot. The normal temperature in Denver in late summer hovers around the low 90s, and everyone feels each degree without the usual air conditioners and fans to circulate the air. The stuffiness and heat didn't help the mood, and since many staff were distracted by their response to the immediate emergency, some tasks were being forgotten. The cleaning staff stayed on for as long as they could manage and did their best to help without electricity, but they couldn't keep up. As time passed, more and more left for the long walk home. The result was trash piling up around bins and restrooms, as Tommy and Bethany discovered, creating health hazards. In response, the airport administration found places to dig trenches for latrines and hung tarps to create some sense of privacy. Some travelers began to become quite territorial and claimed as much space as they could.

Food also quickly became a problem. After an initial period of confusion about how to process payments, concessionaires sold what they had for cash, especially cold drinks, pre-packaged food, and candy. This didn't help the many travelers who didn't carry cash or had only a small amount. To maintain as much peace as possible, airport management asked vendors and airlines to contribute the fresh food they had on hand to help feed the small city that the airport now needed to support. Restaurants had to be persuaded, but in the end, with written promises of compensation, they agreed to provide food for those staff who stayed. This food, though hardly meals, was offered to travelers and staff at no cost to them.

Despite all this, the tension boiled over into heated arguments and, occasionally, fights and brawls. When the power first went out, the entire security department seemed to groan in unison; they instinctively knew this kind of disruption would occur. Similarly, they knew small gangs would start forming, and then those tiny groups would join together and grow larger. So far, they only needed to worry about the tunnels and out-of-the-way corners, but they anticipated a worsening issue. The security department had always been understaffed, which compounded the situation, and they could only maintain order in the Terminals. After some negotiation, airport management recruited Transportation Security Administration staff who were stationed at the airport. With their help, they were beginning to get ahead of the problem.

~~~

The light was weakening, and Tommy was exhausted from all the message deliveries. He sat in a folding chair in the airport offices, chatting with two of the last runners still there, when a worn-out Clarence looked up and said, "Hey, thanks for everything you guys did today; it would have been impossible without your help."

The three of them thanked him in return. Clarence wasn't one of the decision-makers but was at the center of all the information the decision-makers needed to receive and send. While they hadn't quite become friends with Clarence, they genuinely appreciated what he had done for everyone around the airport.

"Things are slow enough now. I only need one of you; the other two can get some rest. Oh, and Tommy, here's your name tag."

One of the runners had only been volunteering for a couple of hours and said he'd take this shift. He asked the other two to find some of the other runners so they could figure out an overnight schedule. Tommy and the other runner agreed to inform them if they saw any other runners. When they left, they settled on two-hour shifts. Tommy chose the midnight to two in the morning shift, thinking he would try to get a few hours of sleep first. As it was, he was almost sleepwalking anyway.

Tommy made his way down to the tunnels, which felt much safer with the help of the TSA agents. On the way back to Terminal C, Tommy decided to check in at the Terminal B first aid station. He had been so busy running around for the airport incident command that he had only seen Bethany a couple of times, and then only from a distance where he could wave hello. The first time he saw her, she looked bored, leaning on a counter with a clipboard in her hand. The second time, her arms were full of supplies as she followed a very competent-looking woman carrying almost the same amount of items.

This time, Tommy found Bethany with her head down, looking at a form and filling out a chart next to it. Without looking up, she said, "Sir, you'll need to fill out the form on the clipboard to your right."

Tommy replied, "Okay, but I don't need any help. Well, except for my worn-out feet."

Bethany looked up and started laughing. She appeared tired but happy. "I'm sorry, Tommy, I've just been so busy helping sign people in and running around getting supplies. How was running?"

There had been no time for Tommy to think about his afternoon. He hadn't given it much thought during his solo walk along the darkening tunnel because he was so tired that he just put one foot in front of the other. "I don't even know. Clarence kept me running from one end of the airport to the other and back again. I even ran out to the hangars and some warehouses a couple of times. But I'm pretty sure I know where every office in the airport is."

Bethany looked at her watch and then shook her head. She had forgotten that her watch didn't work anymore. "This watch!" she exclaimed. "One of the doctors has an old wind-up watch his father gave him, and we've been using it all day. At one point, we used it to time heart rates; at another, we used it to fill out forms where we guessed the time. Thank goodness for his father. He gave it to one of the volunteers to take it around to whoever needed it. Now we call that guy 'The Clock.' Are you finished for the day?"

Tommy looked out the window toward the setting sun. "Yeah, I am. I was heading back to our gate and thought I'd drop by and see how you were doing."

"You know what? Things are slowing down here; let me see if they need my help or if they'll let me go."

She looked around for someone and spotted him. He was a professional-looking man with a stethoscope draped around his neck and was talking to another professional-looking woman. Bethany caught his eye and jerked her thumb toward the nearest exit. He looked at the woman, who nodded, and he smiled and waved goodbye to Bethany.

Tommy and Bethany walked toward the exit, and he asked, "So, what do you think your parents have been doing all afternoon?"

"Mom is probably either reading about Italian Renaissance fashion or compiling notes for an academic paper based on all the traveling we did this summer; she still uses paper, you know, as a history professor.... I don't know what Dad is doing. He's probably beside himself without connections to his company. I guess he's pacing back and forth, compulsively checking his phone even though he knows it doesn't work, and then sitting down to work on his New York Times crossword book for five minutes before starting all over again. Mom hates it when he's like that, but she's used to it; I've never known anything else. What about your family?"

"Wow! I have been so busy since this happened, and I've been away all summer, so I haven't given myself a chance to think about them, even though that's where I'm headed," said Tommy thoughtfully. He genuinely felt bad for getting so involved in his circumstances. He felt fortunate that he both loved and liked his family.

Tommy continued, "My little brother was only at Camp Wallace Creek for a couple of weeks; he's not old enough to stay as long as I did. He's a couple of years younger than me and likes exploring the undeveloped land near my family's house. He's always fishing and bringing home stray dogs. I bet he's loving this. When he grows up, he wants to study amphibians and spends every available minute outside. My mother stays home but might as well work at the community performing arts center; she volunteers there so much. She's probably bored out of her mind like your father unless she's using this as her chance to corner someone and talk them into staging *Where the Red Fern Grows* as an opera. Dad works for a stock brokerage as a recruiter, whatever that means. He says he also works in compliance too. I don't understand it; I'm just not interested in the financial world. Right now, I bet he's using this as an excuse either to work on the yard or go for a long hike; he's a frustrated outdoorsman who enjoys what he does and the money that comes with it too much to give it up and do something he loves more full-time. He's always dragging Mom on hikes, and we love to join him, which frustrates her."

"I wonder if I've met your mother before. I go to ballet classes there. I'm in the fifth level division," Bethany said proudly. "That's so weird. I might know her."

They'd walked the short distance to Terminal C and started toward their gate. As they approached, they saw that Bethany's parents had snagged cots for all of them. Tommy had anticipated sleeping on the ground or in a chair, so he was surprised to find he was a little disappointed. After his experiences at Camp Wallace Creek, he had become used to sleeping outdoors. After thinking for a moment, he felt thankful, realizing that without a cot, he'd be sleeping on a hard floor instead of the soft earth.

Bethany was catching up with her parents, and Tommy was absentmindedly participating while processing his very long day. He'd gone from the Hill Country of Texas to no power in one of the busiest airports in America. The cot came with one of those cheap pressed fabric disaster relief blankets that smelled vaguely of wool, mildew, and petroleum. He took the sweatshirt from his daypack to use as a pillow. The light was nearly gone; the sun had set, and there were no city lights. He heard people at the windows marveling at the night sky; most had never seen the Milky Way. He lay there, prayed, and felt very, very small.

Day Two

The next day, Tommy was awakened by someone's alarm clock. The person must have brought one of those old wind-up travel alarms he'd seen his grandparents use when they visited his family in Sacramento. The sun was already rising, and Tommy looked over to see Bethany's father sitting on his cot. "What time is it?" asked Tommy, still not rested from his midnight to two runner shift.

Bethany's father, Jason, said, "I think it must be about six."

"That alarm clock is pretty rude," said Tommy. He heard either Bethany or her mother groan in agreement. He didn't realize until then that the mother and daughter had almost the same-sounding voice.

Jason offered to see if he could find some breakfast. Tommy decided to join him, and they walked to the center of Terminal C, where the restaurants were. When they arrived, they saw the handful of staff joined by the volunteer food service people just starting to set up. Jason joined in helping them, and Tommy didn't want him to do it alone, so he pitched in, too.

He noticed the food was a real jumble of whatever was available. He asked one of the employees what the thinking was behind the food selection. The staffer told him they were trying to use perishable foods they didn't have to cook—things like fresh fruit, vegetables, bread, peanut butter and jelly, milk, and juices. When Tommy expressed surprise at the milk and juice, the staffer said they would go bad if the electricity didn't come back on soon. Tommy asked if there were plans for lunch and dinner, and the staffer, who said he was a restaurant manager, mentioned they were trying to figure out how to get fires going with old pallets close by where they wouldn't do any damage to the runways, equipment, or buildings. Tommy grabbed some yogurt and bagels for the group and rejoined Jason as they finished. Jason gathered some fruit and some peanut butter cracker packages.

As they strolled back, Tommy asked Jason, "Mr. Brown, what will you do today?"

"Call me Jason. I was going to follow you to the main office and see if I could help with planning. That's kind of what I do, and I thought I might at least shuffle some papers so I don't go crazy pacing around the gate. Amy might kill me if I keep doing it," he laughed.

Tommy said, "Yes, sir. My parents are from Houston and New Orleans, and I was raised to respect my elders. I bet they want your help; the folks walking in and out of the main planning room looked exhausted yesterday. I think most of them work here and are doing everything they can to improve the situation."

"Thanks, Tommy. I hope my experience will help them. I wonder how they're managing their responsibilities at home. I know if I were home right now, I'd be doing everything possible to get back to Bethany and Amy."

Tommy hadn't considered the leadership of the airport and their responsibilities to their own families. He hoped there was a way for them to make it home.

Jason and Tommy joined Amy and Bethany for breakfast. Amy mentioned that she and Jason had talked, and she would babysit their things while the other three volunteered. She was happy to have some time to herself, she said. It would be easier to work on her notes and start writing her paper without the distraction of Jason pacing all day. She grinned as she waved goodbye to them all.

Days Three, Four, and Five

The next three days were a repeat of the first afternoon for Tommy and Bethany. Gate agents were no longer stationed in the terminals, but someone from the airline or airport came during lunchtime each day to give an update. Each day was a little less intense for Tommy and Bethany's family as the airport and the people within it settled into their routines. Most people who were likely to leave did so during the first twenty-four hours, with a small handful departing each following day. Senior management stayed in some rooms set up near the main offices, as did the senior managers of the airlines and larger contractors. As the days went on, the number of regular staff dwindled, but there were still quite a few. They organized a plan that allowed them to bike home to swap with those who decided to stay and help. Bicycles made a significant difference for those staff members and became increasingly important for efficient communication.

Bethany's father, Jason, brought back news from airport emergency operations each evening. Jason mentioned that once the bicycles proved their importance to communications, the airport, government, and businesses established regular communication with the post office, leaving telecommunications companies with non-technical staff suddenly out of work. Indeed, not everyone volunteered for these bicycle duties. Still, since the companies and municipalities offered to pay their usual wages and the population in Denver was healthier than average, the numbers of volunteers were sufficient. Another factor in favor of the early success was that almost everyone believed the situation was a short-term problem and that everything would return to normal soon. Many of the bicycle couriers were having a grueling yet enjoyable experience so far.

Jason also brought back rumors and news from the nerve center of the airport. Tommy was jealous but realized he was just a kid running notes back and forth to the adult operations teams, of which Jason was a member.

During one of their dinners of random food, Jason said, "I heard power was out as far across America as anyone could tell. The governor of Colorado, business leaders, the military, and other government officials were working on developing a communications chain that didn't rely on electricity. They ruled out walking and kept going back to horses and bicycles. I even heard one guy keeps bringing up dirigibles."

Tommy said, "My dad enjoys riding Century Tours, and that long ride takes him all day."

Jason mentioned that the United States was about 3,000 miles wide, and the foursome guessed it would take a month of hard riding for one person to cross the country. Using the back of an envelope, Amy calculated that if they put together a route where riders changed out every eight hours and someone was riding twenty-four hours, a note might be delivered from one side of the country to the other in 10 days.

Bethany exclaimed, "Last year in school, I learned the old Pony Express riders did that back in the nineteenth century!"

Jason said it sounded like the four of them figured out what the governor and the communications team had already figured out. Bike and horse-riding teams headed out on each major interstate highway. He said he heard the governor had already received word from the Governor of Wyoming, and the team was hoping for one of the riders to make it to Santa Fe today or tomorrow. The riders from Wyoming said they were out of power, too, and everyone was planning for the worst, at least in the short term.

Amy asked, "What has your team heard about the hospitals and fire departments?"

Jason said he heard hospitals were in terrible shape. Most hospitals relied on electricity for almost everything, and the early rumors indicated many people were dying due to the lack of electricity to supply oxygen and refrigerated medicines, to name a few. With dark humor, he noted that at least traffic injuries were down.

He went on, "We're hearing fires are starting all over town because people are trying to cook on open fires or using their barbecue grills. The fire chief keeps receiving notes asking for help, but he declines because he fears something might happen here. The night crew said they saw glowing in the distance toward Denver, and the glow has changed location every night. The fire chief told me he's heard the fire department crews are doing what they can, but there's only so much they can do without fire trucks and water pressure. He's heard many firefighters are giving up out of frustration.

"I worry because we may have a rough time if we leave the airport. Law enforcement reports are coming in describing ongoing gang violence and looting moving from one part of the region to the next. Some fires are vehicle fires started by gangs to draw off law enforcement and firefighters."

Tommy said, "You know what? I haven't seen any newspapers either! I bet they need power to print anything."

Jason replied, "We've seen a one-page printed flyer that some old movable type hobbyist must have made. It was minimal and mostly asked for food or money for subscribers."

"This is all so frustrating," said Amy. "We don't know what's going on outside the airport, and the only reason we know anything is because of Jason, with a few bits of information coming from Tommy or Bethany. I mean, I hear rumors, but that's all they are – rumors. We're using pit latrines, and the fresh food is dwindling rapidly. Thankfully, we have enough staff and volunteers to make it a little more livable. Still, even with the doors open, it is almost unbearable inside this terrarium of a building. I hear what you're saying about the lawlessness, but I don't want to live here for the rest of my life!"

Thoughtfully, Tommy added, "I know you're not my parents, and I feel lucky to have found you all. At this point, you're the only family I've got. But I agree with Amy. As I've been running around the airport for the last few days, it is beginning to feel like I'm on a hamster wheel. Jason, what have you heard about the electricity coming back?"

"Yeah, Dad, what's going on?" said Bethany.

"I don't know if you've noticed, but the science volunteers and their families have quietly disappeared. The governor and those in authority have started gathering all the high-level scientists. In the airport nerve center, we've heard they have all been moved to the University of Colorado Denver campus or Metropolitan State over by the arena. I'm told they're using whatever resources they have to figure this out. I keep hearing about a Mass Coronal Ejection, military actions by different countries, or terrorism, all leading to Electromagnetic Pulses. I don't think it's some military action or terrorism, or we'd see military responses. I mean, most of our airplanes, military vehicles, and major business and governmental systems are hardened against that kind of thing happening anyway. I hear that is one of the talking points in their larger meetings. I also hear nerves are frayed already, and some meetings end in yelling and name-calling. These are scientists and some of the best minds in America – yelling at each other."

"I wonder what's happening in Washington, D.C.," said Amy. "At this point, I guess this is all over America. Jason, don't you think we'd have heard *something* by now if it were only regional?"

Amy looked like she was going to cry, and Bethany and Tommy looked expectantly at Jason.

"I haven't heard anything, but I've got to agree with you, Amy," answered a tired-looking Jason.

Tommy asked, "What about us? All four of us are from Sacramento. It's almost a straight shot west from Denver to our home. Why don't we walk there? Maybe we can pick up some bikes and ride home. If Bethany is right, it is only about a two-week ride. Walking shouldn't take much longer."

"If only it were that simple, Tommy," answered Amy. "Jason, Bethany, and I aren't in that kind of shape. Okay, Bethany, you might be, but Jason and I haven't done any long-distance hiking since college. We're soft; sorry, honey, but we are."

"Can't you get in shape on the road? It's got to be better. At least we'll be doing something," said Tommy.

Jason said sternly, "Tommy, you need to be realistic. Getting in shape on the trail is incredibly difficult. Also, if we get bikes or walk, how do we carry our stuff? What kind of stuff do we bring along? We don't know what kind of weather or terrain we'll face. How do we defend ourselves from these roving gangs? That's just what we know about what's in Denver. How about the Rockies or the Great Basin in Utah and Nevada? After you leave the mountains, there's a lot of desert or desert-like terrain we'll have to cover. Right now, it's early August. Your most optimistic suggestion is getting home in two weeks, usually two of the hottest weeks of the year. If we must walk, who knows how long it will take! Doing something might just kill us."

Bethany said, interrupting Tommy's reply, "You're right, Dad." Looking at Tommy, she continued, "We need to think about this. Starting now, without planning, is potentially suicidal. Listening to Dad and Mom, every decision from now on will be a big one for everyone."

With Bethany's statement, the wind seemed to come out of the conversation, and the four of them agreed to sleep on the heavy thoughts.

Early Morning Day Six

Tommy couldn't sleep and was sitting in one of the chairs overlooking the runway early in the morning, just after midnight. The airport was quiet except for the occasional cough and distant snoring; it was dimly lit by the stars and the moon when Bethany came over and sat beside him.

"Hey, stranger!" whispered Bethany.

Tommy kept staring off into the distance.

"Hey, I'm talking to you," she said.

"I'm sorry. Tonight's talk got me thinking about my family. I miss them and worry about them; I miss my bed, my mom's cooking, and my dad's bad jokes. I even miss my little brother and his stupid questions. I want to go home," said Tommy, tears welling up in his eyes.

Bethany looked at Tommy, the moonlight highlighting his profile. "I think I understand. I miss my home, but I have my parents here. I don't know what I'd do in your situation. I say prayers of thanks every night I'm here with them."

Tommy wiped the tears forming and shook his head. "I can't stay here, but your parents are right. I don't know what to do."

"We've got the luxury of time, especially if things keep going the way they are," offered Bethany.

Tommy looked at Bethany, then back at the runway. "Yeah, I guess we do, but that doesn't change how I feel, and I feel lonely."

"Hey! At least you've got us!" Bethany looked around, hoping she hadn't woken anyone with her assertion.

"I know, and I'm grateful. You've become a great friend, and I really enjoy hanging out with your parents every night. We need sleep, and I think talking with you has settled some things enough for me to fall asleep," said Tommy.

"Okay, and by the way, you're welcome," teased Bethany.

Tommy went over to his cot and, after tossing and turning for a few minutes, fell asleep, only to be awoken in the morning by Bethany's mother, Amy.

Day Six

Tommy came back early from his runner volunteering. The day was slow, with a noticeable drop in messages going back and forth across the airport. After the first couple of days, the airport had stopped the overnight runners. He found Amy and Bethany talking in hushed tones, their heads together.

"Good afternoon!" said Tommy, trying to hear what they were discussing without appearing sneaky.

The mother and daughter were startled and looked up to see Tommy. He looked leaner from all of his running over the past four days. He wasn't out of shape; none of the four were, but Tommy showed the most gains in fitness. Papers and notes surrounded Amy. She had tasked Jason with bringing her blank paper to continue working on her ideas from the family's trip to Italy. Bethany tried to avoid sitting on any of her mother's hard work but failed. Tommy guessed Amy looked as she always did when working on a paper—slightly frazzled but happy—and Bethany had the demeanor of someone with more experience than most fourteen-year-olds. She hadn't seen anything significant, but she had encountered many people who weren't in a good place. There were the usual sprains and minor illnesses, but she mentioned that yesterday, the impromptu clinic had started seeing quite a few more people running out of medicines. Most people only carried enough for one or two days in their carry-on luggage. The most significant strain was those who needed refrigerated medicines. The airport and the vendors prioritized these individuals, using the little remaining ice and residual cooling in their walk-in freezers, but all that was starting to give out. Bethany said she saw these people come to the clinic with great concern.

The airport wasn't close to Denver, but Denver is a western city. That was a happy accident for these people. The airport emergency response team sent their concerns to the area's primary emergency response center, and a horse-drawn hay wagon came to take the most critical cases to the nearest emergency room at Rose Medical Center, almost twenty miles away. Bethany was at the clinic when the first group of emergency patients could be loaded onto the wagon. She described the heartbreaking scenes of conscious and semi-conscious patients being loaded onto the wagon, while their family members were told they couldn't ride along, which meant denying people with genuine medical emergencies. She handed maps to these crying individuals and tried to explain how to get to the medical center, having never driven or spent much time in Denver herself. Her volunteering was causing her to mature in ways she and her parents never imagined.

This weighed on her mind the afternoon before when the four travelers from Sacramento struggled to figure out their options. She needed to share her stories and worries with her mother, so she returned to their temporary home to try to come to terms with these very adult experiences.

When Tommy noticed those eyes looking back at him were red-rimmed and saw the mother gently holding her daughter's hand, he tried to step back politely.

Amy said, "Hi, Tommy. You're not interrupting anything. Right, Bethany?"

"No, Tommy, I'm fine; it's just been a tough twenty-four hours," Bethany agreed.

"Are you sure? I can go somewhere else," said Tommy, wishing he were anywhere but there and hoping his worries from the night before weren't part of her rough time.

Amy said, "Really, come on over, help distract us from what we've been discussing."

Tommy sat down, and Amy straightened her papers. The three started chatting about the more mundane parts of their day. Tommy talked about *Watership Down,* and Bethany asked him numerous questions about the story. Amy said it had been a long time since she read the book but remembered enjoying it. She asked Tommy if he'd ever seen the movie and laughed when he said he didn't know there was one. Amy suggested he might want to wait before he watched it. Bethany asked if she could borrow the book when Tommy was done.

Jason slowly walked toward his small extended family with concern on his face. Amy looked up from the papers she had just finished straightening and said, "Is something on your mind?"

"Yeah, I need to talk to you."

Amy stood up and glanced at the teenagers and then at Jason questioningly. Jason nodded. Understanding his silent communication, Amy walked over to him, and they wandered to one of the big windows overlooking the landing strip.

"What's going on? Why the need for privacy?" asked Amy.

"I've been hearing things that concern me and our future here at the airport."

Amy looked at Jason.

"While helping the airport executives and emergency services professionals organize and coordinate the response to this event, I have been hearing increasingly sensitive information as they have come to trust me and my skills. Over the last day, they've been speaking openly in front of me and a couple of other volunteers. This afternoon, I started to hear whispers about martial law…"

"What!" exclaimed Amy. She looked around, hoping no one noticed. Tommy and Bethany were watching the couple with concern. Amy smiled and waved. The teens waved back, confusion on their faces. "What are you saying? They're going to bring in the troops? That sounds preposterous, like some disaster movie."

Jason looked at Amy, widened his eyes, and shrugged. "I think the executives themselves can't believe it, and that's why they whispered it. The situation must be getting pretty desperate out there. That's what I wanted to talk to you about. I think it may be time to get out of here."

Amy stepped back and said, "Wait a minute. We know what we have here; there are actual security personnel and food. I know it gets hot and stuffy in here." Looking around, Amy continued, "Yeah, I guess it is getting progressively grimmer daily. Bethany and I were discussing what's going on with the first aid situation. I mean, we know the staff is starting to dwindle, and maybe the supplies are too, but what's going on out there? It's got to be pretty serious if they're talking about martial law."

"That's why I wanted to talk to you without the kids. This is a complicated decision, and I want to clarify my thoughts before we involve them. I know they're only fourteen, but if they have some input, they may offer insights we're missing. Sometimes naivete helps provide a clearer perspective."

"And sometimes it leads to leaping before you look," added Amy.

"Exactly. I think Tommy definitely needs to be involved, even if he tends to leap before he looks. I understand he's young, but he's here without his parents. We still need to provide structure; we're the closest thing he has to his parents right now." Jason looked at the two young people with care and concern in his eyes.

"You're right about Tommy, but this is a big decision. We must be careful in guiding him and not giving him too much freedom. We have your college roommate on the west side of town. What was his name? Or should we keep going until we get home? What if everything suddenly comes back, and we find ourselves in the middle of Utah or Nevada in the desert?"

"Let's not get ahead of ourselves. First, we need to decide if it's a good idea to stay here or leave in light of the substantial rumors I'm hearing, and then determine how far it's prudent to go," offered Jason.

Cautiously, Amy started, "I'm not keen on leaving, but I'm not crazy about living in the airport for who knows how long – especially under martial law. If we leave, we'll need to get a map. Maybe Tommy can figure out what we can find around here. He's been running all over the airport, and I bet he knows where things are and what shops are still open. We've talked quite a bit about Tommy; what about Bethany? If we decide to go, she will be good at discovering what's happening in the emergency services crowd and might even get us some first aid supplies. I normally only carry some band-aids and moleskin on trips like this."

"It sounds like you're warming to the idea of leaving."

"Not 'warming,' maybe 'not cold,'" said Amy, smiling grimly.

"Let's go talk to the kids."

~~~

Tommy sat awkwardly, reading his book, trying hard not to look at Amy, Jason, or Bethany. Bethany still looked like she had experienced a rough day, and now her parents were talking privately, sometimes with raised voices and occasional laughter. He didn't know how to reach out to Bethany; after all, he was just getting to know her, and most of their interactions had been brief, consisting of little more than an occasional wave.

"Rough day, huh?" Tommy cringed inside when he said the words. He still didn't know what his feelings for Bethany were, but he knew his question was as awkward as it felt.

"What? Oh yeah, I guess," replied Bethany.

"Are you doing okay?"

"Yeah, I'm sorry, it *was* a long day. There were a lot of people coming in and starting to run out of their meds, and we all saw how it was affecting them. Some were physically suffering, others were filled with anxiety, and more than a few were both. Even though we were still handling other stuff we've been doing, you know, trip and falls, blisters, dehydration, this change we started to see recently really got to me. I mean, how do we help these people? We don't have many of the meds they're running out of, and in other cases, we don't have refrigeration to preserve the ones they need. Some of these people are on oxygen or concentrators, living at lower elevations than Denver, and they're coming to us complaining they're suffocating. I'm this worked up, and I can't imagine what the doctors, nurses, and medics are going through."

"Wow! I didn't even know these were things to worry about!"

"It's a whole new world for me, and my grandfather is a doctor. I think it might be a new world for everyone here. I wonder if doctors and nurses who volunteer in disaster zones or go on mission trips can share the knowledge they've gained from working with limited resources?"

"I can only imagine how many people are re-learning how to live right now. This is strange—living without electricity after having it for so long. Hopefully, it will turn back on soon."

"You know, if a teacher had given me this scenario as a writing prompt in school, I would have written that I would miss my video games and other things like videos or movies, but I don't. I miss having light at night, I miss air conditioning. I miss cars. I miss being able to call my grandmother or my friends whenever I want." Bethany's eyes welled up, and she let out a quiet sob, tears falling onto her red and white t-shirt.

Tommy reached out a hand, and Bethany gently grabbed it. "I'm sorry," said Bethany, "I didn't realize how much this is all getting to me. You seem so confident, and you don't even have your parents around to support you. I don't know what I'd do without my mom and dad."

"Don't let this rugged exterior fool you," joked Tommy. "Actually, Bethany, I've been so busy running messages around the airport that I haven't had much time to dwell on our situation, and when I do slow down, it's either to eat or sleep. If you gave me a chance, I might feel the same way you do. Remember last night?"

Bethany looked down at her lap and let go of Tommy's hand. "Thanks. I needed to hear that. There aren't too many people around here our age, or at least I haven't seen very many. It's important to be able to talk this through. Mom listens, but I think she doesn't quite understand."

"My parents wouldn't either. I love them—heck, I even like them," Bethany smiled at Tommy's remark. "It's hard to explain. I mean, they were teenagers once, but that was a long time ago."

"Exactly! Mom is great, but she seems to consider this a problem to be dealt with or solved. I don't think she's experiencing this as deeply as we are, or at least as I am," Amy said, the last part almost to herself.

"Hey guys! We have something we need to talk to you about," said Jason.

"What's up?" said Tommy, somewhat startled. Bethany looked expectantly at her parents as they walked up.

Amy said, "Jason brought back some news we need to discuss. If it's true, it will change how we live in a big way."

Looking around and appearing satisfied with their privacy, Jason began, "There's something I've been hearing through the grapevine, and now the talk seems more serious and more likely to happen."

"What's going on? Is this what you and Mom were talking about by the window?" Bethany asked impatiently.

"Yes, this is what we were discussing. In the planning groups, we communicate with the professionals and government officials; they have been looking stressed, and in some conversations, there have been awkward silences. Most of this concerns plans that extend beyond a few days and involve discussions about law enforcement and crowd management. A couple of times behind closed doors, I've heard the words 'martial law' and phrases like 'bring in the army,' and that, combined with the general direction of the logistical plans I've been helping with, doesn't give me much confidence in our continued freedom or safety. I've talked to Amy, and we're leaning toward leaving before that choice is made for us—one neither of us is comfortable with. We're both homesick, as I'm sure you two are, and we trust our judgment more than some frightened bureaucrat's. While the ultimate decision is up to us, we wanted your thoughts and opinions."

Cautiously, Tommy said, "In the past, I've mentioned that we needed to be ready to head out on our own and even brought up bikes. I don't want to be cocky, but I do want to get home, and I think I've got what it takes. While I've only just begun to get to know you, I think you three do too."

"That's a long way home. I thought we were going to stay here. That's what you said." Bethany looked like she had been slapped with a fish.

"By my guess, we're looking at a thousand to fifteen hundred miles," her father offered.

"Do you have any ideas about how we get there?" asked Bethany.

"We need to get maps and other gear if we do this. It's going to take a day or two, and I don't want to alert or alarm anyone else around here," said Amy.

Bethany suggested, "Hey! I can probably build us a pretty good first aid kit!"

"Slow down, kiddo. We haven't even decided if we're going. This won't be some adventure like in a movie. This will be a long, hard slog, and we don't know what dangers we'll face." Jason looked at his wife with good-natured exasperation.

~~~

Tommy and Bethany talked late into the night about their plans and supplies while Amy and Jason sat in the gate chairs that served as impromptu armchairs in their not-very-private living room during the days the travelers were stuck in the airport. Bethany's parents turned in early, knowing the following day would be a long day of discreet scavenging.

Day Seven

Six days of feeding the many people in the airport was starting to wear on the few remaining staff and the dwindling volunteers. The food supply was running low too. Jason looked at the mealy apples and tough-skinned oranges when he went to the food distribution area. The bananas weren't an option any longer, so he picked four of the best candidates. Next, he went to the packaged pastries and tried to find the least damaged ones.

"Sorry about the limited choices," said an apologetic-looking volunteer.

"Don't worry, I understand. Is there a cooked option this morning?"

"No, we're saving what we've got to cook for dinner tonight. A couple of staff and volunteers are scavenging what they can from different parts of the airport, but I think all the hidden corners have been checked three times."

Jason laughed, understanding and sympathetic. "You're all doing great with what you have. We really appreciate what you're doing under these challenging circumstances."

"Yeah, those corners are hard to search without flashlights."

"I'll bet. Hey, do you have any extra granola bars or anything like that? I think it's going to be a busy day."

"Not right now; come back in a little while, and I may have some from our scavengers."

"Thanks. I would appreciate it if you could find any extras."

Amy looked up from her well-used, impromptu bed. "How did it go?"

"The choices are getting pretty slim." Jason offered her the first choice of the four pieces of fruit and the four sad packages of pastries.

"That bad, huh?"

"Yeah. But the volunteer will keep an eye out for some granola bars for me."

"We'd better get the kids up and make scavenging lists."

After Jason encouraged the two young teens to get up, Bethany and Tommy stumbled over to the area where Amy was glumly chewing on a stale cherry Danish and her orange pieces.

"Jason, were they out of coffee?"

"I didn't see any drinks except for water jugs this morning."

"No milk either?" asked Tommy.

Amy said, "This is what Jason was able to get this morning. Let's start figuring out what we need to get."

"Tommy and I stayed up late last night talking about what we'd need," offered Bethany enthusiastically.

"Yeah, we gave up on you two and went to sleep," replied Jason.

"So, let's hear what you've got," said Amy.

Bethany looked at Tommy.

"I guess since I am the 'camping guy,' I'll start with my suggestions. When I've been at camp, the counselors have us go over the 'ten essentials' before we go on any hike, and they emphasized it this year since we started going on backpacking overnights." Tommy looked at a 3x5 card he took from his backpack. "The list is navigation, sun protection, insulation, illumination, first aid supplies, fire, repair kit and tools, nutrition, hydration, and emergency shelter. Let's start with navigation; we'll need a map or maps of our route and a compass. I think I've got a compass in my big camp pack, but I don't have a map of anywhere we might go. For sun protection, do any of you have sunscreen or hats? Insulation usually means extra clothing or layers beyond what you expect to need. This is a long trip, and we'll encounter a lot of different weather. Do you think we need rain gear? I do. Anyway, illumination normally means flashlights, but we know they don't work. Any ideas? I think we all know who can help us most with first aid supplies," Tommy said with a sideways glance at Bethany, who elbowed him in the ribs.

"Fire might be more important the longer it takes to get to Sacramento. We were taught that it was best to have more than one source of fire, so matches and a lighter each. The repair kit part is harder since we were all on a plane and weren't allowed to travel with knives. Maybe we can find something around here; if not, we'll need to try to find something in Denver. A multi-tool is ideal; all I've got is a pair of pliers and a six-in-one screwdriver. Nutrition is harder now than it was a few days ago. The best kind will be non-perishable. The last item on my list is emergency shelter; my guess is our best bet is some plastic sheeting or some of the stuff they wrap houses in when they're building them."

"Wow! Tommy, that's pretty impressive for a fourteen-year-old," said Amy.

"Yeah, color me impressed," agreed Jason.

"Once he got started last night, he didn't stop," said Bethany. "We talked about a lot more than he just listed. He told me that after his summer camp last year, he started reading any wilderness survival books he could get his hands on. I mean, we all read *Hatchet* at school, but he loves it!"

Sheepishly, Tommy said, "My favorite author is a guy named Bradford Angier, and he liked to talk about Colonel Townsend Whelen. Those authors from the sixties and earlier sure had some interesting names. I read somewhere that you can't rely on everything he wrote, though, but I sure like the way he wrote."

Jason, still impressed with the young man, started to ask questions to clarify what Tommy said, which then led to a discussion of job assignments. Bethany was the obvious choice to gather the first aid supplies, which everyone agreed needed to focus on hiking first aid like moleskin, as well as wilderness first aid items. Amy volunteered to continue acting as the home base for everyone and keep track of items as they came in on a checklist she started to make while Tommy was talking. Jason also wanted everyone to double-check their own bags and see what they already had before he and Tommy went scavenging.

Bethany was in a hurry because she wanted to get to her medical station on time, so she rushed through her bag with an occasional groan or small celebration. She came over and shared her finds. She already had a small first aid kit, inspired by her grandfather, as well as a small tube of sunscreen. She mentioned she didn't have many extra clothes since she thought she was just traveling from Rome to Sacramento. Jason and Amy said they expected the same for their clothing. Tommy said he had a rain jacket and a sweatshirt, and he wondered if the other three had anything like that. Amy said she packed a zip-up fleece because she got cold on planes, and Jason said he carried one too, just in case Amy got cold. Bethany was wearing hers in the morning coolness. Tommy said, "Well, that's a start."

Bethany continued that she didn't think there was anything else except for a couple of snacks she saved over the last few days, "just in case."

Jason thanked her and let her go so she wouldn't be late. He looked at Amy and Tommy and said they'd better check their bags too. Each dug into their bags. Tommy's bags were the two he carried onto the plane in San Antonio. Amy and Jason had the kind that rolled on wheels and fit in the overhead compartment on the plane. Jason also brought along one of those day packs that didn't look out of place in an office. Amy pulled her travel purse out of her large carry-on shoulder bag and started to go through it.

Tommy had already gone through his orange backpack several times and shared what he packed with Jason, but he hadn't looked in his Camp Wallace Creek pack except once or twice, and then only for a second to get something. He loaded his Wallace Creek pack the way his parents had taught him in case he got separated from his duffel bag and trunk. He packed underwear, socks, a t-shirt, his rain jacket, an extra pair of shorts, and his toiletry bag (which was almost used up in the six days he'd been in the airport). He pulled out a light fleece blanket his mother encouraged him to carry and transferred his towel to his backpack. The Wallace Creek pack actually looked a little deflated.

Jason and Amy packed their roller carry-ons very similarly to Tommy's Wallace Creek pack. Neither put a blanket or towel in their carry-ons, but they each carried an extra couple of days of clothing. Amy also had a now useless travel-sized hair dryer. Jason's business backpack was filled with the kind of things one would expect someone in finance to carry: a laptop, some paper files he couldn't be without, his passport, other identification, his medications, pens, pencils, a couple of small notepads, a book on leadership, a magazine with the latest business finance trends, and an airport novel. Amy's shoulder bag was fuller now than when they landed, due to her fleshed-out notes from her family's trip to Italy and her research on Italian Renaissance fashion. Jason snuck more notepads to her so she could work on her notes and start a first draft of her latest academic paper. Throughout their days and evenings in the airport, whenever Tommy saw Amy, her typical complaint was that it was maddening she didn't have access to her reference materials to cite them. Her laptop was in the bag, along with the usual pens and pencils; she kept quite a few brochures tourists get from museums and historic locations, as well as a few books in Italian that she had bought. When Tommy asked about these, she'd get excited and tell him about the author, and the topic was invariably about Italian fashion—usually historic, but sometimes more modern. Tommy didn't laugh because he had gotten to know Amy in the bedraggled state that living without power in an airport brought. Bethany insisted her mother was always very fashion-conscious and well-dressed. Inside her travel purse was her passport and other identification, medications, a small amount of makeup, safety matches, a mirror, nail clippers, an emery board, some cinnamon gum she had squirreled away, a small tube of sunscreen, and a lightweight linen scarf.

As the three of them sat assessing their resources, each seemed to be perplexed; a bit pleased, disappointed, and sobered.

Jason said, "Well, I think we've got our work cut out for us. I just don't know quite what that is."

"Really?" asked Tommy.

"Okay, let's take what we've got and see what things we need to get to fill in any holes in the list Tommy gave us," said Amy.

After some time, the threesome came up with a list, and in reviewing it, all three realized in their own way how unprepared they were.

"Well, at least Bethany will bring us some good first aid supplies," offered Amy.

"I thought I was really, really well prepared," said Tommy. "I didn't realize how confident I was."

Jason said, "That's a pretty sobering list of things we don't have."

The three castaways put together a scavenging and shopping list for Jason and Tommy that included a compass and map, more sunscreen, more matches, sewing kits, more substantial food than snacks, water bottles for Jason, Amy, and Bethany, and finally some sort of tarp or plastic sheeting for shelter on their way until they could scavenge or buy a tent. They also decided to keep their eyes open for anything else that might seem useful. Amy said if it didn't make sense, it was possible to leave it at the airport before they left.

"Tommy, you've run all over this place doing errands for the command center. What do you think will be the best way to take care of this list?" asked Jason.

"Well, I guess I am going to be the best at scavenging, so I can try to get us some sort of shelter. While I'm at it, I can look for a compass and map. Maybe you can buy us some of the other stuff? Oh, by the way, here's some cash to help if you need to buy anything..." Tommy offered some of his money, keeping some for the compass and map, as well as some for emergencies.

"Keep your money, Tommy. That sounds like a smart division of our time and resources. Keep your eyes open for more food, matches, and anything that might work for water bottles."

"Okay! And good luck!" said Tommy over his shoulder as he ran off.

"He's a good kid," said Amy.

"Yeah, I hope we can live up to his hopes for this long walk we've got ahead of us. He sure seems like he has a good head on his shoulders for such a young kid."

~~~

Tommy started out trotting to where he thought he might find some construction supplies, hoping to find something with which to improvise a tarp or two. He also figured it might be the best place to scavenge items he hadn't thought of. As he ran along, he realized he and Bethany's family were about to embark on a huge undertaking.

"Hey Tommy, what are you packing for?" sneered Charley.

Tommy groaned. He was less than thrilled when he found out he and Charley were assigned to the same bunkhouse. Every summer some boys didn't return, and others took their places, but Tommy had never been forced to cope with such an intense bully at summer camp before. Most of the summer was still quite good despite Charley.

"The wilderness experience," Tommy finally responded.

"Why would anyone want to do that?" sneered Charley.

Charley resisted any activity that might include hiking, claiming that was why motorbikes were invented. In fact, Charley tried to avoid doing anything that might make him move around very much.

Defensively, Tommy said, "I like to go see new things, and while I'm hiking, I get a chance to clear my mind."

"You mean the little mind you have needs clearing?" said Charley.

Charley came over and started picking up random things, asking what they were for. When Tommy answered, he dropped them on the floor and laughed as Tommy picked them up until Tommy finally exploded.

"Just stop! This is my stuff, and if you don't know what any of it is, then you're too dumb to appreciate the hike anyway!"

"I know what all of this stuff is; I just wanted to make sure you did before you hurt yourself or the rest of the guys hiking with you!"

"I'm really looking forward to getting away from you, you big idiot!" Tommy yelled.

By this time, a couple of counselors hurried in and walked toward the two boys. Tommy quickly shoved all of his gear into his pack and ran outside with it.

When Tommy got outside, he immediately began regretting saying anything to Charley, much less calling him names and raising his voice. He thought he might never regain the trust and respect of the other older boys.

Tommy shook his head, trying to forget this bad memory. He mostly redeemed himself with his cabin mates and had several long talks with their bunkhouse counselor. Those conversations began during his hike with the group of seven other older boys, where he apologized and took responsibility for his lack of self-control. The other boys said they understood and didn't like Charley either. A couple suggested he should have punched Charley. The bunkhouse counselor thanked Tommy for his apology and reminded him that even if he didn't like Charley, he had to control himself.

While he was lost in memories Tommy didn't realize he was almost at his goal until he nearly ran into the fence that kept airport customers from entering the construction area. The dimness didn't help matters much, but mostly it was Tommy's distraction. One day, while running errands for the control room, he discovered this place, and since he was ahead of schedule that day, he tried to see if he could get inside and explore a little bit. He had always enjoyed sneaking into construction sites as a kid, pretending he was building his own house or getting friends to join him to build forts and play capture the flag or other games. He also liked to bring home construction debris, pull out the nails, and put together different projects. His father still used a step stool he built from some 2x6s he cobbled together.

"There it is!" he thought to himself as he found the loose fencing he carefully reattached so it was easy to get back in but looked secure. Tommy curled the fencing back and crawled into the construction area. As he stood up, he looked around and noticed it didn't look the same as the last time he was behind the fence. He decided to be very careful while he searched for some shelter materials.

It took Tommy longer to look around, but he went to where he remembered finding some supplies stacked up, ready to be used by the construction crew. As he poked around, he found some promising materials and was trying to decide whether to take the black plastic sheeting like his father used in the yard to reduce weeds or the house wrap. He remembered the wilderness experience counselor saying he liked the house wrap because it was lightweight, but he didn't like it because it was too stiff. The counselor's solution was to scrunch the house wrap into a ball. He said it made it less noisy and easier to pack. Tommy decided to take a couple of the shorter pieces that must have been the ends of some rolls—enough to act as a tarp to cover Bethany's family and him if they needed shelter overnight or while they were hiking when he thought he heard voices.

"Let's take him to the table," said one of the voices. The voice was high-pitched, nasally, and very... New York.

Trying to squeeze between two piles of used pallets and shrink as much as possible, Tommy heard another voice—this one sounded like some surfer dude—say, "Yeah! Let's take him to the table and see if he's tough enough."

While wriggling around to get a hidden view, muffled sounds of struggling and protest made their way to Tommy.

After hearing a loud crash followed by a thump, Tommy saw feet waving in the air and heard the first voice say, "That's good, hold him down tight… Liam, stay close so you can do your special trick."

Tommy scrunched and then wriggled some more, and after a couple of moments during which he heard the group getting better situated, Tommy himself adjusted and saw most of the young men from below one of the piles of pallets. He wasn't able to see who was being held down, but he saw one young man on each limb pulling down, forcing the captive boy to arch his back on the metal work table. There were two more boys holding a rope across his bare upper chest and another two with a rope pulled taut across his waist at the belt line. He saw the young teen he assumed was Liam standing on the other side of the table working on something in his hands. Finally, the New Yorker was standing near the head of the captive, fiddling with something near his head. All of a sudden, Tommy remembered where he'd heard that voice! It was the older boy from the transit system that he and Bethany barely escaped. He looked around and spotted the boy he nicknamed "Pearl Snap" in his mind; he was one of the boys restraining the captive's head. Tommy didn't see Charley anywhere and wondered if he was doing something else for this gang or if he was one of the others holding the captive down.

"Okay, let's get to work," said the older boy in a tone that was a little deeper and huskier. He unbuckled his belt and slid it out of his jeans. He folded the belt in half while walking from the head of the captive to the middle of the table. He was blocking Tommy's view now, except for his legs. The older boy took a step back, and then Tommy saw him swing the belt and slap it hard across the captive boy's belly. Tommy flinched.

"Welcome to our version of red belly," said the older boy. The other boys in the room started to laugh, and the older boy shouted, "Shut up! Unless any of you want to take a turn on the table!"

The boys mumbled their apologies and tightened their grips.

Tommy realized he hadn't heard the boy on the table react. He wondered if he was really that tough or somehow gagged.

Suddenly, Tommy heard the slap of another swing of the belt. Still, there was no sound from the victim. Tommy refocused on the situation, first taking stock of his own hiding spot. Feeling well hidden, he looked back at the scene unfolding in front of him. This time he saw the boy on the table tense up as the older boy started his swing, but he didn't react.

"Liam! He thinks he's pretty tough, doesn't he?"

Liam laughed quietly. "Yeah, he does. Is it time?"

"You've seen this before, haven't you, Charley? Do you think you're tough enough?"

Tommy's face went white with shock. He thought Charley was part of this guy's gang. He wondered what had happened. Was this some sort of torture session for an error Charley made? Was this a sick and twisted initiation ritual? He loathed Charley, but no one deserved to go through this! Tommy's head was spinning.

Charley spat something out of his mouth. Tommy guessed it was something he had been biting down on to endure the pain.

"You're not going to beat me! I'll make my way through all this."

The determination and defiance were clearly evident in Charley's voice.

"We'll see," said the older boy with a sneering self-confidence that was unearned by his slight frame and nervous twitching. "Liam, I think it's your turn."

Liam looked around. He put on a pair of brass knuckles. Then he inserted a mouthguard like those worn by boxers or football players. He clinked the brass knuckles together.

"Let's go, pretty boy!"

"You won't get anything from me!"

Liam reared his well-muscled right arm back and swung it into Charley's stomach. There was an audible "Oof!" but that was it. He did it again and got even less of a response from a better-prepared Charley. This seemed to really make Liam angry, and he just started wailing on Charley's stomach. Tommy saw blood starting to appear on the brass knuckles. Then Liam hit Charley in the face. The older boy told Liam to calm down; this wasn't about torturing him.

Tommy thought, "Torturing him? This isn't torture?"

Liam took a breath, nodded his head, and started to beat on Charley's stomach again. Then he heard Charley taunt Liam. Liam looked at him and approached, getting face to face. So quickly Tommy barely saw it, Charley reared his head back and head-butted Liam so hard that Liam reeled back and fell down.

The older boy hollered, "Enough!" He told his goons to let Charley go. He helped Charley off the metal table. Charley gingerly moved forward and unsteadily stood up. Liam was sitting on the floor holding his nose.

"Congratulations, Charley! You've proven to me and the rest of the gang that you've got what it takes to be my number two. No one is tougher or smarter than you."

"Thanks, Boss." Holding his shirt in his right hand, Charley then walked over to Liam, kicked him hard in the ribs, and said, "I'll remember what you tried to do to me."

Horrified, Tommy looked at the exhausted but still defiant Charley. He felt a mixture of revulsion, respect, and confusion. The initiation acts the boys had subjected Charley to were reprehensible, yet he withstood them and even triumphed. Tommy couldn't understand why anyone would want to be part of a group like that or even rise in the hierarchy. Still, he was impressed by Charley's toughness. Tommy thought he'd better sneak back into a safer hiding spot. As he carefully did so, he heard the other boys congratulating their new number two. Tommy shook his head and waited among the pallets, trying to blend in and appear as just another pallet.

~~~

"How did the scavenging expedition go?" Amy asked when Tommy arrived.

Tommy's hands were full of scraps of house wrap, and his backpack was stuffed with other things he had managed to find. He felt a bit awkward with the people who had also set up camp in the airport looking at him as if he were homeless, which, in a sense, they all were. He decided that the opinions of those who were staring at him didn't matter; he and Bethany's family would never see them again anyway.

"Sorry for taking so long; I was trying not to get caught," Tommy said as he reached their little airport campsite. "I think I found a lot of helpful stuff. We might need to thin things out, though."

"That's okay; better to have too much than too little," Amy replied.

Tommy walked over to the pile Amy had started organizing as the rest of the extended family brought in supplies. Jason picked things up in the conference room on his way back, and Bethany scored a big pile of medical supplies and other useful items that she hoped wouldn't be missed for at least a couple of days. The pile was way too big, and each of them knew it. Tommy figured that when they left, after doing some sorting, like at Wallace Creek before the hiking trips, they'd leave the discarded but useful items in a discreet but discoverable place so the materials might still go to good use.

He looked down at the items he had scrounged. The main piece of house wrap measured about nine by twelve feet, with a pretty uneven edge on one of the nine-foot sides. He hoped it would be enough to cover all four of them. He also brought a couple of smaller pieces that he figured could be cut into ground cloths. For rope, all he found was a half-roll of bright pink braided nylon line his dad called mason's line. It was pretty thin, but he hoped it would do the job until they found something better, like more parachute cord or actual rope. He didn't find anything to use as tent stakes except some long carriage bolts, but again, they had to suffice. He felt really lucky to have found a carpenter's pencil, a permanent marker, and a utility knife with a couple of extra blades. He looked around for more tools, but they all appeared too heavy or of limited use. He found a mostly used pack of matches and a barely functioning lighter.

Tommy looked up to see Amy and Jason talking. He hadn't even heard Jason approach.

"Hi Tommy! How'd it go out there?"

"Hi Jason! I think it went pretty well. I got us a tarp and ground sheets, and I even found matches and a lighter. Oh, and I found this utility knife!" said Tommy, sounding more triumphant than he felt.

"Hey, a knife! That's awesome. With airport security these days, it's tough to find something like that. We sure have a big pile of stuff; I don't think we can carry all of it. How about you?"

"Yeah, I was just thinking about a shakedown. You know, a way to spread everything out and get rid of what we don't really need."

"Do you think we can do that without attracting a crowd? This pile is already suspiciously large. And I thought we were trying to be discreet."

Tommy felt sheepish. He had forgotten about keeping their work discreet to avoid causing more problems for everyone.

"Maybe behind that pillar?" he suggested, pointing behind Amy and Jason, just outside of their "home." "How about over at the kiosk for the airline?" Tommy offered uncertainly.

"Either of those will work. Why don't the three of us do a quick sort right here so we don't have to carry so much to where we're going to do our real sorting?"

After Tommy and Jason finished their pre-sort, they both sat back with satisfied sighs and looked at a much smaller pile. The discard pile included more than half of what Tommy, Jason, and Bethany had scavenged. They hoped the other travelers left behind might find some use for their discards.

"I wonder how much more we'll lighten our load?" Tommy questioned.

"It'll be interesting to see. I'm surprised at how easily we whittled down what we've worked so hard to collect. I think this stuff is going to be easy compared to what we each brought."

"Hey! Has anyone tried to track down our checked luggage?" Amy said.

Tommy and Jason looked at each other, initially with blank expressions, then chuckled and shook their heads.

~~~

Tommy and Jason stashed the keep pile and sneaked the discard pile to a nearby obscure corner. Finding that corner was a little more challenging than they had initially thought, since most of the area they were in was open and surrounded by windows. Eventually, they succeeded and used some discarded luggage carts to move them, trying to appear official to any onlookers.

The next task was to see if Jason could use his contacts and official pass to get them into the area where they hoped their checked luggage might be. They thought it was unlikely their luggage had been processed onto their plane since the aircraft they were supposed to board to get to Sacramento hadn't even taxied to the gate where they had set up camp. Both Tommy and Jason hoped they would find their checked bags in one of the trailers airports use to transport luggage to planes or on the portable conveyor belts that lifted the bags to the belly of the airplane. An unspoken concern for both of them was that their bags may have already been looted.

Airport emergency operations staff were happy to grant Jason and Tommy access to the area where their luggage was most likely sitting, as a thank you to Jason. The duo wasn't surprised it was probably close to the concourse where they had set up camp. They weren't excited about the hike all the way back to where they started. Tommy didn't remember when they decided they ought to just wait until the next day to actually start their real search. On the way back to their concourse, they stopped by to visit with Bethany. While they were chatting, they told her they didn't need any more medical supplies. She asked them to wait a minute.

"Okay, that's done," Bethany stated when she returned.

"What's done?" asked Tommy.

"Oh, I just put the stuff I was going to bring to our sleeping area back into the supplies. I also asked if I could leave early with you two, and they said 'Sure!' It's getting slower and slower here. I think the doctors and nurses have been trying to transfer the chronically ill and seriously injured to a better nearby medical facility. Maybe the Children's Hospital? I don't know, it's close, and I think they're taking anyone from here, even if they're not children."

"That can't be very close; Denver isn't exactly handy to the airport, if I remember right," noted Jason.

Bethany replied, "When they were talking about moving those patients, it sounded like a big deal. Someone said it was over fifteen miles away. I think they managed to round up some horse-drawn wagons, but I heard it still took most of a day to get them there. Dad, I thought you knew about this; it went through emergency operations."

"Oh, honey, there's so much going on in those rooms that I don't know most of what's happening. I just try to help where I can."

The trio headed back to their temporary home.

When they arrived, Amy was sitting in the middle of all their collected materials with a notepad and a frazzled look on her face.

"Thank goodness you're back!"

"Yeah, I thought this would wait until later," said Jason.

"I just wanted to get a head start."

"Okay," said Jason, looking around. "There aren't many people around. Let's move this stuff over against the window, behind that pillar next to the pile Tommy and I started."

The freshly arrived trio began to move the supplies and were quickly joined by Amy as soon as they cleared a path for her. It didn't take long. After a quick discussion, they decided to bring their carry-on luggage over too.

"Why don't Tommy and I sleep over here tonight, and we'll sort through everything after we get our checked luggage? That way, we can have a better grasp of all our resources," suggested Jason.

The rest of the group agreed and hung out, looking through their packs and bags until dinner time, when they went to the serving line two by two. Bethany and Tommy went first, followed by Amy and Jason.

"They're sweet kids," said Amy, looking up at Jason while they walked hand in hand to what turned out to be a meager dinner. "I hope this long walk is successful, but what I hope for even more is that everything gets fixed and we can return to normal."

Jason looked at his wife, who had tears welling up, and said, "I hope you're right, but I just don't think that's going to happen. We're lucky to have Bethany with her big heart and very fortunate to have run into that amazing boy. He's resourceful and respectful. We just don't see that very often."

"Do you really think he knows what he's talking about? He certainly seems very sure of himself, maybe too sure."

"Everything he's talked about so far sounds good, but I think a lot of what he's saying comes from reading books and listening to camp counselors. Sure, I think he's camped with his family, but that's not what we'll experience, even optimistically. This is going to be a very long and tough walk. I'm sure we'll run into some unpleasant people along the way. We'll face awful weather and hard nights on a journey this long.

Still, even if it is book smarts, he knows more than I do about this subject, so I'm willing to listen."

Amy tightened her hold on Jason's hand and wrapped her other arm around him as she rested her head on his shoulder.

Day Eight

Jason woke as soon as the sun rose over the horizon and shone into the concourse. He nudged Tommy, who resisted the morning. Jason said, "Come on, Tommy, we'd better get to work on finding our stuff."

Tommy grudgingly accepted Jason's prompts and sat up bleary-eyed with messy hair. He thought to himself that he really missed his morning showers; they were something he looked forward to that helped him wake up and start the day fresh.

The duo walked over to the food distribution area and picked up some fruit. The fruit looked worse for wear and he definitely would have skipped it in the first days of this strange new world they were experiencing.

While they munched on their apples, they refreshed their memories about the directions they were given at the emergency center. The route wasn't difficult, just specific. You were supposed to go down this hallway, find a certain door, go down some steps to another hallway, and find another door. Fortunately, Jason had one of the spare backup keys the airport kept on hand for when the power went down and the ID card readers wouldn't work. He was also told there was a seven-thousand-foot tunnel and one million square feet of space in the baggage system. When he told Tommy, they both shrugged it off as marketing exaggeration.

Almost every door was locked, and a couple showed evidence of someone trying to pry them open without success. They finally reached the last door before the baggage system closest to their concourse.

Tommy didn't know what to expect—maybe something like a big garage, a couple of tractors with luggage trailers, and some conveyor belts—but what he found was much more. In the dim twilight provided by the small windows in the garage doors, they saw conveyor belts, or something like strange, complicated conveyor belts with little trolleys attached to them, lots and lots of conveyor belts. There were tractors with trailers, about ten of them to service the planes. "Garage" didn't begin to describe the actual facility; it was more like a giant warehouse with an underground tunnel apparently built for cars or trucks. Even after all the time that had passed without power, it felt even more eerily silent. It looked like everything behind the public part of the airport had just been abandoned; when everything stopped, the employees of the airport had simply stood up and gone home in the middle of whatever they were doing.

It was then Tommy realized there must be thousands of pieces of luggage all over the airport in these tunnels, just stopped where they were when the power went out. He looked at Jason wide-eyed and saw he must have been processing the same thoughts, realizing they weren't exaggerating in the emergency center. Tommy hoped their luggage had made it to this small corner of what must be a massive system.

Jason said, "Well, I guess the best place to start is those trailers."

The two of them went over to the first tractor and pulled back the tarp to begin their search. As their eyes continued to adjust to the darkness, it quickly became apparent that this particular trailer and the one attached to it were headed for Atlanta, Georgia. Five tractor setups later, they still hadn't found the one they were looking for, but they had become efficient in their search, requiring just pulling back the tarp and looking at the first tag they saw for the destination. Jason told Tommy their airport code was SMF and to keep his eyes peeled for that abbreviation.

"Hey, Jason! There's a sheet of paper taped to those trailers over there that says SMF!"

The duo rushed over to the trailers, bypassing all but the second-to-last trailer set up, and pulled back the tarp. Their relief and excitement at finding the right trailers was evident in their actions, but they still wanted to locate their luggage, so they quickly got to work. They divided the two trailers between them and started their search. The trailers were almost full, which made sense to Tommy because all they were waiting for was the connecting flight to land. When the power went out, he expected to see the plane at any moment. Tommy paused and realized the plane never made it to the concourse. He hoped the plane had landed safely and was taxiing to the gate when everything stopped. He took a moment to say a prayer for the passengers and crew, as well as the rest of the airline travelers at that terrible moment. After a sad sigh, he started on his trailer. He called back to Jason to ask for a description of the Browns' luggage.

Jason said their luggage consisted of just three black roll-on suitcases—nothing particularly special except that Amy had tied royal blue ribbons with white stars on them so they'd be able to identify their bags on the luggage pickup carousel. Tommy knew he was looking for his orange footlocker, which would be easy to spot, but he dreaded searching for the Browns' suitcases because it seemed like everything else would fit Jason's description aside from the ribbons. There were a few different colored suitcases and an occasional odd item like a golf bag, but those were obvious. He decided he'd better get to work on his side of the first trailer they chose. The work actually went pretty quickly, and they found Jason's bag toward the end of one trailer and Bethany's at the beginning of the other. However, they didn't find Amy's or Tommy's big orange trunk.

"Amy's bag is the most important one of ours. She packed many things she found for her work in hers. We even moved about half of her clothes to my suitcase."

"I thought *your* bag was heavy," exclaimed Tommy.

By this time, their stomachs were telling them it was lunch. As the two sat munching on week-old pastries and overly soft fruit, they shared their wariness of climbing into the trolley system. From what they saw, each trolley was big enough to hold two suitcases, a foot locker, or a golf club bag or ski bag, with sides just awkward enough to climb over. The conveyor system had a pretty low ceiling too, so they needed to constantly crouch while climbing over from one trolley to the next.

Jason threw the trash into a trashcan that might never get emptied, and Tommy joined him at the beginning of their dreaded task. Tommy was chosen to go first since he was younger, more limber, and therefore quicker over each cart side. Jason followed him to help bring back the luggage, if they found any.

Tommy climbed in and looked into the darkness and down the conveyor, in the direction that incoming bags were headed to get dumped to the waiting luggage handlers. He didn't see anything remarkable, least of all his own orange trunk. He scrambled over and into the next trolley, took a cursory look at the suitcases, wishing he had a flashlight in the dark caverns of the luggage handling facility, and moved on to the next one. It went on like this; sometimes there was an empty trolley, and then he would wait for Jason to catch up. They'd rest for a minute or two and start again. Tommy was thankful Jason remembered his water bottle, which they shared during their stops. They each took a sip, conserving the water since Tommy left his bottle back in the area where the trailers were parked. After what seemed like an eternity, Tommy realized the suitcase he had just looked at and was getting ready to crawl over to the next trolley was actually Amy's. He tipped it up to double-check and saw the royal blue ribbon. He was surprised he had almost moved past it and now felt how heavy it actually was. Amy must have filled the bag to its limit. He yelled to Jason that he had found it, and Jason cheered. Tommy waited for him to reach the trolley, and they discussed their next steps. Jason decided he would wait with Amy's bag while Tommy clambered along to find his trunk, unless he got out of sight, in which case Jason would move ahead to spot Tommy in case he needed help.

Looking back, Jason seemed to be less concerned as Tommy kept moving forward. Tommy understood his relief, especially after feeling how heavy Amy's bag was and realizing how important it must be to her. He wondered how they would be able to get her suitcase back to their home in Northern California. Tommy turned around and looked forward, and seeing no sign of his bright orange trunk, he hiked his leg up and over to the next trolley. After a while, he saw what looked like a switchback turn. He motioned to Jason and kept on. After he made the turn, he looked ahead, and his heart started racing. He thought he saw some orange just a few trolleys ahead. He raced ahead, tripping over the lips of each trolley, excited and not caring. When he got to the trolley, he couldn't believe his eyes; the familiar decals were there, the familiar scuffs and scratches were there—he'd found it! He let out a giant whoop! It was the first time he felt real joy since the event, a personal sense of accomplishment; he found his trunk! He heard Jason yelling, asking if he was okay, and Tommy jubilantly yelled that he'd found his trunk. Jason told him he was excited for him and asked if he needed help. Tommy said he didn't and started to heave his trunk back the way he had just struggled. At each trolley, there was the heave over the lip followed by a ka-chunk of the trunk falling into the next one, over and over again. When he caught up with Jason, they slowed down to be careful with Amy's bag, one of them going ahead and the other raising it to them, both carefully lowering it to the bottom of the next trolley. Jason told Tommy he thought he remembered there were several fragile items in there and they thought it was best to be overly cautious, even though they were exhausted. They followed with Tommy's trunk, not as carefully. They then realized that if they put Tommy's trunk first, Amy's suitcase would be easier to load into the following trolley, then they could slide the trunk with the suitcase on it and have less to raise to the next empty trolley. They continued this way, alternating Tommy's trunk and Amy's suitcase, saving some energy and pausing when the dry heat of a Denver late summer got to them in the stillness of the conveyor system. They finished Jason's water what seemed like ages ago. Jason and Tommy finally reached the last few trolleys, and the temperature slackened with more space around them, with the cement helping to cool the air. They relaxed, knowing their major exertions were almost over; they almost felt the water from Tommy's water bottle pouring down their throats.

"Nice job, Tommy!" said Jason, crawling out of the last trolley.

"You too, Jason! That was a lot harder than I expected," said Tommy.

The two of them enjoyed the water from Tommy's water bottle, conserving some for their long walk back to their temporary home in the terminal.

The return to the terminal was tedious, with Tommy and Jason leapfrogging the four pieces of luggage from one spot they perceived as safe to the next. When they finally reached the door of the concourse, Tommy went to gather Amy and Bethany to help bring their luggage to their place in the terminal. Amy felt a little nervous because they hadn't left anyone behind to guard their belongings. Her worry dissolved when she saw her suitcase.

"Oh, Jason! I thought I'd never see it again!"

"I'm happy we were able to find it for you, but you have some difficult decisions to make when we start packing for our journey."

She looked at Jason, joy tempered by sadness in her eyes. "I know; it's just that now I can make those decisions instead of having them forced on me by circumstance."

The foursome returned to the rest of their belongings and began the process of sorting through and deciding what was worth carrying almost 1,200 miles to their home. Some decisions were easy, while others were difficult, especially for Amy, who had both professional and personal attachments to many of the items she acquired on the family's trip to Italy.

Jason helped her by offering space in his luggage that he had set aside just for her.

Tommy reminded them of the ten essentials, and Jason good-naturedly pulled him aside to let him know Amy was struggling with her choices enough, and his timing was poor.

They had decided earlier to limit themselves to a backpack and one other piece they could drag or otherwise bring along with them. Tommy chose his daypack and backpacking pack, while each of the Browns picked their carry-on from the plane and a suitcase with wheels. Before their family left for Italy, Jason made sure to get suitcases with heavy-duty wheels to cope with the cobblestones in some of the cities they visited on their trip. All three of the Browns were even happier he'd gotten those new suitcases.

The plan was for each of them to carry the most important items in their smaller bag in case they needed to leave their other, heavier bag behind for some reason. This meant they'd have at least one water bottle, a fire starter, snacks, extra clothing, and a knife, if they could scrounge one up. Tommy found Colorado maps for each of them, but he was unable to find any compasses other than the one in his gear. Flashlights seemed unnecessary, but each of them decided to carry some form of one, "just in case." Each person carried a personal first aid kit made by Bethany, while she carried a more complete one. They each also had sunscreen; after all, it was late summer, and they needed hats to protect themselves from the sun. Tommy found a pair of sunglasses for himself, while each of the Browns already had theirs. Additionally, each person packed their own extra items into their bag.

~~~

Tommy sat down in one of the chairs that overlooked the runway and thought about his time at the airport. He knew they were leaving soon. They were at the end of one of the wings on the last concourse, and during their many days there, he often did what he was doing right now—looking outside and staring at the plains stretching on forever. Occasionally, he went over to the other side of the concourse and gazed at the mountains, which always seemed like they were within reach, their white-speckled peaks visible even in late summer. The plains kept drawing him back; the swaying golden grasses and the endlessness of it left him speechless and allowed him to think or not think at all, whichever he seemed to need the most. Even though he despised the life at the airport, he knew he would miss these odd vistas he absorbed like a fish in a very strange fishbowl.

He looked forward to starting his long walk home, but he was anxious as well. He prayed the journey would be uneventful, just one day of walking after another, but his intuition told him that even in the best of times, there would be many opportunities for learning—learning about himself and the wider world. He had only ever flown over most of the route that Jason said made the most sense for their journey home. Tommy had skied in the Colorado Rockies only once, and he didn't remember much except for the skiing and the food. He loved looking out the porthole windows of the plane when he flew, and what he was able to remember from the flights he took to and from summer camp increased both his excitement and his worry. The mountains looked beautiful and inviting yet steep! They resembled a bowl of dragon's teeth—jagged and uninviting, but with whispers of adventure like the fantasy novels he loved to read. Beyond the mountains lay the Great Basin, filling half of Utah and most of Nevada, based on the maps Jason shared with everyone. From the plane, it looked dry and monotonous, dotted with brush. When Tommy first considered walking home, he naturally thought of taking the interstates. It appeared to be a straightforward path down I-70, then onto US-50, and finally the homestretch down I-80. However, Jason convinced everyone that a route further north would be better. It wound along through Winter Park and eventually to US-40, then Steamboat Springs and Provo, Utah, following small roads to the west until they finally joined US-50 near a small town called Eureka, Nevada. They planned to stay on US-50 until they got home.

Both routes made Tommy hopeful that they might be able to get some bicycles and shorten their time getting home. Every time he thought about how long the trail looked, he almost lost hope, but he wanted to get home, and it seemed like the electricity was never coming back.

He leaned back in his seat and looked at the endless openness of the plains facing east, feeling as if he was preparing to turn west into the mountains for a never-ending journey, and hoped he was making the right decision.

Day Nine

As it turned out, the group left the following morning. Each of them left quite a bit of stuff back at the airport. No one was more disheartened than Amy, but all of them were certain they'd never see their luggage again, even though they had carefully stashed it in a quiet corner behind the locked doors of the baggage handling facility that Jason and Tommy used to access their checked luggage. They all checked and rechecked the security of their suitcases, or in the case of Tommy, his footlocker. Tommy carried his overnight backpack and daypack, Bethany brought her carry-on suitcase and backpack, while Jason and Amy decided to bring her large suitcase, his carry-on suitcase, and their business-style backpacks. Amy also decided to bring her purse to try to squeeze in as much as possible. Jason and Amy planned on alternating who would take care of the larger suitcase, hoping they could count on the heavy-duty wheels working for most of the planned route since it was almost entirely on roads.

Jason woke early, a habit formed from a life of getting to the office before anyone else, allowing him to concentrate on his more complicated tasks before the normal hustle and bustle of office life began. He nudged Amy and struggled to wake Bethany and Tommy in turn by shaking their shoulders harder until they muttered, "I'm up, I'm up!" The group stumbled around in the predawn light, putting on their shoes and gathering their bags as they quietly began their walk through the three concourses and two interconnecting tunnels. The small groups that had started to form during their time in the airport were mostly shut down by security or had moved on out of boredom and frustration with their limited success, so Tommy and the Browns didn't have to worry about them, but they still remained wary and kept their eyes and ears open.

After they got through the first tunnel, they looked to their left and noticed the sky beginning to lighten. As they walked through the second concourse, they took in the dim forms of a couple of others with the same idea and walking the same path. Tommy and the Browns noticed the airport didn't feel as full as it had for the last couple of days but hadn't put the clues together until that moment. Jason guessed that after the first exodus of the sick, the airport lost about ten people a day. It didn't sound like much, but over time it added up.

By the time they emerged from the second and final tunnel, the sun had begun to rise, but had not yet broken the horizon. They were now joined by about half a dozen others in the terminal. The terminal felt luminescent as the rising sun glowed through the unique tent-like roof. It was spacious and airy even this early, their footsteps echoing off the dull, bright floors. As they stepped out of the main entrance into the cool morning air, the reality of their endeavor began to settle in. For all of them, the slight breeze on their faces felt good. Aside from going to the latrines, they hadn't really been outside since they arrived. Turning to their right, they walked east toward the road on which they'd begin. As they reached the road, Tommy looked out at the parking lots, which showed no signs of life, filled with motionless, dusty cars in the wide-open, treeless plain surrounding the airport. The road up to and away from the sidewalk also had cars on it, obviously left by their drivers after the event. Some of the nearby ones had been moved; Jason said this was done for the horse-drawn wagons that took emergency patients to local medical care facilities and later brought deliveries of food and water that the airport provided to the trapped travelers. There was some evidence that people had tried to break into the cars, but the security presence must have dissuaded them this close to the airport.

The three members of the Brown family struggled with their rolling suitcases and carry-on bags as Tommy readjusted his packs after the group's walk through the airport. As they moved onto the still night-cooled road that would carry them away from the stuffy airport and toward their homes, each of them, after some time arranging their individual gear, started to make reasonable but slow progress. After several minutes, the group realized the direction they wanted to go was up a bank as part of an overpass that led them away from the airport. They looked up at the late summer golden grass interrupted by gray rock drainage trenches and groaned. To get up to their new road, the Browns struggled up the dirt and grass slope with their wheeled burdens. Tommy came alongside Jason, nodded at him, gripped the handle, and helped him drag Amy's big suitcase up the hill. Once they got past a dirt road and back onto the asphalt, they started to walk in earnest. After fifteen more minutes, they began to curve to face the mountains far off in the distance. It really began to feel like they were on their way; they shook off the awkwardness that so often accompanies the first part of any journey and saw their first big goal: the beautiful purple, dark blue, and white speckled mountains.

Yet, the eerie scene before them could not be ignored. Vehicles remained substantially still in the positions they occupied when everything electric stopped, each ten to twenty yards apart. Occasionally, a car showed evidence of someone breaking in, either with broken windows—sometimes shattered by large rocks—or a pried-open door. Jason wondered aloud if the thieves were picky about which cars they broke into. With that evidence in front of them, the group pricked up their ears and started to pay attention to anything peculiar in their path. With their heightened attentiveness, the walkers began to see open bags with clothes strewn in the direction of the wind, lying on the ground in the wide open space.

The silence was particularly unnerving. The normal sounds of a city were no longer present. The silence was not absolute, though; they heard birdsong and the wind, something people don't typically hear on major thoroughfares. Even for Tommy and Bethany, who grew up in a place smaller than Denver, it still unsettled them. They knew what a city was supposed to sound like, and this wasn't it. Maybe it was their heightened sense of hearing playing tricks on them, but they all heard the crunching of glass and the sharp sound of metal bending, and they stopped and crouched down.

"What was that?" exclaimed Amy.

"You heard it too?" said Jason, looking around. "I guess we all did."

"I bet it was these thieves taking more from the cars," suggested Bethany.

"Let's be careful through here."

Tommy, Bethany, and Amy nodded their heads and resumed their walk, keeping their eyes scanning the surroundings and listening more carefully. The idle chatter stopped as they walked quietly along, jumping at any sudden movement or noise. Everything that drew their attention turned out to be natural occurrences: wind-blown fabric, birds cawing, or car doors swinging on their hinges. Jason quietly noted they needed to be watchful for dogs, particularly strays that became sick, feral, or had recently escaped from their owners and no longer knew how to behave. Very rarely did the group see cats, but the cats usually kept their distance.

The group continued to pick their way through the abandoned cars on the highway, passing under a highway sign, and then pausing in the shade of an underpass. It was still well before lunchtime, but the sun was starting to warm the late summer morning. During their first real break, they wondered if they had enough water and asked if Tommy had plans for safely refilling their bottles. Tommy took out his map of Denver and looked it over, appreciating how his perspective had already changed in the few hours they had been on the road instead of just romanticizing about walking home. He guessed there might be some ponds nearby, but the nearest location on the map that looked like a usable water source was about ten miles away. Tommy suggested they might find some water at an abandoned business if they became really concerned. Jason voiced his worry that those were perfect places for gangs to set up their headquarters. The group tried to be careful not to get dehydrated while conserving their water as much as possible. Tommy estimated the creek was about five hours away.

As they passed by the defiant big blue Mustang sculpture atop a hill, Amy noticed that the lower sections were already completely covered in graffiti, and some particularly motivated individuals had climbed even higher on the horse to paint there. Tommy said he thought that was ugly and disrespectful, but Amy argued that many people liked and even collected pieces of graffiti.

"I won't be one of them," said Tommy.

Leaving the statue behind, the group regained its relaxed nature and chatted as they walked along. Bethany abruptly told the group to stop and get low. They huddled behind a car, and Jason asked what was going on.

"I heard something and then I saw something moving in that big dump truck up ahead."

Jason looked around the car and spotted the dump truck in the distance. Tommy tried to look as well, but Jason pushed him back. After watching for a minute or two, he saw some heads pop up from the dump bed of the truck, followed by a lot of waving of what he guessed was clothing and whoops of joy.

"I don't want to attract their attention. I'm afraid they might try to steal something or attack us. Maybe we can sneak around them," offered Amy.

"Let's try going over there," said Jason, pointing to a rental car parking lot north of where the small group was heading.

Crouching, Jason ran as quickly and quietly as he could to a car between them and the roadside. He signaled for Bethany first, then Amy, with Tommy following closely after. The next open space looked like it was almost one hundred yards away, leading to a line of vans parked against a curb, when they realized the whole lot was surrounded by a high chain-link fence. Bethany pointed to the corner of the lot where a tree stood next to a stagnant pond. Jason nodded and took a couple of breaths to prepare for the run.

Before he took off, he whispered, "Keep your eyes on the dump truck and follow each person in front of you when they get about a quarter of the way there. Don't stop, just run. Peek at the dump truck if you think it's safe, but run."

Jason turned around and took off.

Each of them started to run when the previous person reached the spot Jason indicated. Tommy was last, and as he ran over the summer-dried grass, he avoided the little shrubs in his path. He looked to his left and saw that nothing was happening with the dump truck. He almost tripped but caught himself. When he looked up, he realized he was just behind Bethany, who was nearly catching up to Amy ahead of her. The three of them arrived at the lonely tree almost simultaneously.

Amy and Jason were out of breath, their faces blotchy and red. Bethany looked a bit flushed but seemed fine, while Tommy didn't even feel winded.

"I guess all that office time has caught up with us," said Jason.

"Hey! Do you think that water might be worth a try?" asked Tommy, pointing to the pond.

"It looks pretty rough, Tommy," said Amy.

"Tommy, take one of our disposable bottles, fill it up, and let's see what it looks like," said Jason.

Tommy took his almost empty water bottle and finished it. With the others hiding behind the tree and bushes, Tommy snuck over to the pond and gingerly pushed his bottle into the water. He saw something green go into it, pulled it up, and dumped it out. He had an idea: he was going to take his shirt and wrap a layer of it over the mouth of the bottle to try to filter the water. This time, he tipped the bottle in more carefully, using the shirt to strain the water, and saw that his idea worked. He crept back to the others, who gently made fun of his shirtless water gathering. Tommy laughed but showed the Browns the result of his effort.

"I'm not sure how safe that water is to drink, Tommy," said Amy.

Tommy said they needed to boil it if they wanted it to be safe. He was still happy with the result of getting some water when he wasn't sure they would see any for another ten or twelve miles. Jason encouraged his family to give Tommy a water bottle each so they would have extra water if they needed it.

After Tommy collected water for the foursome, he put on his shirt, which was dirtier in some ways and cleaner in others. The group decided to creep along the fences of the car rental companies for two to three hundred yards to remain less obvious to anyone looking their way. Again, Jason led the way. They encountered windblown litter against the fences and stepped over rocks and bushes lining the unused roadside. When they came to a stormwater-filled ditch, they decided to take advantage of the limited cover to sneak back to the much easier-to-walk-on road.

"That was close," Tommy said to Jason.

"We're not past them far enough yet."

Tommy looked back and still saw some activity in the dump truck. He crouched again and continued west with Bethany's family.

~~~

After about two hours and five treeless miles, the little group looked at what Tommy expected to be a creek and was disappointed by what appeared to be a low marshy area. Luckily, the group was able to collect some questionable water from roadside ditches they hadn't yet boiled to make safe. They looked longingly at a gas station and restaurant area that had been vandalized and stripped of anything usable, and decided it wasn't worth the risk of even approaching the parking lot. Tommy offered to go down into the marshy area to see if there was any water. He returned to where the other three had decided to rest under the bridge in the shade and told them that when he dug a little into the ground, some brown water came up. Jason decided to try to filter their water using some extra cloth in a scavenged pot and boil it to see if the water they collected was safe to drink. Jason built a small fire under the bridge and brought their collected water to a boil in three separate batches before extinguishing the little impromptu fire. They carefully filled their water bottles, hoping that once the water cooled, it would be drinkable.

This stop, which Tommy saw as a little blue line intersecting the highway on the map, was the first spot the group planned to stop if they were slow or if the going turned out to be rough. After their early slow start and the delay around the dump truck, the four actually hiked at a pretty good pace for people with mixed levels of activity since the event. Tommy fared best since he ran all over the airport, while Bethany and Jason fared about equally, and Amy did well even though she was the most sedentary of the group. Each of them was nursing hot spots on their feet from where their shoes were rubbing, and their hands were tired and shoulders sore from carrying their luggage. Despite all of that, they each felt strong and decided to keep walking until they reached the next little blue line on the map, hoping for a better water source and maybe a nice place to set up camp.

As the group got back on the road, they started on a big curve leading them south. For the next few miles, they began to see what looked like hotels and restaurants in the distance to the southeast and east as they walked along in the hot afternoon sun. They were wearing hats, and Jason and Amy had on light-colored long-sleeve shirts, but the heat still bore down on them. There was a slight breeze keeping all but the most persistent bugs away and helping them avoid overheating. Tommy was the first to cautiously sip the water they collected from the roadside ditches. He made a slight face, scrunching up his nose. Jason asked how it was, and Tommy choked out a response that it tasted kind of flat, but drinkable if he needed to avoid dehydration. Jason and Bethany tried it next, and their reaction was similar. Amy laughed at them, reached into her purse, pulled out a little white bottle with yellow accents, opened the lid, and squeezed several yellow-tinted drops into her bottle. When she drank her water, she winced slightly and said it wasn't too bad. The other three looked at her in shock. She smiled and showed them her bottle; it was lemonade flavoring! She added that she had done some scavenging of her own. The others excitedly asked if Amy would share, and she did. The group laughed at their fortune, each thanking Amy for her foresight and resourcefulness.

With a lighter step, they hiked on for another hour until they reached the next little blue line on their map. As they got closer to their planned stop for the night, the first sign of the hoped-for creek was cottonwood trees in the distance. This was the first time the little group had seen anything other than low bushes and grass since they left the airport. As they approached, they noticed it was some sort of nature or fitness trail alongside an intermittent creek. Tommy excitedly saw that even though the water wasn't always above ground level, it was trickling along, meaning this was the freshest water they had encountered since the airport. He dropped his bigger bag and ran down to the creek.

"Watch out!" yelled Amy.

"I'm fine."

Tommy tripped and went sprawling, his water bottles flinging out of the side pockets of his backpack. He sheepishly got up and dusted himself off.

"I didn't realize you meant to look out and not trip," said Tommy, hanging his head and looking at his scraped elbow. He continued to clean himself up, while the rest of the little group cautiously followed him down to the creekside, dragging their rolling suitcases behind them. Tommy collected the bag he had dropped and joined the others as they filled the pan to start the sterilizing process. Jason started a small fire. After they sat down for a minute to rest and cool off, Tommy and Bethany told her parents they were going to check out the area. After the usual "be careful" and "don't go too far" from their parents, the two younger members of the group walked toward the southwest, where it looked like there might be something to explore.

It turned out they stumbled upon a place that appeared to be an old campground or mobile home park with sidewalks, several cul-de-sacs, and even an old, run-down, mostly collapsed office. They ran back to Amy and Jason and excitedly told them about their discovery. Jason and Amy were cautious, but they agreed to accompany Bethany to investigate further. Tommy stayed behind tending the little fire and the water sterilizing process while guarding everyone's luggage. The area was nice enough for them to discuss setting up for their first night under some trees on the flatter ground available. Jason even mentioned he bet it would be more comfortable than sleeping next to the creek, as well as less buggy. Jason returned and told Tommy they decided to move up to the old campground.

The four of them finished sterilizing enough water to last the night and, realizing they ought to have their dinner next to the little campfire, prepared a meager meal. They wanted to be careful not to use up their scavenged food on the first night out. They were cautiously optimistic about their chances of finding food as they went along, but they knew they would be walking along the highway for another day or two to get to the western edge of Denver, and they didn't know if there were places to scavenge, buy, or barter for food. The group didn't even know what to expect once they actually got into the more inhabited parts of the city.

After they ate, Tommy went over to the trees where the group decided to set up their sleeping area. He took the sheet of house-wrap he had cut down to use as a ground sheet, laid his sleeping pad down, and spread out his sleeping bag to let it air out and fluff up. The others followed Tommy's lead, using humanitarian aid blankets instead of cozy sleeping bags and pads. Fortunately, there were some leaves on the ground that they could pile up to help soften their makeshift beds. They decided not to pitch the larger pieces of house-wrap they carried for a tarp to remain a bit more inconspicuous while reducing their setup and breakdown time. With their backpacks leaning against nearby trees, they chatted about their day for a little while until the stars came out and they each fell asleep in turn.

Day Ten

When Jason woke before the others, as was his habit, he opened his eyes to a garbage-strewn mess. He rubbed his eyes and shook his head, not wanting to believe what he saw. He shook his wife awake, and she stifled a gasp, looking back at Jason with her eyes wide and her mouth even wider. She mouthed, "What happened?" to Jason, and he shook his head, putting his finger to his lips to ensure they didn't wake the two young teens still sleeping. He stood up, getting out from under his blankets, and started looking around barefoot. He quickly pieced together what had happened: some animal—a raccoon, or several squirrels or rodents—had gnawed into their soft packs and ransacked them looking for food. Everyone's soft bags were chewed to some extent. The suitcases looked like they had been attempted but with no success.

Jason groaned and said to Amy, "It looks like we're going to have to do some sewing."

"What do you mean?" whispered Amy in response.

"Animals got into our bags."

"Oh no! Did they get the food?"

"That and maybe more; I can't tell—there's too much to figure out until we get the kids up and sort through this mess."

"Do you think there's enough food left for breakfast?"

"I really don't know. Let's wake up Bethany and Tommy and share the bad news."

After Bethany and Tommy were roused from sleep, everyone started to clean up the mess, trying to organize as they went along. Each of them picked up something off the ground, trying to figure out what it was and to whom it belonged. Whenever Bethany or Tommy found a more personal item, they blushed and quietly took it over to where it belonged. Sometimes the items found were partially or mostly destroyed, and it often took questioning the group to even figure out what they were. After a little while, it seemed like everything had been picked up. It didn't look like they had lost all their food—enough remained to be more careful, but also enough to last them through the day. The meals were now going to be more utilitarian. Each of them had lost a piece or two of clothing and noticed some damage to other things. Amy found her deodorant and soap were missing. There was some damage to all of their soft bags, backpacks, and purses. Tommy and Amy both carried small sewing kits with them, and after the group finished a meager breakfast, they started to work on their repairs in pairs. Those who didn't do any sewing packed up or prepared their belongings to be packed up once the repairs were done. Amy's repairs were the best, thanks to a lifetime of fashion-fueled sewing experience. Tommy's sewing wasn't pretty, but it was consistent and durable, reflecting his camping experience and his love of putting souvenir patches on his packs and jackets. Jason and Bethany needed a lot of help, with Amy finally getting frustrated with Jason's two left hands and taking over from him with an exasperated sigh. Bethany was just inexperienced, and once she got the hang of it, she seemed to do okay.

Late in the morning, the foursome finally got back on the road heading toward the west side of Denver as the day began to warm up. A little over a mile into their walk, while they were gathering and sterilizing water from a roadside pond, Jason spotted what he thought was a grocery store in the distance. After discussing it, the group noticed an overpass a short distance away with a road leading in the right direction. They walked to the side road and started on the surface road toward what they hoped would be a resupply point. After about half a mile, the group began to notice different shops popping up along the side of the road. Many of the restaurants had odors of spoiling food wafting out to the walkers. Some were vandalized, and it looked like any food that might have been useful had been taken along with whatever the looters wanted. It wasn't much, but it certainly showed that the breakdown of law enforcement was having an effect, even in this area that seemed to be home to the people who helped a large city like Denver run. They passed a health food store that appeared mostly untouched and were surprised to see it surrounded by cars parked bumper to bumper, with several people standing or walking behind the cars, visibly armed. There was one opening in the fence of cars that seemed to act as a gate for people entering and exiting the store. Since the incident with the dump truck, this was the little group's first time seeing other people, and it was a reality shock they had not expected.

Jason looked at the other three and shrugged, then walked up to the gate and the guard who was standing nearest, carrying a shotgun, and greeted him. The guard asked Jason to identify himself. Jason told the man his name and was asked for his driver's license.

"Really?" asked Jason.

"Locals only; IDs are the only way we know," said the guard.

"I'm not from here, but we were stuck at the airport and have decided to try to walk home to Sacramento, California."

"Wow, that sounds awful. I'm sorry, but we can't let you in."

"Is there nothing you can do?"

"Nope."

"Is there someone we can talk to?"

"Yeah, but you're talking to him. I'm in charge for this shift. We're all volunteers trying to protect what we have."

"Do you have any ideas? We lost a lot of our food last night when some animals got into our bags."

"Gosh, I'm sorry. Maybe that store over there?" said the guard, pointing to the health food store. "Not many people seem to go there."

"Thanks, I hope we can figure something out."

"Good luck."

Jason walked over to his small extended family and shared what he had learned. They decided there was nothing to lose and walked across the street.

As they approached the health food store, they expected to be stopped as they had been at the supermarket across the street. They didn't see anyone until they reached the doors, where a man who looked like a manager unlocked the door for them. He welcomed them, and when they asked, he said he was the manager and was committed to keeping his store open for the needs of the community. He apologized for the empty shelves. He mentioned that he had to raise some prices but wanted to be fair and try to keep supplies on hand until he was restocked or ran out.

They noticed there were sandbags and plywood in place to protect the store's windows and doors, which they guessed was for nighttime. Tommy asked the manager about it, and he confirmed that was indeed the purpose. He explained that a rotation of his few remaining staff slept in the store every night. They also noted a clerk who was assisting the small number of customers while restocking and keeping an eye on the checkout.

They grabbed a cart and started shopping. The hungry hikers were careful because they knew they would have to carry whatever they bought, and they were also worried about the cost and how they would pay for it. After checking their pockets and bags, they found they did have some cash, even some foreign money from the Browns' trip to Italy. Jason joked that at least they were carrying unspendable money.

They shopped carefully and found a surprising amount of fairly fresh food in good condition; they were able to get some lemons and limes that were acceptable. They focused their shopping on dehydrated fruit, vegetables, and other items that made sense for their long walk. They all agreed the whole experience was somewhat strange given their recent past and the stifling lack of air conditioning in the hot late summer. The little group approached the checkout counter, where the clerk worked with a lined sheet of paper and did all of the math by hand. He must have practiced a lot since he was pretty fast. When he told them the total, they happily found they had enough to pay! They thanked the manager on their way out and ate their lunch before packing their bags so they didn't have to carry extra weight.

Satisfied and happy, the four returned to the road and rejoined the highway a short time later. Tommy reminded everyone they were approaching a major change in direction. They were walking south to reach the interstate and were looking forward to turning west and heading toward the mountains. Tommy and Jason expressed their concerns that, since they were approaching a big intersection, there might be an informal market, hucksters, or thieves. Tommy took out his map again, and the other three gathered around him. They stopped to consider where they wanted to try to camp. Amy saw a couple of parks just north of the interstate and wondered aloud if those were reasonable spots. Jason, Tommy, and Bethany all thought the one a little further west was the better choice since they felt pretty good after their grocery shopping and lunch. Tommy put away his map, and they resumed their walk.

As they approached the intersection with the interstate, it looked much less busy than any of them had expected. This was the first time they saw major evidence of collisions and abandoned cars that must have resulted from the event. As they took the on-ramp, they noticed there was only one group of people going through vehicles as chaotically as possible. One or two of them left the vehicle they were all working on, moved on to the next one, shattered the glass without checking if the doors were open, and then swung the doors wide. If the trunk was still locked, they went back to the previous vehicle to grab what looked like a pickax to violently open the trunk, hitting it as many times as necessary. Then the rest of the group descended on the now-opened vehicle to pick it clean like a swarm of locusts.

Jason and Amy looked at each other and then motioned for the two teenagers to duck down as they gathered behind a large truck. After deciding they needed to continue toward the mountains on this road and that getting to the side streets would be difficult, they planned to try sneaking past this new gang, just as they had with the first gang by the dump truck they passed the day before.

The plan was for Tommy to lead, moving from the largest vehicle possible to keep the small group shielded from the wild-looking gang. Amy was to follow, then Bethany, with Jason bringing up the rear. They figured this way, Tommy might spot or flush out any potential threats, while Jason could keep an eye on all of them. Their first move was to reach a silver sport utility vehicle. Tommy ran ahead, motioned for Amy, and then moved toward the front of the vehicle. Amy did the same for Bethany, and then Jason followed. As they had experienced from the beginning of their walk, the luggage was their biggest difficulty, but otherwise, it went just as planned. They kept moving this way for about 500 yards. The first semi-trailer truck they encountered initially brought them relief due to its size, until Bethany pointed out that their legs were clearly visible on the other side. Carefully, they got past the trailer part, using the wind fairings to their advantage and resting behind the large tractor. From that point on, they avoided semis whenever possible.

Tommy suddenly realized they weren't going to be able to sneak past the gang this time. One of the gang members spotted Amy as she crouched and ran toward the car Tommy was hiding behind. The gang member ran toward the small group, and Tommy recognized his old campmate, Charley. Charley saw Tommy at the same moment and ran toward him instead, grabbing the backpack Tommy wore across his chest with a devilish grin. Tommy struggled to pull away, off balance but using all his strength. Charley seized one of the straps on the pack, dug his heels into the pavement, and yanked. Tommy, still off balance, decided to try spinning to his left. It worked! Kind of… Charley managed to reset his grip on the strap.

Tommy yelled, "Why?"

Grinning evilly, Charley yelled back, "Why not?"

Seeing his opportunity and regaining his balance, Tommy grabbed the strap himself and pulled Charley toward him. When Charley was close enough, Tommy forcefully shoved him back. This put Charley off balance just enough for Tommy to finally pull away and dance out of reach.

The rest of the gang refocused and began to approach the Browns.

Bethany imploringly cried out, "Mom!"

Tommy, his heart in his mouth, realized this was the same gang from the airport, the same gang in the dump truck, and he saw that Charley was now behind the gang leader, and all of a sudden…

"Toooommmmy! Your moooommmy is calling! Toooommmy! Mommy's boy! Tommy Mommy!"

The gang broke apart and started running toward them.

Jason yelled, "Run!"

The little group sprinted toward the mountains, with all three of the Browns desperately pulling their roller suitcases behind them. Tommy ran in front since all he carried were two backpacks, allowing him to focus solely on running. He looked back and saw Jason and Amy struggling with both Jason's suitcase and Amy's larger, much heavier bag. Tommy ran back and told Amy to drop the bag, and he would help Jason. She looked at Tommy with wild, terrified eyes and nodded mutely, then dropped the handle and ran. Tommy and Jason were able to pick up their speed. Bethany was just ahead of them, struggling herself.

Jason, as quietly as he could manage but still loud enough for Tommy to hear, said, "I'm going to drop my suitcase and get Bethany to drop hers, so we can save Amy's."

Tommy nodded just in time to see Jason drop his bag and yell to Bethany to drop hers. Tommy and Jason immediately sped up, and after processing what Jason told her, Bethany dropped her suitcase and was able to run at almost her full speed. Tommy saw the two women running —their hair flailing and blowing in the wind—as he and Jason picked up Amy's suitcase and increased their speed again.

All the while, the call of "Tommy, mommy's boy" persisted, growing louder as the now-expanded gang joined Charley's deriding chant.

The little group kept running, their legs and lungs burning with effort. Amy and Bethany struggled to keep their footing through tears streaming down their faces, still valiantly running as fast as their burdened feet would allow. Jason's instinct was correct; by dropping the two pieces of luggage, the gang slowed down to loot the bags, with most members stopping. Only Charley and a few others continued the chase and the chants.

Looking over his shoulder, Tommy saw and heard the chants of the chasing gang losing their power. He watched as the gang dropped the chase altogether and Charley turned around when he realized he was the only one running after the little group.

Tommy seized the opportunity and yelled to the Browns, "Keep going, they've stopped!"

The little group continued on, each of them encouraging the others as they started to fatigue. It felt like they were running forever when Jason looked back and told the others he didn't see the gang anymore. They kept jogging, finally slowing to a walk when all four of them turned around, unsure of how far they had run, knowing only that they had escaped the gang, dodging immobile cars, and heading toward the mountains. Amy looked at Jason and broke down.

"I can't do this!" she said, her face in her hands.

Jason embraced her.

"I can't."

"We've got to keep going; there's no place else to go," Jason said tenderly, apologetically.

"I can't do it. The walking is so hard; my feet hurt more than they ever have. I have blisters on my blisters. We lost your suitcase… and Bethany's, and almost lost mine and all my…" Amy broke down again.

She continued, "I can't lose you, I can't lose Bethany; they almost got Tommy!"

"We can't stay here. What about the Muellers?" Jason offered consolingly.

"The Muellers?" Then, comprehending, "The Muellers!"

"Yes, they moved here a year ago."

"Where are they? Do you even know?"

"I actually have their address. I got Mickey and Cheryl a postcard in Milan and was going to send it; it was one of the few I actually forgot to mail. Here, let me get it." Jason reached into his messenger bag and pulled it out.

"Tommy, do you still have the map of Denver?"

Tommy got the map out, and they figured out that the Muellers lived on the west side of the city, luckily not far from where the little group was heading. They also guessed their approximate location after looking for cross streets or highway signs.

Jason looked up at Amy.

"I think I can do it."

"Shall we try to camp in the park we found on the map too?" asked Amy.

"Yes, but let's be very careful."

Bethany nodded in silent agreement. She looked numb from the experience. As they walked to the highway exit, looking bedraggled and each reflecting on their close call with theft at best, and who knew what kind of violence at worst, every one of them was also taking a mental inventory of what they personally lost, as well as what the others lost. It was easier to start with what they still had. Amy still had her large suitcase and her bag holding her purse; Tommy still had his large backpack and his daypack, while Jason kept his messenger bag, and Bethany saved her daypack. While these were small sacrifices for what might have been a much worse encounter, they still felt monumental in this new world the four of them were experiencing for the first time. Even though each of them left things back at the airport, there was at least some semblance of security where they'd left them. This loss was personal and important since they chose each piece with careful consideration of the requirements for the walk or a deep desire not to leave it behind. Some items were necessities, like clothing and toiletries; some were sentimental, like Bethany's teddy bear she had kept since infancy; and some were hopeful, like Jason's laptop computer. Their personal losses and the inevitable difficulties of their journey were beginning to sink in.

Bethany was walking along, arms hanging beside her, her backpack on her back, with a long and vacant stare, occasionally letting big, slow teardrops fall from her cheeks. Tommy approached and gently asked her how she was doing. She looked at him, her eyes swimming, shook her head, and broke down in sobs. Tommy embraced her without saying anything, and she let her head fall on his shoulder, her sobs shaking her whole body. Jason and Amy looked back and came to embrace them both as the late afternoon sun began to lose its heat. The four stood still with nothing to say.

~~~

The little group didn't like the look of the park; it seemed to have been taken over by unsavory-looking people—something more like those who had no place else to go, creating a disorganized city made of cheap tarps, cheaper tents, plastic sheeting, scrounged lumber, and old signs. They found a small pocket park not far away that seemed to have been bypassed by the park campers.

Bethany still wasn't talking much, just gently acknowledging others with nods, head shakes, and occasional quiet monosyllables. However, she seemed to listen and pay attention to everything and everyone. Of the four, she appeared to be the jumpiest, startling at the smallest sudden sounds or movements. Once they settled down—Tommy giving up his sleeping bag to Bethany and Jason and Amy sharing Amy's blankets—the group, which had become even more family-like, fell asleep quickly, exhausted by their ordeal, and slept well because it seemed they had found a good place to camp in seclusion.

Day Eleven

Amy stood still, her coffee in her makeshift cup, breathing the morning coolness deep into her lungs. She had always loved places on the edge of mountains, and even after the horrible experience of the day before—perhaps because of it—she appreciated it even more than usual. Amy noticed the smoke rising from the little community's campfires. She made a tiny campfire to warm some water for coffee and oatmeal, small enough that it didn't give off much smoke at all. Jason had taught her how to make these fires early in their relationship so their location wouldn't be given away while on a hunting trip; a skill passed down from his grandfather during their camping and hunting trips. She looked back at her husband, daughter, and their "adopted stray dog" of a son, whom they had come to love as one of their own. The night's rest must have been necessary since Amy was the only one up. Jason, uncharacteristically, was still asleep under the blankets they had shared the night before. She heard Bethany's quiet crying in the middle of the night, causing her heart to ache with a longing to hold her daughter as she had when she was a toddler and tell her everything was going to be okay. Tommy was using a makeshift tarp as a blanket and had added an extra layer; he seemed to be sleeping alright.

Amy knew that what she had said to Jason the afternoon before was still true. She was unable to go on. There was no way she had the physical or emotional strength to make it home to Sacramento. Her life in the halls of academia had poorly prepared her for such a journey. Looking west, she made out the mountains between the suburban trees. She hoped that if things didn't return to normal, they would be able to figure out a way to return—whether by stagecoach or steam engine train. She shook her head. Who would have thought, even two weeks ago, that an idea like that might reasonably come to her mind? But here it was. Still, she hoped the Muellers would be accommodating, at least until they got their bearings and could more constructively figure out a way forward. She wondered how many others were trying to determine their future. Was it worldwide? It certainly was nationwide; that much she had learned from Jason. He had shared with her that he thought it was a global phenomenon. The estimated number of dead she had initially heard, and then hearing from Jason that those numbers were probably low, was staggering. How were people dealing with that? How many families were more lost than they were, even though they had never left their homes? The beginnings of this new world were turning out to be brutal.

Amy shook her head again and decided her little family needed to get moving if there was any chance of reaching the west side of Denver by tomorrow evening. She gently shook each of the sleepers and whispered in Jason's ear that the coffee was fresh, hearing a comforting and agreeable groan from him. She sat down with him, both of their cups in her hands, looking forward to seeing old friends, while concerned about the next couple of days and what their future held.

~~~

Getting back to the road took a little while as they wove through the side streets. As they walked, their senses were heightened from their experience the day before. Jason and Tommy were very defensive, while Amy and Bethany were quite skittish, jumping behind the nearest cover whenever they perceived a sudden sound or motion. By late morning, they cautiously moved onto the on-ramp, crouching below the line of the cement safety barriers and occasionally peeking over them to see what lay ahead. Numb from their experience the day before, the group had not noticed that once they got onto the interstate, the level of foot traffic increased from almost none to a small but steady number of people using the interstate as a quicker way to navigate the city. They also spotted a few bicycles for the first time. Jason was surprised he hadn't seen any evidence of horses or horse-drawn vehicles since the airport, where they used horse-drawn hay wagons to transport people to medical care facilities. He mentioned this to Bethany, who expressed her surprise as well.

The plan and hope was to reach the intersection of the two major interstates in Denver. Tommy guessed it was about ten miles away from where they started. Even at two miles an hour, he hoped they would reach their goal by mid-to-late afternoon. Jason and Amy were nervous about gang violence in the area and wanted to stop either a mile or two before or after the intersection to reduce their risk. They all agreed to make the decision at the South Platte River.

After an hour of walking, the group came to an overpass and saw smoke rising from underneath. As they grew closer, it appeared there was an area with a couple of repurposed food trucks or trailers serving food. This was the first underpass they had encountered in a couple of days that wasn't turned into a camp. Jason walked up to one of the trailers, and they told him they were serving grilled tacos. He asked what they cost, and they responded with, "What do you have?" This startled Jason because, up to this point, everything had been done with the cash they still had.

"What do you mean?" asked Jason.

"Do you have anything we might use or want?" replied the guy behind the window.

Jason smelled the taco meat cooking and saw a woman behind the trailer making tortillas over a metal disk placed above a campfire. He also noticed fresh salsa sitting behind the window. The cookstove behind the guy in the trailer was now serving as a makeshift countertop.

"Let me go talk to my family."

Jason walked back to his makeshift family and shared what he had seen.

"Do we have anything to barter with?"

"I don't know. The last time we bartered was after we graduated from college, just scraping by when we went to the flea market. Do you remember that?"

"Yeah, I do. Is there anything we can trade? Do we want these tacos?"

Tommy said, "They smell amazing, but we're only a day, maybe two, from your friends' place. We lost so much yesterday. Do we really want to trade away what little we have left?"

Amy looked at Tommy. "Wow, that was a very mature question. I think you're right. But maybe we've got something to buy one taco and at least get some news or a rumor."

"I could try to offer them some cash or maybe some matches or a lighter. They have a campfire, and I'm sure they'll want it more than we'll need it."

"It's worth a try," said Amy.

Looking at Bethany, he asked, "What do you want, kiddo?"

Brightening, Bethany said, "A beef taco with onions, cilantro, and lime, if they have it. Thanks, Dad!"

Jason walked back over, and the others saw him going back and forth with the trailer operator. They looked around and noticed a couple of tables with people who appeared to be working as traders or laborers eating.

Jason returned with a little red and white paper boat containing a couple of tacos, which he handed to Bethany. She took one, squeezed lime on it, and tentatively offered the other one to Tommy, who happily accepted it.

"He took a ten and a lighter and gave me a second taco," he said, shrugging but smiling.

"Did you find anything out?"

"Not much. The guy said there's a growing open-air market at the intersection of Interstate 70 and Interstate 25. Everything is supposed to be bartered, but he did mention a few vendors were accepting cash. He said that's why he took mine. I asked about gangs, and he said he's been hearing a lot about the gang we just escaped from yesterday, and there are rumors of other, larger gangs throughout the city, especially in the already rougher parts of town. He mentioned that many police aren't coming in to work, but those who are are on foot, bike, and mounted patrol near their stations and the downtown area. He said every time he's been at the interstate intersection, he's seen plenty of police."

"That sounds promising," said Amy.

"I guess as we get into more populated areas, things will be safer... unless they aren't. I bet we can gauge what it's like just by looking around and paying attention," said Tommy.

"I hope so; I don't ever want to go through something like we did yesterday again," said Bethany.

The group, feeling a bit of relief, packed up and walked west.

They decided to stop at the South Platte River where it crossed under the Interstate, and as they went down the off-ramp, they saw a large encampment of people under the bridge next to the river. From where they were standing, none of them saw an easy way to get to the river at all, either upstream or downstream. After discussing whether they ought to walk along the roads beside the river, the little group expressed their reservations about straying too far from their route to the Muellers. Tommy volunteered to run up or down the river to search for a place to get drinking water and left the group on the off-ramp. Amy thanked Tommy for volunteering but said he'd be in more danger alone. Each member of the group looked at their water supply, and each had about half a bottle. Jason said he'd rather pay for water at the intersection's open-air market, so the little group pressed on and walked up the on-ramp.

They found out they were only about a hundred yards away from the impromptu open-air market. The market was mostly on the roads but spilled over onto the roadside. It was full of people with pop-up canopies, blue tarps, and ramshackle shelters made from whatever was at hand. There were vendors selling all sorts of goods, but the busiest ones were those offering food items. The food included fruits, vegetables, sacks of flour, beans, and rice, while others sold dried meats. A couple of vendors even sold chickens, beheading and plucking their feathers as they were purchased. There were also others selling already prepared food to waiting customers. The whole atmosphere was one of barely controlled chaos. People mostly bartered, trading one good or item for another, though a few vendors accepted paper money, with silver and gold always welcome. Occasionally, you'd see police walking around or someone dressed in a police or security guard uniform acting as a guard or bouncer for particularly busy locations.

Each of them was easily overwhelmed by the busyness and the large crowds but got into the spirit of the area fairly quickly. They looked for a booth that wasn't too busy so they could get a better idea of how things worked. As before, Jason was the first to approach. They walked up to a place selling military surplus and various bags and packs. The guy running the place wore mismatched military surplus clothing, aviator sunglasses, and had a stubble-covered face. He had just finished selling a backpack to the person in front of them and asked what they wanted.

"Can you tell us what's going on?" asked Jason.

"Sure, sure. What do you want to know?"

"How do we pay for anything?"

"What'cha got?"

"Is it really that basic?" Amy whispered to Jason.

"Will you take cash?" Jason asked.

"No, I don't take cash. Almost no one does. I will take silver unless you have something else to trade," said the vendor, eyeing Amy's unusually large suitcase.

Jason looked at the items on display.

"Is this everything you have?"

"Everything is for sale if the price is right," the vendor replied.

"I'm surprised there are any cops here. Are they actually on duty?"

"They're on duty all right, their own duty," he said, looking around. Then in a quieter voice, "We pay them to be here; the city is barely functioning. If they aren't here, our paying customers aren't here. We were just getting everything taken from us as 'protection' from the gangs. A couple of police sergeants showed up and offered to help... for a price."

"Okay, thanks," said Jason, handing the vendor a twenty-dollar bill.

"That's not much anymore, but I'll take the gratuity," the vendor winked.

The Browns and Tommy walked away, each feeling better informed about the current state of the city after Jason shared his impressions with the rest. They decided to try to find some water and maybe food before they left the area. The group drifted from stall to stall, browsing through the different offerings. When one of them found something of interest, they caught the attention of the others and pointed to it or showed them their find. For each, it felt something akin to normalcy, even though they were at an interstate intersection browsing through an impromptu flea market. It felt good to be among a throng of people doing relatively normal things: buying, selling, haggling. The hustle and bustle of people moving and talking was reassuring.

Until it wasn't.

~~~

Bethany was looking at a red insulated throw, thinking how nice it would be at night after the sun went down, when she felt a hand curl around her upper right arm. Before she could even turn her head to see what was happening, the hand tightened around her arm so much that it hurt. She tried to twist her head to see who had grabbed her when the hand jerked her hard, and she heard a deep, gruff voice tell her not to make a sound. Bethany struggled to keep her feet as she was dragged out of the stall. She felt another hand grab her other arm and begin to lift her so that she was barely able to touch the ground. As the three of them left the stall, she caught a glimpse of her mother's head and attempted to yell, but the first man's free hand clasped over her mouth.

Amy was browsing in another part of the stall, not knowing what she was looking for or even what she was looking at, just enjoying the feeling of doing something normal like shopping and browsing, touching new and used items in the flea market, hearing the sounds, and smelling the aromas of the cooking food. Amy knew Bethany was looking for another layer to sleep a little warmer, and she found a fleece throw with cute stripes in colors she was certain Bethany would love, which she wanted to show her. She looked around to find Bethany... but she was no longer there. Amy panicked and started rushing around the stall until she found Bethany's abandoned backpack. Fearing the worst, she went outside the stall. Still not finding her daughter, she yelled out her name. Getting no response, she called for Jason and Tommy, wildly looking around for any of the three.

The first guy who grabbed Bethany was wearing a yellow tank top with a team logo and dirty blue jeans, his wiry arms, neck, and face dusty with streaks of sweat. The second guy had a salt-and-pepper mustache on his round face and a dirty white t-shirt that barely covered his distended belly, paired with black jeans. Both men smelled of sweat, cigarettes, and the stale scent of cheap alcohol. Their hands felt dirty and gross on her arms. When they whispered to each other, their breath was foul.

Bethany heard her mother's calls and tried to wriggle out of her captors' grips, but they tightened further, causing her to yelp into the rough hand covering her mouth. She bit down hard, feeling her teeth catch the skin of his palm. She clamped down harder. He yanked his hand away, and the other guy cuffed the back of her head. She jerked forward, looked around, and was surprised that no one was witnessing their commotion. The first guy roughly placed his hand back over her mouth, firmly grabbing her cheeks with his thumb digging into her right cheek. Bethany realized she was being dragged, so she picked up her feet to make moving her as difficult as possible. As the two men trying to abduct her struggled against her resistance, she kicked the second guy's right knee with both feet. She felt a crunching in his joint, and his knee collapsed. He let go of her arm, crying out. Bethany took advantage of the sudden shift in her weight and broke away from the first guy's grasp. She was free!

Amy found Tommy first, who ran to her when she called, followed closely by Jason, looking around with great intensity in his eyes. Bethany was nowhere to be found. Amy started to grab anyone around her, asking if they'd seen her daughter. No one had seen her. Jason and Tommy began to go from stall to stall. Every once in a while, Tommy jumped up and swung his head and eyes, sweeping the area for any sight of Bethany. Then both of them spotted a commotion out of the corner of their eyes.

Bethany quickly backed away, then spun around and started to run back the way they had come. Ducking low, she darted through the crowd, zigzagging with her head down. Before she realized it, she ran into her father. Jason grabbed her shoulders, pulled her up, and hugged her tightly.

Jason yelled to Tommy and then to Amy. They found Bethany!

"They got me, Dad! They got me, but I got away! I was afraid, but I beat 'em and I got away!" Bethany broke down sobbing in her father's arms.

"You're a tough kid, and I'm proud of you, honey!"

Jason felt her shaking and put her down carefully so they could start walking away from the area until they found a spot where they could keep their eyes on everything around them. Tommy and Amy joined them,

Amy shedding tears of relief, pulling her own suitcase and carrying Bethany's backpack. Bethany bravely shared her story with everyone, gradually gathering herself with her mother holding her hand and stroking her hair. Amy apologized several times for not keeping a better eye on her, and Bethany kept telling her it was okay. Tommy saw the strength in Bethany's tear-filled eyes as she told her story and answered her parents' questions. She knew she had come very close to some very bad things happening to her, but she kept her wits and was able to get away and back to her father just in time.

The little group didn't see any more threats or abductors, and after resting, they decided to get going. Jason slipped away and returned with a homemade peach pie for everyone to share in celebration of Bethany's safety and bravery. During the group's stops, Amy asked people who seemed trustworthy about places to camp on their way to the western outskirts of Denver and received a couple of recommendations. The group started walking west, chatting about what they felt might be the best place to camp for one more night before reaching the Muellers. Amy looked exhausted but happy after the frightening ordeal as they left the informal market.

~~~

The extended Brown family discussed several nearby parks and urban lakes but decided against them after noticing what those kinds of places were beginning to attract. They opted to take a chance on a church they had heard was near one of the parks, hoping it might provide better and safer assistance for those in need.

They walked a couple of miles further down and then a couple of blocks off the highway to reach the church. It was getting late in the afternoon, and the sky was beginning to darken. The little group was exhausted after their day and hoped for a nice yard or park to camp in an area that might be a bit safer. As they approached the church, they didn't see anyone camping, but they did notice some people enjoying the cooling evening at the park across the street.

Tentatively, they walked up to the door of the church, and Jason knocked. A gentleman opened the door and welcomed them, telling them the door was always open and that they were just starting preparations for their evening meal. Looking at each other, they followed the gentleman.

He introduced himself as an elder of the church and asked where they were from.

"We're from California and got stuck at the airport on our way home. Tommy here was traveling home from summer camp in Texas, and we were on our way home from Italy on a working vacation," Jason explained.

"We're happy you've made it safely to our church. We've been hearing reports that there are parts of the city without rule of law. By the way, we have several people here whom we are hosting and helping since the event."

"How are you making dinner?" asked Amy.

"Oh, we have gas stoves and ovens, and we've been lucky enough to have church members with gardens and other goods, so we can make soups and stews. Tonight we're serving ham and bean soup with cornbread. Here's our lead pastor."

Everyone introduced themselves to the pastor and his family. His kids were running around the meeting hall, and his wife immediately excused herself to corral them. Amy and Bethany followed, offering to help. Tommy and Jason asked if there was anything they could do.

The lead pastor said he was unable to think of anything and asked if they wanted to sit and chat while the church members finished preparing dinner. The young man and the older man said they would enjoy the conversation.

"First, though, is there any place nearby where we can sleep?" asked Jason.

"We hope you'll be able to stay with us here in the church."

"We don't want to impose."

"You aren't imposing," the lead pastor said gently. "We're here to serve and share what's meaningful to us."

"Share?" Tommy asked, curious.

"Yeah," the pastor replied with a warm smile. "Have you ever heard of the Great Commission?"

Tommy shook his head. "I don't think so. My family goes to church sometimes, like for Christmas or Easter. Is it related to that?"

The pastor nodded thoughtfully. "In the Bible, in Matthew, Jesus asks his followers to go out and share their faith with others, inviting them to learn more about God's love. It's about spreading a message of hope. Have you ever heard the word 'gospel'? It actually means 'good news.'"

Tommy blinked, taking it in. "I didn't know that," he said, his voice uncertain.

Tommy's family wasn't big on church. They'd show up for holidays, weddings, or baptisms, and they always said a quick prayer before dinner. He'd heard friends mention something about Confirmation Classes, but it wasn't something his family did. Sundays were usually just a free day, and he figured his parents liked it that way too. He had more questions but felt a bit shy about asking them.

Jason inquired about where they would stay.

"I'll show you after dinner. You can leave your bags here by where we're sitting."

"How many people are staying here?"

"Well, we've seen a lot of variation so far; we only just started to do this after a week without power. The first couple of nights, there were a lot of people from the area who showed up to eat some hot food and share companionship and news. The elder you first met when you arrived was actually the one who came up with the idea. He biked over to our house, presented the idea, and I talked to the other elders, who were enthusiastic about it. Most of them help when they can, and the others have assisted by spreading the word for volunteers. I guess we have about thirty folks or so who aren't from the church. There are usually a few looking for a place to stay—some homeless, some looking for community and conversation, and some like yourselves, travelers. Although you're the first we've seen who are planning to walk such a long way."

"We don't think we're headed back to California just yet," said Jason. "We've experienced a rough few days, and my wife especially wants to stop at some family friends and reevaluate."

"I still want to go," offered Tommy quietly.

Jason didn't seem to notice, but the lead pastor looked at Tommy and raised an eyebrow.

The lead pastor asked, "What do you think has happened? What do you think is going to happen?"

"I volunteered at the operation center in the airport and got to hear an awful lot about what was going on, and I'm still not sure anybody really knows what happened. We'd get reports from the mayor's office, the governor's office, and military and police; we even heard some pretty reliable rumors from high-level scientific meetings involving academic, government, and industry scientists, and it sounds like they have no clue either, which is causing quite a lot of tension among them, with shouting matches and accusations flying around during particularly heated meetings. As far as what's going to happen, I really think we need to plan on not having electricity ever again, but hope we do get it back, and the sooner, the better."

"Really? That's news to me, but most of us at this church aren't part of any real power in the area. We're just normal people. We've been lucky; it seems there is still some local police presence around here. We've heard other stories like what your family experienced."

"Oh, I'm not related to the Browns," interrupted Tommy.

"Oh? I hadn't heard that; I apologize. I guess you've been through a lot together; you certainly act like a family. How did you find each other?"

Tommy told the story of their early days together, with Jason adding details whenever Tommy forgot something or disagreed about a specific point. Together, they recounted their journey from the airport to the church. The lead pastor listened attentively, asking occasional questions. At the end, he thanked them for sharing and expressed how much he learned about the situation they were all facing.

"Jason, do you know how widespread this electrical outage is?"

"From what I heard, it is definitely at least across several states. Based on what I saw at the airport, my guess is that it covers at least all of North America and maybe even the globe. I haven't heard any engines or planes of any sort, and Denver is an international airport. I can't even imagine the loss of life this has caused and continues to cause."

"I was afraid you were going to say that. Thanks for the reminder; we'll certainly add all those people and their loved ones to our prayers this evening. Speaking of which," the lead pastor glanced down at his self-winding watch, "dinner ought to be ready."

~~~

Tommy and the Browns collected their meal with everyone who showed up for nourishment. The group was diverse, including the obvious homeless, many church members, community members, and what appeared to be a handful of travelers like themselves, but with nearer destinations in mind among other people of various backgrounds.

The travelers to California joined the lead pastor and his family in conversation. Amy and Bethany quickly struck up a friendship with the pastor's wife and kids, while Tommy and Jason continued their discussion more lightly, everyone getting to know one another better.

The lead pastor stood up and began the meal with a table grace and prayer: "Dear Lord, bless this food to the nourishment of our bodies and us to Thy service. And let us keep in our prayers the people who are suffering and dying and their loved ones in this trying time. In Christ's name we pray, Amen."

Amid the murmured "Amens," the hearty meal of bean soup and cornbread was eagerly enjoyed by everyone in the room. The Browns and Tommy couldn't remember enjoying such a simple meal. The warm, freshly cooked food was clearly appreciated by all those around them as well.

After dinner, most of the church members said their goodbyes. While it was still light enough to see, the little group gathered their suitcases and bags and followed another volunteer to a room that looked like it was used for youth Sunday school. There were several cots laid out, more than enough for the four of them, and to their surprise, lanterns. The lanterns were the kind people used for power outages, made of decorative glass. Each one had a different color of lamp oil: one had red oil, another had green, and a third had blue oil. Fresh, clean pillows and neatly folded blankets were laid out at the end of each cot. The church member said good night and mentioned that a cold breakfast would be served at eight the following morning.

Tommy and Bethany flopped, or what passed for flopping, onto the cots. Bethany playfully laid her head on the linens, took a big sniff, and let out a contented sigh.

"Clean sheets always smell so good to me!"

Her mother replied, "I've always liked them too, but I never thought I'd get teary over them. It's been so long."

Jason pulled two cots together and sat on one of them, joined by Amy. The four of them just sat there with silly grins on their faces, looking at each other and enjoying something they had taken for granted until recently.

They chatted about everything and nothing until the sun went down, preparing their beds and absentmindedly looking through their gear. It was only a few days, yet they were amazed at how beat up their bags and suitcases were. Tommy asked Amy to help him sew up a couple of rips. She was pleased by the request and happily showed him how to sew the rips better, even helping him with a patch made from a piece of a torn pair of pants he had accidentally packed at the airport. The church thoughtfully provided a wash basin, which each member of the little group gratefully used. As the light began to fade, everyone started to yawn. Jason looked around at his sleepy, mismatched family and encouraged everyone to get to sleep. The other three, even the young teenagers, didn't need much convincing to lay down in the clean sheets, which felt magical after days of sleeping on the ground and on the airport cots.

Day Twelve

In the morning, the four of them slept in until the sun shone on their faces and then made their way to the dining area. They were warmly greeted by a couple of volunteers from the night before, who asked how they had slept. Amy appreciatively told them it was the best night of sleep she had ever had, and Bethany eagerly agreed, telling the volunteers how much the clean sheets meant to her. The volunteers expressed that they hadn't heard such glowing reviews of their work and how much it meant to them to hear it.

Breakfast turned out to be cinnamon biscuits and scrambled eggs from someone who kept chickens in their backyard. There was no milk or juice, so Jason and Amy chose coffee, while the two teenagers drank hot tea. The four of them kept marveling at the generosity and how much these small things meant to each of them. It cannot be understated how energizing this small respite was for the four travelers. Jason mentioned they needed to think about heading to the Muellers, who he hoped they would reach that day. He noted that when he looked at the map, he thought it was only about five miles away. Tommy and Bethany pleaded with Amy and Jason to wait just a little bit longer, dreading the hike ahead. Amy pointed out that the longer they waited, the hotter the hike would be. Reluctantly, the teens saw her point, and with comically exaggerated moaning and groaning, they went back to their temporary room and packed up for the day ahead.

When everyone was ready, they made their way to the lead pastor and his family, who had returned to the church while they were packing, to say their goodbyes. Jason and the lead pastor exchanged promises of updates and contact information, including phone numbers, in hopes of a future with electricity. Then they put on their packs, grabbed Amy's suitcase and Tommy's other backpack, and started back to the road to walk to the Browns' old friends.

~~~

The late-summer grass in the neighborhood was getting pretty long and beginning to dry out, but there were one or two scattered houses along every block with neatly trimmed lawns. The little group even waved to a guy who was mowing his lawn with a reel mower in front of a pale-yellow house with white trim and carefully tended bushes.

"That's how they're doing it!" exclaimed Tommy.

"Yeah, my dad used to make me mow our lawn with one of those about a million years ago. I swore I'd get a gas mower if we ever owned a house, and now that mower is going to be a really awkward paperweight," said Jason.

Tommy chuckled at the thought of a riding lawn mower atop a well-kept desk.

The little group kept walking down the otherwise well-kept street.

"It's been a while," said Amy, looking at Jason. "I hope they can help."

"I bet they will," offered Jason. "Mickey has always been a great friend, and you and Cheryl always seemed to get along so well."

"Yeah, but I haven't spoken to Cheryl in ages."

"Mickey and I keep in touch at least once a month. We'll be fine."

"Do I know the Muellers?" asked Bethany.

"Yes, they're the family that left Sacramento a year ago. They have a couple of boys, but we haven't visited their house here in Denver since they moved," replied Jason.

"Here it is! Wow, it looks just like the pictures Cheryl sent."

They walked up the sidewalk edged with long grass to the front door. Jason tried to ring the doorbell, then sheepishly smiled at his wife before knocking on the door.

"Hello?" came a tentative and confused-sounding answer.

"Hey Mickey! It's me and Amy; we walked all the way from Sacramento!" joked Jason.

The door opened, and a grinning man in shorts and mismatched socks looked out with a shocked expression on his face.

"Well, I'll be…"

"Don't just stand there; invite us in!" insisted Jason with a big grin on his face.

"Come in, come in. Honey! You'll never guess who just walked through our door!"

A pretty, casually dressed, middle-aged brunette hurried in, gasping as she rushed over to hug Amy and then Jason. "Bethany! I didn't know you had a son! Is he adopted?"

"I'm not a son, I'm just tagging along with the Browns," said Tommy bashfully.

"Tagging along? All the way from Sacramento… Hey, there's no way you walked from Sacramento; you were just in Italy. What's going on, Jason?" said a confused Mickey.

"I'll tell you what, Mickey Mouse, you'll never guess what happened to us after our trip to Italy."

Cheryl steered everyone into the family room, and after everyone sat down, Jason shared the story of what had happened since the event. Amy offered occasional quiet corrections, while Bethany and Tommy enthusiastically contributed where they could. Cheryl and Mickey were rapt listeners, expressing their shock, sadness, disappointment, and laughter—asking questions throughout the story. They shared how glad they were that Tommy found the Browns and voiced concerns with Amy about Tommy's reappearing antagonist.

"He's no big deal; I've been dealing with him all summer," said Tommy bravely. Even if he didn't completely feel it, he wanted to believe it, anyway.

"The boys are over at a friend's house and will be back any time," said Cheryl.

"How old are they now?" asked Amy.

"Oh, Brad is a senior and will be eighteen this year, and Curtis is a sophomore and will be sixteen. It's hard to believe we'll have another driver in the house!" said Cheryl, who quickly realized what she had said and put her hand over her mouth. Everyone laughed at what had become a theme of the day – reflecting on the habits of a lifetime, now changed so drastically.

The adults then started catching up since the last time they had seen each other. Bethany and Tommy excused themselves and went to the backyard porch swing. The two teenagers sat next to one another in silence, absorbing the sounds of an engineless world. It felt like this was the first time they had stopped and taken a breath since they left the airport. The night before at the church was the first glimpse of what they were now experiencing, but this moment felt more real, more present. They heard birds and insects up close and the sounds of kids playing several houses down, with the adults behind them in the house occasionally laughing. Mrs. Mueller opened the sliding glass door, its unique sound announcing her arrival, and asked if the kids wanted anything to drink as they were going to open a bottle of wine. They inquired about what was available, and she said she had water and sun tea, but she could make limeade with the last of her limes. The two of them agreed that sun tea sounded great, as neither wanted to take the last of the limes.

Mrs. Mueller's interruption broke the reverie, and the two of them started to chat about nothing and everything. They talked about the walk so far and how amazed they were at what they had experienced before they even left Denver. Bethany expressed her concern about what they might encounter between Denver and Sacramento and hoped they might stay here until the electricity came back on.

Tommy, however, didn't want to stay there; he didn't think the electricity would come back on anytime soon. He just wanted to get home to his mom and dad, something Bethany already had. He had feelings for Bethany and her family, and over the past few days, they had come to mean so much to him. He didn't want to hurt their feelings or betray their trust. Certainly, he was concerned about his ability to make it that far. If Jason was right, it was almost 1,100 miles to their home—much more walking than Tommy had ever imagined doing in his whole life, much less all at once. He and Jason guessed it might take them two months if they never found a ride in a wagon or bikes for part of the trip. Whenever he felt overwhelmed by the challenges ahead, he remembered a saying his grandmother used: "The best way to eat an elephant is one bite at a time." He adapted it in his mind to the more familiar phrase, "one step at a time."

"Hey, are you there? I said it sounds like the brothers are back."

Tommy shook his head. "Sorry, I was thinking about our walk across Denver and how nice it will be to rest."

"Let's go meet them. It'll be nice to meet some people our age."

The moment Bethany and Tommy walked into the house, there was an obvious change. The air felt charged and electric, as if the volume had been turned up. Brad and Curtis were in the kitchen asking their mother what snacks they were allowed to have. The two younger teens didn't know which was which, but they both looked flushed as though they had run home. They were both blonde and athletic, with one taller than the other. There were grass stains on their shorts, as if they had been playing some sport too. When Tommy looked down, he saw both boys were still wearing cleats.

"Hey, how's it going? Where did you come from?" said one of the brothers.

"Boys, I'd like to reintroduce you to the Browns and their young friend, Tommy. We've known the Browns forever, and they've gotten stuck here in Denver on their flight home. They met Tommy in the airport terminal. Tommy is from Sacramento, too." Looking at their guests, she continued, "These are my boys, Brad and Curtis. Brad is the taller one in the soccer jersey, and Curtis is the shorter one wearing the blue shirt."

"Mom!" protested Curtis. "I'm growing."

"Growing rounder, not taller," chided Brad.

"Snacks sound great! Can I help make something?" offered Bethany.

Tommy awkwardly offered to help, too.

Cheryl Mueller, feeling the great mood their guests and sons brought to the house, directed the teenagers to put together an impromptu snack platter filled with crackers, cheeses, and sausages. There were a few sad grapes, but a couple of different olives and pickles on the platter for everyone to enjoy while they sat in the family room to get to know one another better.

~~~

The three teenage boys snuck away from everybody else outside to play catch with an old football they kept on the back porch. The late summer evening began to cool off as it does on the front range of the Colorado Rocky Mountains. The heat still lingered in the buildings and on the roads and sidewalks, but a coolness was settling in around them, with the trees and shrubbery absorbing it first. The birds twittered their happiness, finding their evening meals of flying insects and worms on the ground, some taking their daily baths to cool off and clean their feathers for warmth later in the night. The squirrels chittered away in the trees at the three boys throwing a football to each other, interrupting their evening nut gathering and letting their neighbors know all about the rudeness of the humans.

The conversation was mostly teenage boys getting to know one another – what sports they enjoyed, what games they liked to play, what the girls were like where they lived, and other things that helped each boy understand where the others were coming from and whether they could be trusted, tolerated, or avoided. The three boys naturally came to think of the new boy as someone worth exploring deeper with more inquisitive questions, the answers to which teased out each other's character.

"California is a long way away. Do you miss your folks, or are you enjoying this break?" asked one of the brothers.

"It is a long way. I do miss my parents; I guess that's weird?" He scratched the back of his head. "But yeah, I want to go home. The sooner, the better."

"How are you going to get there? The Browns sure seem to want to stay here until the electricity comes back on or some sort of transport like a covered wagon or something," said Brad.

"They've been very good to me. They've almost become like family, but they aren't. I don't want to upset them, so it's a hard decision I have to make. I don't think Jason or Amy believe I'm mature enough to make that choice, and I think they feel a certain sense of responsibility to take care of me," said Tommy, throwing the ball to Curtis.

"I'd want to get home to my mom and dad too, even if Brad was still living with them."

Ignoring his brother's dig, Curtis said, "If it were me, I'd be trying to figure out a way to get home, too. I bet your mom and dad are going

113

crazy worrying about you. Hey, do you know if there's any sort of mail happening?"

"No, I think I heard Jason saying there were rumors going around at the airport that the post office was trying to get mail going again, but that has to be a huge job. I wonder how many packages have gotten lost in all this?"

Brad offered, "Maybe your parents have tried sending letters to you. Have you tried to send them anything?"

"The last thing I sent them was a postcard from summer camp telling them I'd be seeing them in a few days."

"Well, you definitely need to write them a letter," said the high school senior, trying to sound wise beyond his years.

"Is the post office still picking up your mail?"

"It stopped for a few days, but we've been getting mail in our mailbox, even though there are fewer and fewer every day."

"I will write that letter as soon as I wake up tomorrow."

Day Thirteen

"Good morning! Sleepyhead!" exclaimed Mrs. Mueller to Tommy as he came down the hall yawning.

"Am I the last one up?"

"No, honey, you're the first one up from your hiking club. Mickey and the boys are in the garage doing chores and fixing things. Ever since the event, we've been trying to be very careful with everything we have."

"I guess we're all a little tired."

"That was pretty obvious last night. After you came back in with the boys, all four of you got really boring, really fast."

"Sorry."

Laughing, Mrs. Mueller said, "Don't be, honey. After we heard all of your stories, it was amazing you made it as late as you did. Come to think of it, I'm surprised not to see Jason yet. He must really be wiped out."

"This *was* the first night any of us had been in a real bed since the beginning of summer. I don't know why *I'm* awake; I mean, I'm a teenager!"

Mrs. Mueller laughed again as Tommy walked out to the garage.

One of the boys was edging the lawn with an old manual edger, and the other was cleaning up behind him with some old, beat-up looking hand lawn trimmers. There was a broom leaning against the garage door frame, and Mr. Mueller was loudly reminding the boys that even if there was no power, their lawn was still going to look neat and tidy. His two sons groaned and kept their heads down.

Tommy felt a hand clap his back and heard a satisfied sigh.

"I've never had coffee that tasted so good! Thanks, Mickey!" said Jason.

"It wasn't me; thank Cheryl."

"I'm really happy you two have that double burner camping stove! I used to call you old-fashioned for using the white gas version of it too."

"Hey boys! The yard looks great! Why don't you take Tommy and show him around the neighborhood!"

They didn't need to be told twice. They rushed into the garage, dropped their yard tools against the wall, and grabbed Tommy by the arm.

"Wait! I haven't eaten breakf...."

"I'll sweep up!" yelled Mickey after the three boys as they ran off.

The three boys wandered around the neighborhood, the Mueller boys pointing out local landmarks, friends joining the charismatic duo for a block or two and then going their own way. Tommy eventually got a feel for the whole area; in some ways, it was very much like his own home neighborhood, so far away.

Brad asked, "Did you write that letter yet?"

"No, I didn't even get a chance to eat breakfast," said Tommy lamely.

"We grabbed something to eat on the way out to help Dad. We'll go home and get you breakfast so you can write that letter without your stomach growling."

"Hey!" said Curtis, "Have you thought any more about heading home?"

"Yeah, if I could do it, I'd go right now. I think if I packed carefully, I could get everything in my big backpack and make life a lot easier. I still worry about them, though."

"Why don't you write them a letter too? We could give it to them the morning after you leave," said Brad.

"I mean, it's a possibility," said Tommy tentatively.

"When we get home, after you write your letters, we'll pull some maps out of Dad's car. He always keeps some in his glove box 'just in case.'"

~~~

While the Browns and the Muellers decided to go for a walk around the neighborhood in the cool of the evening after dinner, Tommy excused himself with a wink to the brothers and said he wanted some time to himself. He went off to the basement room he was using, next to the brothers' rooms, and started to go through his stuff and write his letters.

Tommy had heard of thru-hikers but had never read or watched anything about them. The experience and knowledge of hiking a long trail along the Continental Divide, Pacific Crest Trail, or Appalachian Trail were not going to translate to his experience of walking from Denver to Sacramento. He regretted paying more attention to wilderness survival topics and almost no attention to thru-hikers.

He tried to think about what someone like that might pack in their bag. He wanted to pack as lightly as possible, but he also wanted to be comfortable. He guessed no one hiked one of those long trails without electricity for a long time. He figured he would need long pants at some point in the journey and set aside the pair he had packed for horseback rides back at Camp Wallace Creek, along with the long-sleeved shirt he had packed for the same purpose. The sweatshirt he packed for the airplane would hopefully be enough as the season became cooler. He packed a pair of underwear, a spare t-shirt, and shorts. He included two pairs of socks in the clothing bag. He couldn't forget his rain jacket either. He had one of the makeshift tarps from the airport, which had proven its worth on the walk from there. He retrieved his sleeping bag and ground sheet from Bethany and assembled his sleeping kit.

Tommy included one of the pots the group used for cooking, and he had the water bottles they scavenged, along with a bottle and hydration bladder he already owned. He snuck upstairs and filled the bottle and hydration bladder, keeping the two scavenged bottles empty, hoping he could fill them along the way if needed. He wondered how they still got water out of the faucet since the airport had hauled it in on wagons after the first day. Back in the room, he packed the lighter and the matches they found for fire-starting. His biggest worry was food. He had learned how important it was in this new world without electricity. The brothers promised to sneak some down, at least for the first part of the walk.

Tommy remembered his conversation with Brad and Curtis, especially Brad; they were enthusiastic about helping him with a shortcut to save time. The brothers took Jason's planned route on highways to Steamboat Springs and pointed out that there were lots of back roads getting him to Kremmling, hopefully saving Tommy several days of hiking along such exposed roads. Tommy still had his compass from summer camp and the map he found in the airport, as well as Mickey Muller's marked-up map.

Going through his gear, Tommy realized he was carrying too much, and the items he packed into his daypack to leave behind were overflowing. He also felt more confident now that he had carefully planned his route with the help of Brad and Curtis. Thinking he was as prepared as possible, Tommy decided to write those letters and read *Watership Down* while he waited for everyone to get home, especially the brothers.

~~~

Dear Mom and Dad,

Hopefully this letter gets home before I do. I got stuck in the Denver Airport and I have decided to walk home. I met a great family named the Browns who are from near Sacramento. They have helped me a lot here in Denver.

We've had a crazy two weeks here. I helped run messages all around the airport for the first few days after the event happened. Mr. Brown helped at the main office and their daughter, Bethany, helped at the first aid station. She's the same age as me and really pretty. Mrs. Brown watched our stuff while she wrote notes about their trip to Italy.

I've got a long walk I need to start in the morning. I hope to see you in two months. When I get a chance, I'll write to let you know how its going.

Love, Tommy

~~~

Dear Amy and Jason,

First of all, thank you for inviting me into your family. I don't know where I might be without all three of you. You have provided me a place to reflect and you have given me so much. Your guidance and confidence in me has helped me better understand my own potential.

I know you won't approve of me heading out on my own, but I cannot stay here in Denver when my family is in Sacramento. The walk from the airport was difficult and I can't blame you for wanting to stop but try to understand me. You have each other and Bethany, you have your family. I need my own parents and brother.

The distance is enormous and the time to get home is equally scary, but I have the will to get it done. I will think of you often and do cherish our time together. Hopefully we will get to meet again. In the meantime, I will write as often as I can.

I need to go now.

Sincerely,

Tommy

~~~

Dear Bethany,

From our first awkward meeting I knew you and your parents would be extremely important in my life. I have decided to go home. As much as I value you and your parents, I need to get home with my own family.

I will be thinking of you often on the long walk ahead and promise to write to you as often as I can. I've taken down the address of the Muellers and hope whatever I write will find its way to you.

The quiet moments we have had together, getting to know one another, has been a new experience for me and I am so glad I got to know you. I hope we can see each other again soon.

Sincerely,

Tommy

Day Fourteen

The sun was slowly rising behind Tommy, and he appreciated its warmth even though it was still late summer. He'd been walking toward the Moffat Tunnel for a couple of hours and hoped he was walking faster than a couple of miles an hour; if that was true, he aimed to reach the tunnel by late afternoon. He'd left the letters on his bed and asked the Mueller brothers to take care of everything he'd left behind. He hoped the early departure would put as many miles as possible between him and Denver before anyone woke up. The route wasn't exactly the same as the one Jason recommended, but it was close enough that he hoped Jason, Amy, and Bethany could guess how he planned to get home in case something went wrong. Looking back, he undeniably felt the tug of the warm bed and the comfort of Jason and Amy's care, but the pull of his own family and adventure was greater. He hoped he wouldn't experience too much adventure, though.

The sun filtered through the trees down to the creek where Tommy found water to fill his bottles. He decided to fill his other bottles too, just in case. So far, the day held no real surprises, but he didn't want to take any unnecessary chances. He seemed to be making pretty good time and hoped to take a nap after lunch. The brothers really came through for him. Their father, Mickey, was a hunter and backpacker, so they snuck some dehydrated meals for him and gave him some water purification tablets. He even got some of their father's homemade jerky and dried sausage.

Tommy still filtered the water through a bandanna to help reduce the texture as he drank it, just like he did on the road out of the airport.

Lunch consisted of a sandwich, some chips, an apple, and cookies. He made lunch himself while everyone was on their evening walk. Tommy figured he would be eating a lot of dehydrated and canned food, so he wanted one more meal that wasn't either of those things. He savored the ham in the sandwich and the juicy apple as he looked back the way he had walked. He stayed on the side of the road, ready to jump into the ditch or the trees, just in case he saw something. The previous days of walking from the airport to the Muellers taught him the value of caution. He didn't need to worry, though; he hadn't seen anyone so far on his walk. With the concern that the Browns might try to follow him and talk him out of his idea, Tommy decided not to take a nap. Instead, he tucked his half-eaten apple and the cookies into the belt pouch of his backpack and headed back on the road to try to make it to the tunnel before nightfall.

Tommy had never hiked this far in his life, and he was starting to feel it all over his body. His shoulders hurt, his legs were weak, and all he could think about was putting one foot in front of the other. His world had become walking, barely seeing anything but what was directly in front of him. Fortunately, the road was clear, with few navigational challenges. His feet were sore. His back ached. He looked up at the sun and thought he might have sunburn on the tips of his ears. One foot, one foot, one foot, one foot in front of the other.

The road split, and he looked up. There it was! The entrance to the tunnel. It was behind a fence he would have to jump, but he'd made it twenty-five miles! He made it! He tried a quick hop, a quick jog, but his legs didn't want to cooperate. Tommy thought about sleeping inside the tunnel but decided against it when he felt the cool wind blowing out of it. He found a good spot a hundred yards in front of and above the entrance. The ground was flat, and he found a couple of sticks long enough to make a tent with the tarp. He built a fire but used three precious matches to get it started. His dinner was a dehydrated backpacking meal meant for two, and he wolfed it down like it was a snack. He'd never been so hungry or sore. Not walking had never felt so good, but anytime he tried to get up, it was a struggle. There was one bottle of water left, and he needed it for the morning. He hoped there would be water nearby or at least on the other side of the tunnel. The map showed the Fraser River on the other side, but he didn't know if it was a reliable river or just a blue line on the map. Tommy didn't even remember falling asleep.

Day Fifteen

The sun woke him up, shining in under his makeshift tarp. At first, he was confused. He shouldn't have seen the sun under his tarp; it was way too early for the sun to be up. Suddenly, he sat up. "What time is it? Oh my gosh, oh my gosh, I slept too late!" he thought to himself. He scampered out of his sleeping bag, not even remembering getting into it. All of a sudden, he realized he didn't hurt like he did the night before. There was some residual soreness in his shoulders and feet, but otherwise, he felt fine! He looked around the outside of his tarp as he stood in the late morning sun, half expecting to see Jason and Amy standing there with disapproving looks on their faces, but there was no one there except for a ground squirrel looking for scraps and finding them in the backpackers' dinner bag, which it shredded into a thousand shiny bits scattered around the campfire ring. Tommy laughed out loud, startling himself with his own voice, and realized he better be more careful or things might end up like they did the first night they camped outside the airport. Remembering, he looked at the repairs Amy made on his backpack. He wished they had joined him, but he was still resolved to make it home before it snowed.

Packing up was easy. Tommy gave up trying to clean up all the thousands of pieces of trash. Based on the map, he knew he was going to be passing *under* the Continental Divide, the imaginary line crossing the United States from Mexico to Canada where a drop of water on one side eventually flowed to the Pacific Ocean and a drop on the other side eventually flowed to the Atlantic Ocean. It was an important landmark for Tommy since it meant he was, in some way, heading downhill all the way home from that point on. Passing under it was kind of funny since he was going to be walking through the tunnel that passed under the Continental Divide. Just then, he realized he didn't have a headlamp to make that walk. He had never made a torch, but he had seen drawings of them in comic books and thought he could make one. He looked around for a stick and tried to see if there was any cloth lying around with which to wrap it. Finding the stick proved to be really easy; the cloth was more difficult. He finally found what looked like an old t-shirt lying in a pile of other rags. The t-shirt was partly soaked in oil and grease; it looked like someone wiped their hands clean with it. Tommy felt lucky to have found it, but he wasn't happy with it. He wrapped it around the stick and then secured it with some bailing wire he found while looking for the t-shirt. Standing outside the tunnel, he lit the homemade torch with one of the last of his matches, being careful to keep the match from blowing out. The dry part of the t-shirt flared brightly and burned quickly away, leaving only ash, but the oily part stayed lit and kept going for a minute until it burned up too. Tommy stood there, mouth agape, not knowing what to do until the thought struck him. "Use the oil-soaked rags, and more of them, then you'll have a real torch!" He quickly went over to the pile of rags and found a big can of something that smelled of old oil, kerosene, or grease. He tightly wrapped the stick with double the cloth this time and secured it with the bailing wire again, then carefully dipped it into the mouth of the can. As he pulled it out of the thick liquid, he saw that whatever it was wasn't a uniform liquid, but an imperfect mixture of everything he smelled. The tip of the torch was covered in some sort of greasy goo. He prayed this time his torch might work.

It worked, kind of. As it continued to burn, it got better. Tommy learned to keep the stick tilted after a few drops of the noxious liquid dripped hotly onto his outstretched hand. As he stepped into the tunnel, he wondered how long it was and hoped the torch might last the whole way. He didn't know how long a homemade torch like the one he held might last anyway.

It turned out the torch lasted about half an hour. As the flame slowly flickered out, he grew concerned about his decision to walk through the tunnel. While the torch was still lit, he heard the scurrying sounds of small animals ahead of him, which he imagined were rats or other rodents. He hadn't encountered any bats, but that didn't stop him from thinking about them. When the torch went out, he stood there contemplating his options. He really only had two practical choices: continue on, running his hand along the wall for some frame of reference, or go back. Giving up and sitting down wasn't in his nature, but a tiny voice in his mind suggested it. He looked over his shoulder and didn't even see the entrance. He thought to himself, "How bad can it be? I'm sure it isn't very far." Tommy turned back around and determinedly started walking, half stumbling toward the western end of the tunnel.

Two and a half hours in, he thought he heard a ghost, or at least he heard moaning and the clanking of chains. The sound frightened Tommy, but he talked himself out of his fear until he was breathing normally again. As he continued forward, more slowly and cautiously, he occasionally heard the moaning again. He realized that what he thought was the clanking of chains was actually an occasional metallic ringing coming from the rails of the train tracks, sounding like a hammer on the rails. Breathing a little easier, Tommy continued forward. Gradually, with his light-deprived eyes, he started to see shapes in the darkness. Along with those shapes, he kept hearing the moaning, which became clearer with every step. The clanging, while not stopping completely, diminished significantly.

As Tommy approached the end of the tunnel, he realized he was hearing a human voice in agony. His stomach tightened with fear at the thought of approaching a dying person. He didn't see anything in the brightening of the tunnel and began to wonder if it was some trick of his ears or an echo. Then he saw a pile of rags outside the tunnel, lying in the middle of the tracks. The moaning, now much softer, was coming from the pile of rags, and he saw a hand loosely holding a rusty old rail spike. Tommy cautiously walked up.

"Hello?" asked Tommy, his voice quavering.

The pile moaned a little more loudly and shifted for the first time since Tommy saw it.

"Hello? Are you okay?"

"Unngh…"

Tommy walked up to the pile of rags and saw they were soaked in blood. It was a person! He noticed cuts all over the person's body and was afraid he saw bone.

"I'm coming up to help you," he said, not knowing what he'd do to assist but feeling compassion for a hurting fellow human. "Holy... Are you okay?"

"Go away!" said a young man's voice.

"You're very hurt. I can help," he replied, relying on his limited wilderness first aid training to remain calmer than he felt.

"I don't want any help. Go away."

Tommy frantically looked around and saw a beat-up day pack he vaguely recognized. "Is that your bag?"

"Leave it alone. Leave me alone." The body attached to the voice collapsed further. Tommy was surprised, but it did. There must be nothing left of that body.

"Are you still with me?"

There was no response.

Tommy approached the pile of rags and blood and gently shook what he guessed was the shoulder. He received no response. Thinking back to his training at Camp Wallace Creek, he carefully shook the shoulder as hard as he dared. Again, there was no response. Looking around, Tommy didn't know how to proceed. He figured the pile in front of him was close to death and that whatever he did wouldn't make the situation worse and would hopefully make it better.

Tommy ran toward what he hoped was the river and was relieved when he found it. He pulled all his water bottles and his hydration bladder out of his pack and filled them. He then returned to find the person hadn't moved. He walked up to the pile and shook the shoulder again. Receiving no response, he checked the young man's vitals and, finding them okay, took his backpack off and dug out the first aid kit Bethany had filled to overflowing. He took it and one of the water bottles over to the person. He started with the arm attached to the shoulder, cleaning it with the water. As he cleaned the arm, he saw the obvious result of a brutal beating —cuts and bruises all over. The number of cuts was overwhelming, and he gingerly taped the larger ones that were oozing blood. As he moved to the other arm and the legs sticking out of a pair of very dirty shorts, he continued to find more injuries. He was worried the other arm might be broken but decided to put that off since it didn't seem to cause any additional discomfort.

Tommy finally turned his attention to the person's face. By this time, he had pretty definitively decided his patient was a teenage boy, as he suspected, and was startled to realize it was Charley! He almost dropped Charley's head in shock. Charley was clearly unconscious but not unresponsive; he occasionally moaned or reflexively pulled away from Tommy's cleaning. With a strong ambivalence rooted in compassion for another human and revulsion for a weeks-long, sometimes violent antagonist, Tommy gingerly cleaned Charley's barely recognizable face. It was clear Charley had been the focus of a brutal beating. His face was swollen, cut, and bruised. Charley flinched so hard that Tommy almost dropped his head when he started to clean an ugly gash on his left cheekbone. Tommy guessed he must have broken his face. Realizing there would be no train in the near future, Tommy tried to stretch Charley out as comfortably as possible and pitched the tarp over him.

Now that Charley was out of the sun and the elements, Tommy tried to stabilize his left arm. The arm seemed fairly stable, but it was quite swollen. Tommy found a couple of sticks and used the self-adhesive wrap Bethany had put in his first aid kit, along with some rag padding he found on the side of the railroad, to splint the forearm. After splinting the arm and with Charley stretched out on Tommy's fleece blanket, Charley finally relaxed.

Tommy walked over to the daypack beside the railroad and realized it was the annual daypack from Camp Wallace Creek, but it was so dirty that Tommy didn't immediately recognize it. He picked it up and brought it over to the tarp.

He was beginning to unzip it when Charley weakly snapped at him, "Leave my bag alone."

Tommy dropped the bag, more shocked by hearing Charley than by what he said.

"Okay, okay, I was just looking to see if you had any more first aid supplies."

Tommy offered the unopened pack to Charley, who feebly grabbed it and hugged it to himself before immediately passing out again.

Tommy decided to leave Charley alone and ate his lunch of cheese, jerky, and dried fruit from the Muellers. The water he had gathered in the bottles was used up tending to Charley, so Tommy decided to go collect more. When Tommy returned, he saw Charley settled into a deep sleep. Tommy hoped Charley would wake up in the afternoon so they could move the tarp to a more comfortable spot than right on top of the train tracks. In the meantime, not wanting to leave the obviously very hurt Charley, he decided to build a fire and read his book.

There was stirring accompanied by moaning under the tarp, so Tommy went to check on Charley. It had been a couple of hours, and Charley was sitting up and blinking.

"Good morning, sleepyhead!" even though the sun was getting ready to dip below the mountainous horizon. Tommy hoped his attempt at light-heartedness might go over well.

"Tommy? Tommy from Camp Wallace Creek?"

"How are you doing, Charley? You were pretty beat up when I found you."

"I, uh, I hurt all over. What's this on my arm?" asked Charley, looking at the splinted forearm.

"I think your arm may be broken. You were unconscious, so I wasn't able to check it very well, and I thought 'better safe than sorry.'"

Flexing his hand and wincing, he said, "I think you might be right; my hand sure doesn't feel right."

"Do you mind if I check you out a little more? I didn't want to do too much."

Charley looked at his body and then at Tommy. Warily, he said, "I guess so. You better not take this chance to hurt me!"

"I'm not like you. That's not what I do."

Tommy checked Charley out more thoroughly since he was awake and could tell him how things felt and if anything hurt. The two of them were less confident Charley's arm was broken, but Tommy thought Charley might have broken a rib or two. When Charley stood up with Tommy's help, he winced, but after they checked, they found a cut on the bottom of Charley's left foot, soaking his sock with blood. They were baffled because when Tommy found the nearly unconscious Charley, he was still wearing his hiking shoes from summer camp.

The two adversaries gingerly made their way to the river, and Tommy helped Charley as much as he allowed him to clean up. They used Tommy's soap, and Charley managed to clean up pretty well. He had cuts all over his upper body and face. Charley let out a loud yelp when he tried to clean his face; the area around his cheekbone had swollen considerably, partially closing his eye.

Tommy, sitting by the river, noticed Charley's mustard-colored shirt for the first time, too busy tending to him to notice before. "Hey, is that your Camp Wallace Creek shirt?"

"So, what if it is?"

"I'm just glad to see you wearing it."

"It's the only one I've got left."

"We ought to clean it."

Turning away and wincing from the rib pain, Charley said, "I can do it."

Tommy offered him the soap again, and Charley grabbed it, almost dropping it in the river.

"Hey! Careful."

"I got it, didn't I?"

Charley sullenly cleaned the shirt while Tommy sat back down, his eyes on Charley.

While Tommy was waiting for Charley, he looked up and noticed what seemed like the base of a ski area. He thought he might be able to make it over to the area and buy or scavenge some supplies to get himself to Steamboat Springs or at least to the next town.

When the two teenage boys made it back to camp, they moved the tarp to a flatter, more comfortable spot. Charley was barely more help than nothing at all, alternately hostile, in pain, and defensive. Tommy explained to Charley that they'd have to share the tarp. Tommy regretted not bringing the larger homemade tarp he had made for the Browns, but this tarp was still big enough—barely. He tried to get Charley to use his sleeping bag, but Charley insisted the light fleece blanket was enough.

Tommy chose a chili mac backpackers' meal to prepare. Charley wolfed down his portion of the two-person meal, awkwardly cradling the bag with his broken left arm and using the shared spoon with his good, but still battered, right hand to get the food to his mouth. He ate so fast that Tommy felt compelled to make another one, this time chicken and rice. Charley ate it as well without so much as a "thank you."

"Did you even taste it?" asked Tommy, trying to elicit some sort of appreciation.

"I ate it, didn't I?"

"You did; you ate it."

Tommy asked Charley if there was anything in his bag that might attract animals. A suspicious Charley asked why, and Tommy recounted the story of his and the Browns' first night away from the airport. Glumly, Charley replied no. Tommy decided not to push his luck and just hung his own bag, trying to keep it away from the ground squirrels and other rodent-like animals he feared might get into it again.

After some jockeying and lots of wincing and moaning from Charley, the two were finally able to lie down to try to sleep. Charley never seemed to find a comfortable position but eventually settled into a restless sleep after a couple of hours. In the middle of the night, after a few tentative patters, the clouds unleashed a torrential downpour. A bolt of lightning and its accompanying crash, seemingly close enough to touch, woke the boys. Both tried to act like they weren't really scared, their eyes wide and breathing fast and heavy. Water streamed down the sides of the tarp, with two streams running through the tent—one at an angle by Charley's head and another, parallel, at Tommy's feet. The wind whipped around, and the rain blew in one open end of the tarp or the other. After an hour of sitting miserably on their individual pallets, the boys, cold, wet, and tired, tried to create a little area of dryness, improvising with portions of the sleeping bag and blanket, rearranging the ground cloth into something like a nest. Still feeling their animosity toward one another, the two boys tried not to touch each other. Exhausted from the previous day or two, Tommy didn't know how long Charley had been hurt. Charley fell asleep, leaning onto Tommy's shoulder. Compassion winning out over loathing, Tommy let him.

Day Sixteen

Morning came as the two boys fell asleep, leaning against each other. The rain was still coming down when Tommy woke up first. He gently laid Charley down, and he curled into the fetal position, starting to snore gently. Looking around, Tommy didn't know what to do. He was sure his backpack was soaking wet, and he didn't know where Charley's day pack was. He felt dejected. Growing up, Tommy loved rainstorms, setting up a cozy blanket on his parents' porch with cookies and hot cocoa, but right now he hated the rain and missed his home so much. Tommy stifled his tears and, turning, looked at the mouth of the tunnel. Just beyond the entrance, he saw it was dry except for a little rivulet running along the downhill side of the tunnel itself. It was completely dry! He decided to try to run for it. He made it into the tunnel, a little wetter for the effort but standing in a much drier place.

Even though he was disappointed that he hadn't thought of it sooner, he felt very proud of himself for moving to a more comfortable location. Tommy then looked around for something with which to make a fire and ward off the cold and damp. Leaning against the uphill side of the tunnel, he saw some partially broken wooden pallets. He decided to break them up and build the fire against the wall to try to reflect more heat toward himself. Patting his pockets, he realized he had used the last of his matches to make the dinner fire last night. He looked across at his drenched backpack hanging in a tree and groaned. He took a deep breath and ran over to his pack. After the wet trip back and forth, Tommy looked through his pack and couldn't find his lighter. He was sure he had packed it! Out of desperation, Tommy decided to use some of his parachute cord to build a fire bow drill.

Tommy was using his bow drill, pushing the bow back and forth, frustrated and unsuccessful, when Charley walked up behind him, grimacing with each step.

"Hey, mountain man! Do you want to use my lighter?" he offered weakly.

"What?!" Tommy nearly fell over as he looked up and saw Charley grinning with a lighter in his hand.

Finally getting the fire lit, Tommy and Charley huddled over the meager flame, warming their hands.

"Thanks for the lighter."

"No problem."

"Did you get any rest last night?"

"Not much, but some."

"Me too." After a pause, he asked, "How did your day pack hold up?"

"You were right, a mouse got into it. It's a small hole, though. I threw the mouse a million miles away."

"You threw it?" Looking at Charley, he added, "Never mind. Did it mess anything up?"

"No."

The two boys sat next to the fire for a while, warming up and drying off. Occasionally, one or the other added another piece of an old pallet to the fire. Each of them dozed off for a while, waiting for the rain to stop. Eventually, late in the morning, they made the hot cocoa that Tommy had brought.

Sipping the hot cocoa and trading the cup back and forth, careful to use their own side, Charley said to Tommy, looking down at the fire, "Thanks. Thanks for taking care of me."

Shocked, Tommy replied, "Sure."

"I mean it, you know."

"Yeah, I had to help."

~~~

The two boys spent the rest of the day trying to keep dry in the railroad tunnel. During a lull in the rain, Tommy ran out with Charley limping behind him to tear down the tarp and grab their sleeping gear. They ended up laughing the whole time at how absurd their situation was. Good-naturedly, Tommy started calling Charley "Limpy," and Charley began calling Tommy "Mountain Mama's Boy."

By the evening, the two boys had rested enough to be in a good mood. They reset the tarp to reduce the blown-in rain just as the cold front accompanying the rain really set in. Tommy was still in his shorts but was wearing his sweatshirt and rain jacket. Charley got his thin Camp Wallace Creek poncho out of his day pack, having to tear open the plastic bag it came in.

Cold but dry, the two boys tried to figure out a better sleeping arrangement. The best idea they came up with was to reset the tarp, this time with the edges touching the ground perpendicular to the prevailing wind in the tunnel. They put on all the clothes they had, used the thin blanket as ground cloth, and shared the sleeping bag fully opened. It wasn't much, but it was all they had.

Day Seventeen

The night passed without incident, the rainstorm finally stopping sometime late at night without the boys noticing. They slept soundly, occasionally struggling with one boy or the other pulling the sleeping bag over himself and leaving the other boy half uncovered.

After waking up, the two boys restarted the fire that had gone out overnight. They made the last two packets of oatmeal Tommy had while moving around, trying to get warm. Charley was still not fully healed, but he was doing much better; the exposed cuts had all scabbed over, and the bandaged ones looked like they would heal well when Tommy re-bandaged them. They faced the grim reality of running out of food and decided to head into town or the Winter Park Ski Area to try their luck there. If things went smoothly enough, they hoped to keep going. Charley decided to tag along with Tommy at least to Steamboat Springs, saying quietly, "If you'll let me."

They still hadn't discussed why Tommy found Charley in such rough condition. Tommy decided to leave the topic alone until he felt it would be met with less hostility.

They walked across the bridge and found the base area of Winter Park Ski Area deserted. The whole area looked untouched in the over two weeks since the event. Charley wanted to break into one of the buildings, but Tommy persuaded him to try the doors first to see if they opened.

The door to the main restaurant in the base area was open, but when they walked in, they were hit with the smell of rotting food. As quickly as they could, they found the main serving section of the cafeteria and grabbed as much food as they could fit into their pockets. Tommy took the food bars, while Charley picked up the candy bars. The two of them separated to search for more items that might help.

Half an hour later, Tommy found Charley with a bottle of liquor. He had clearly already been drinking and took a big swallow.

"You want a drink?" he said unsteadily to Tommy.

"No! What are you doing?"

"There aren't any parents around. I can do what I want!" She took another drink. "I've been doing it a lot since the airport!"

"Don't! It's stupid! We need to head to Steamboat! Hiking there drunk will be awful."

Already slurring a little, Charley said, "Itsh medishinal! My face all...already feelsh better."

"Charley. Put the bottle down. I don't want to hike with a drunk."

"You're not my mother! You're...you're Mountain Mama's Boy!"

"Put the bottle down."

Charley defiantly took another big drink and unsteadily set the bottle on the ground, the entire time staring Tommy in the eyes.

"Let's get out of here."

After Charley turned around and woozily started walking toward the door they came in from, Tommy walked over to a cash register and put some money on it, guessing at the amount they owed.

As Tommy walked out, he saw the tipsy Charley talking to a guy in work clothes sitting on his mountain bike.

"So, you're walking to Steamboat, huh?"

"Yep! All the way!" said Charley.

"Alone?"

"No, no, no…. I've got a hiking pardner!"

Tommy walked up and said, "Hi! How are you doing?" in an exaggerated tone.

"I'm doing alright, Tommy! I just met this really great guy!"

"I'm Jacob," he said, offering his hand to Tommy.

"I'm Tommy," he replied, shaking Jacob's hand.

"Your friend sure seems relaxed," Jacob said, pointing his thumb at Charley.

Hanging his head, Tommy replied, "Yeah, he got into some liquor back there."

"Oh? He'll be fun to walk with. Hey, aren't you two a little young to be out here on your own? Do you have any parents around?"

"My family is in Sacramento, California. I don't know where Charley's family is. But I got stuck in Denver on my flight back home from summer camp, and I decided to walk home."

"You don't want to wait for something else? Like a wagon train or for everything to start working again?"

"I guess I've just lost hope that we'll get electricity again, and I really miss my family."

While the two were talking, Charley wandered over to a post, threw up behind it, sat down leaning against the post, and dozed off.

"What about him?"

"Oh, we went to camp together in Texas. I just found him at the mouth of the tunnel. He was pretty beat up, and I patched him up as well as I could."

"Yeah, he looks pretty rough. Hey, was he part of the gang that came through here a couple of days ago? I heard they went into town and made some pretty stupid decisions."

"I think so. They gave me and some friends of mine a lot of trouble at the airport and in Denver. I know he was part of a gang. I guess they hurt him, or he got hurt and they left him behind."

"Why did you take care of him? Hearing all that, I'd think he was more trouble than he's worth."

"I don't know. My folks taught me you're supposed to take care of others."

"I hope you don't regret it."

"Me too."

Jacob asked Tommy if he had a map. Tommy's map was a little soggy, but Jacob took a pencil out of his pocket and gave him some recommendations for getting to Steamboat. He wished him good luck and told him to be careful in Winter Park.

"Wait! You're going?"

"Yeah, I've got to get to work. If this ever gets past us, I want the lifts to be ready to go."

"You work on lifts?"

"Yes, I'm a lift mechanic. But I have to get going."

Tommy watched Jacob get on his bike and ride off. He then turned around to find Charley and try to get him moving. He found him leaning against the post, still dozing. Shaking him, he got him awake again and made him drink some water. With some resistance, he got him to start on their walk.

After his conversation with the lift mechanic, Tommy hoped they could get to Steamboat in a few days if they were able to hike all day. Looking at the sobering Charley with all his injuries, he wasn't optimistic. He thought Charley would also be difficult because he had never seen him do anything very active at Camp Wallace Creek. The most active Tommy ever saw him was with the gang he joined at the airport and the harassment he and Browns received across Denver. With the shortcuts Jacob gave him, Tommy hoped they would reach Hot Sulphur Springs that night, but he felt he might be overly optimistic.

As the boys came into view of the town of Winter Park, away from the resort, they saw what looked like a few men standing at a sawhorse blockade. On the side of the road were what appeared to be several fresh graves. Straightening his shoulders, Tommy said they should walk straight up to the blockade since they had nothing to hide. Charley replied that Tommy didn't have anything to hide. At that response, Tommy just kept walking, with Charley following him.

"Hello!" said Tommy, waving, before the men at the sawhorses had a chance to respond.

"Hello, boys. You aren't from around here. At least I don't recognize you. What are you doing here?" said a big blond man wearing a plaid shirt, blue jeans, and work boots. He was holding a shotgun that leaned against one of the sawhorses.

"I'm heading home to Sacramento, California."

"That's a long walk. Where are you coming from?"

"Denver. I got stuck at the airport when the event happened."

"Who's your friend?"

Looking over at Charley, he signaled for him not to talk. Tommy said, "He's a friend of mine from summer camp."

"He looks pretty rough for summer camp. Those injuries look newer than a couple of weeks."

"He got beat up by a gang. You haven't seen them, have you?"

"As a matter of fact, that's why we're here. They thought they were pretty tough and tried to throw their weight around. We reminded them about the 'rule of law.' They told us one of their friends was coming to help them. That ain't you two, is it?"

"No sir. We're just heading to Steamboat and then west until I get home."

"What about him?" he asked, pointing to Charley with the barrel of the shotgun, his finger off the trigger for now.

Tommy looked back at Charley and shrugged.

Charley said, "I wanna go home to Salt Lake City. I miss my mom."

Tommy was surprised. He had never talked to Charley about himself or his family. He didn't even know why he was dragging Charley along with him other than obligation and compassion. He'd have to ask him more about that later.

"We thought we'd walk together so we'd be safer."

"How can we be sure you two boys aren't here to break out your friends and cause more trouble?"

Tommy thought that was a good question and didn't have a solid response. He was trying to come up with an idea when the still tipsy Charley abruptly said, "How about you escort us to the other side of town?"

"I don't know about that."

"It wouldn't take more than one or two of you at the most. You've got guns and we don't. We're both carrying packs and aren't able to run very far."

"We don't know if you've got guns or not."

"You can search my bag and his," offered Charley, looking up at Tommy, who nodded.

The big, blonde man approached and had two of his fellow watchmen point their guns at the boys while he searched their bags.

"You seem to be missing one set of camping gear."

Tommy said, "Yeah, my friend was lucky to keep his day pack."

The big, blonde man looked at the two men keeping their guns trained on the boys and nodded, saying, "Go ahead and take these boys across town. If there are enough men there, send at least one with them to Fraser."

Tommy thought it was okay since the first shortcut Jacob had told them about was after Fraser. He wondered if this was how each town they were going to pass through would be. He had never relied on any actual negotiation skills; of course, he'd read about them in books but didn't think he'd need them until he was out of college.

The walk through Winter Park and on to Fraser was uneventful. With the awkward accompaniment of their escort, leaving Winter Park and arriving at Fraser was less dramatic. They didn't have an escort through Fraser, which didn't really change anything other than making it less tense. Throughout the entire time, there was ready access to water, so they took advantage of it and drank whenever they needed to.

On the other side of Fraser, Tommy kept his eyes peeled for the first open fields with a road crossing the main road they were on. He found it easily enough and started to turn onto what must have been a less busy road.

"Can we stop? My foot hurts and so does everything else," Charley asked.

"Yeah, I guess."

Tommy took the opportunity to look at his road map and guessed there wouldn't be a lot of water until they got to Hot Sulphur Springs, which he estimated was about thirty miles away. He asked Charley for his water bottle, then filled all of his own from the Fraser River. When he got back, Charley asked if he had any painkillers. Tommy was surprised he hadn't thought of that himself and dug into his first aid bag to offer Charley some of what Bethany had collected at the airport. After that, Charley thanked Tommy, and the two of them got back on the road.

The boys didn't need to worry about water; they'd find some source or another every couple of miles, so Tommy emptied his extra water bottles. They walked past pastures and by a golf course with overgrown fairways and greens. They strolled through a rural neighborhood, waving to people on their porches or walking their dogs. As they passed houses, they often saw fresh gardens planted nearby. They also noticed that while the people were friendly, they usually kept some sort of firearm nearby. Without electricity, the boys observed that people were more cautious. Tommy wondered aloud to Charley if they might continue to see signs of fear as they walked along. He also wondered how many people made similar decisions to escape into the countryside.

Along the walk on the highway, the boys saw fields of hay, some harvested into big marshmallow-shaped rolls. Cows dotted the landscape of ranch homes and second homes all along their route to Tabernash and then on to Granby. In Granby, a sprawling mountain town, the teenagers walked over a high bridge spanning train tracks and a flowing river. They decided to keep moving and walked along the road as the mountains began to close in around them. After a short while, they saw a now-useless power station of some sort and decided it might be a good stopping point.

After most of a day walking, Charley was barely able to continue, and Tommy was concerned he had pushed him too hard. The boys didn't make it to Hot Sulphur Springs, but they got pretty close. Much of the hike was in the open sun, and after the hard rain, the whole area was much more humid than usual. Tommy didn't want to admit it, but he was tired too. The two boys walked a short distance west of the road into a cluster of large cottonwood trees and set up camp. Tommy estimated they were near the pass Jacob had told him about since they hadn't started any major decline in their walk. Still, Charley did better than Tommy had feared, but not as well as he had hoped.

The boys ate in silence and went to bed under the tarp. Tommy was in his sleeping bag, and Charley was under the blanket. This time, Charley listened to Tommy about taking care of his day pack, borrowing some parachute cord from Tommy to hang it as high as he could reach.

Day Eighteen

After the sun rose and the boys took down their makeshift camp, they began their journey toward Steamboat Springs. A few hours into their walk, they kept catching glimpses of mountains higher than the valley in which they hiked. As they closed in on Hot Sulphur Springs, they both felt hungry and tired of the energy bars they had found in Winter Park. They decided to search for a grocery store in town. The first open place they saw was a gas station, and they walked in. Inside, they discovered the town didn't have a traditional grocery store. It was still pretty early in the day, well before lunch, and the boys asked about food. The person at the counter, who was also the owner, told them what he had and how much it cost. When the boys hesitated, he offered to feed them if they would split a cord of wood for him. The boys jumped at the chance.

"Okay," said the owner, "I've got a splitting maul and a hydraulic splitter. If you both work at it, you'll be done in no time since it's all pine. If you stack it, I'll give you some pie."

Setting down his pack, Tommy offered to take the splitting maul. Charley, with his injured arm in a sling, was happy to let him. The owner showed them how to operate the hydraulic splitter. Charley awkwardly lifted a small log onto the splitter and then pulled the lever back and forth until the log split. He continued to split the log until there were four pieces of firewood. Tommy was much faster with the splitting maul and was able to split three logs for every one Charley managed, but together they split a whole cord of wood in just a couple of hours. They took another hour to stack the wood, restacking the first half-row after the shop owner showed them how he wanted it done.

When the boys came in to eat, it was almost lunchtime, and they were very hungry. The owner's wife came in and insisted they wash up. They enjoyed a lunch of sandwiches made with leftover roast elk and homemade bread, accompanied by pickles and apples. The promised dessert was raspberry pie, which the owner's wife proudly told the boys was made with berries picked from the family's backyard. The boys thanked the couple profusely, and to show their appreciation, Tommy offered to wash the dishes while Charley joined him, not wanting to seem unhelpful.

During the meal, the owner, who grew up in the area, told the boys about another shortcut that would save them some miles. Instead of walking to Kremmling, he mentioned a turn to the north just before they got there. He provided them with some landmarks to help them find it. As it was getting late, the boys wanted to at least make it to the turnoff. His wife gave the boys a couple of extra sandwiches each, and the owner let them shop for groceries at pre-event prices. Tommy and Charley were able to buy some food to change up their meals. The owner's wife encouraged them to buy some mixed spices and suggested they try to make stew when they had the time.

After they said their goodbyes and got back on the road, the two boys hiked for a couple of hours under the mountain spires and then took a nap in the shade of a roadside tree. After their nap, they continued walking, observing long, limbless pine trees lying in tall piles, waiting to be turned into lumber or firewood. They made good time, and when they reached the turnoff, they looked up the dirt road and didn't see any trees along it at all. They decided to refill all of Tommy's water bottles, and Charley even offered to carry two of them. Noticing homes around the turnoff, they decided to keep hiking a couple of miles before stopping for the night. When they did, Charley offered to build a fire while Tommy pitched the tarp. All Charley was able to find were thick, dried twigs from dead brush. He built a meager fire, and the two disappointedly decided not to make stew. Instead, they each ate one of the sandwiches they had been given earlier.

Sitting next to the fire, Tommy said to Charley, "I didn't know you were from Salt Lake City."

"I didn't know you were from Sacramento."

"How did you get to Camp Wallace Creek?"

"My dad lives in Houston and doesn't want much to do with me, but he went to Camp Wallace Creek and thought it might be a good experience. He came once during the summer."

"What did you think of Wallace Creek?"

"It was okay, I guess. I liked it better than his apartment in Houston. He made me read books and write reports when I was in the apartment. I do that all year in school; I don't need to do it during the summer too."

"That sounds awful! Was there anything you liked to do at Camp Wallace Creek?"

"Yeah, eat."

The two of them laughed. They agreed the food wasn't very interesting, but it was better than what they heard other camps were like from the other boys.

"You know what?" offered Charley, "I liked the craft lodge and riding and taking care of the horses. Curry combing them was relaxing, and I liked the way their coats smelled. There's nothing else like it. This summer, I made matching wallets for me and Dad. I never got to give it to him."

"You can mail it to him when you get home."

"No, I can't. When I got beat up, the gang took them both. I kept money hidden in them. They found the one in my pocket, and my dad's I kept hidden in my sock fell out, and they grabbed that too."

"Why were you a part of that gang?"

"I don't know. They were like a family until they weren't. They made me work harder than I ever have in my life, and they appreciated what I did, unlike my dad or my mom. My dad's a lawyer, and my mom's a hairdresser in Salt Lake, and they don't have time for me..."

Interrupting, Tommy said, "If your parents are too busy for you, why do you want to go home to your mom?"

"I don't know. My grandparents are there too, and they're awesome. My grandfather does projects with me, like fixing things around the house and making furniture out of wood. Once we built some porch chairs that we still use in their backyard. My grandma makes the best homemade meals. Her Irish stew is so good; she showed me how to make it, and I was disappointed we didn't get to have stew tonight."

"When we were in the airport, I was out scrounging for stuff for my walk home, and I saw you. I saw you when you were held down on a table...."

"Yeah, that was tough."

"But they congratulated you. Didn't you become the number two guy in the gang?"

"It wasn't worth it; it didn't last long," said Charley, looking off into the distance, back toward Denver.

"What happened?"

"Just after that, we left the airport. Right before I saw you for the first time, we teamed up with another gang, and they pushed me down several spots. Most of the members of that gang were adults, and we were all just teenagers. We needed their help, but they also kept us down while using us, making us go first into dangerous situations. It was scary... and exciting. I got a lot of stuff from cars and took from people, but I no longer have any of it."

"You've got your day pack, and you're still alive."

"Yeah, that was rough."

Uncertainly, Tommy asked, "You haven't told me what happened."

"Yeah, I don't know..." Charley ran his good hand through his dirty hair. "We heard that if you went into the mountains, there was a lot of money and other things. We stayed on I-70 and were doing pretty well. We didn't go to the places with guards out front, but we'd go into some of the neighborhoods close to the highway, and we scared a lot of those people and got a lot. One of our guys got shot by someone inside one of the houses, but we patched him up. There were several other gangs we kept fighting with, but we usually won or held our own until we got to the spot where we turned off to Winter Park. We didn't want to go to Winter Park, but there was a group of people at that road who blocked it off with cars, and they only let regular people and traders through. They had hunting rifles and shotguns. Some of them had the kind of guns soldiers fight with. The best we carried were a few handguns and some knives. Our boss decided to try turning. We didn't even know where we were going; none of us brought a map. We just knew we had to get off I-70. It felt like we were walking straight up at first, going back and forth, and then we got to Berthoud Pass. I made some sarcastic comment – I know, I know – and I was mean to the boss's girlfriend. I was tired and hungry and wasn't thinking straight. At that point, they tied a rope around my neck, and the boss called me his hound dog since I howled too much. The way down from the pass was more back and forth; sometimes we got to cut straight down, but that was almost worse because it was so steep. Every time he wanted to stop, he made me howl so everyone knew it was time to rest. I didn't like that too much.

"The last time I howled, he said I didn't howl loud enough and kicked me. I kicked him back, and then it got crazy. All I remember is hands and feet coming at me; someone used a chain, and that's how I broke my face. I guess they beat me so hard they thought I was dead and left me on the road. I woke up and didn't know what to do. I was afraid a bear might find me, so I tried to follow them. At some point, I caught up to the slowest group, and they saw me. They rushed at me, and I ran into the woods. I climbed a fence trying to get away, unable to see very well, and then I tripped and fell over the entrance to the tunnel. I think I'm lucky to be alive. That must have been when I screwed up my foot and my arm. I remember my ribs hurting after I blacked out from the beating, but I was able to climb the fence with no problem. It all gets a little hazy. I don't know how long I was lying on the railroad tracks when you found me."

"Wow. I had no idea."

"I thought I was tough. I guess I wasn't tough enough when the gang turned on me."

"Did you ever do any, you know…?"

"Drugs? No. There were some guys who did, but they all looked really bad after a few days. I did drink, though. I liked the way it felt while I was drinking, but I always felt bad the next day. When I saw rum at the resort, all I thought about was drinking to blot everything out. I was embarrassed, angry with myself, and in pain."

"What now?"

"I've been thinking about that a lot while we've been walking. I don't fully know yet. This summer at camp and in Denver, I made a lot of wrong choices. I know that's not how I usually act. You've been a surprise. I thought you were a goody-goody. You're just a nerdy, athletic, outdoorsy guy; I didn't know you were a real person. I was wrong about a lot of things. You've been a better friend to me than anyone else has in my life, and I treated you really badly all summer long, attacking you and that girl several times."

Charley stood up and looked around. It had gotten dark while he told his story. He put his hand out to Tommy, who took it, and then Charley pulled him up.

"Thanks, Tommy."

Charley went to the tarp, got under the fleece blanket, and pulled out another blanket the shop owner back in Hot Sulphur Springs had given him from behind the seat of his truck. He was snoring lightly before Tommy even got to the tarp.

Day Nineteen

Tommy was awakened by the cold, wet nose of a curious cow, and he was so startled that he woke Charley up. They ate some of the oatmeal they had bought in Hot Sulphur Springs, and Tommy said he hoped to make twenty miles today, but he knew most of the hike would be exposed to the sun. The shop owner back in Hot Sulphur Springs warned them there wasn't much shade, but he had only ever driven the dirt road, so he wasn't sure. Tommy wanted to wake up early, but neither boy had a wind-up alarm clock, so the cow woke Tommy and Charley instead. For most of the morning, both boys were lost in their thoughts about what Charley had shared and how it changed everything for them. Tommy had a very different perspective on Charley but still wasn't ready to fully forgive him or trust him for what he did all summer and, even more, for what he did to Tommy and the Browns since they landed in Denver.

Charley mulled over what he had shared with Tommy. Everything he said was true, but he didn't mention that he actually enjoyed all of his bad behavior until he was beaten up. The beating changed things for him, and so did sharing his story with Tommy. Listening to himself, even with his omission, he realized how awful he had been recently. His grandfather would be very upset with what he did, and he didn't even want to imagine the tears his grandmother would shed if she ever heard of his actions. He loved his family and hoped they loved him, but he felt like a burden to them and wanted to figure out a way to connect with them; this time, he wanted that connection to be positive.

At their lunch break after hiking for five hours, the two discussed cooking and eating stew over their last roast elk sandwiches. The shop owner shared some of his jerky along with onions, carrots, and potatoes from his own garden. Tommy purchased a few seasonings and spices, but not much. Charley remembered that the longer the stew cooked, the better it would be. They decided to soak the jerky in water while they walked to soften it as much as possible. The rest of the walk was uneventful; their packs felt lighter because they knew over half their hike that day was behind them, and they would soon be eating the stew they had been dreaming of since their wood-chopping day. Their mood was lighter too, even joking with one another and trying to out-pun each other.

The biggest challenge of the day turned out to be finding a place to set up camp. The boys were accustomed to the suspicious stares of a few people from their porches or while doing chores on their land, but the spot they found to camp was surrounded by homes they wanted to avoid in order to prevent any confrontations. When they finally found their spot for the night, they were able to prepare their stew. As they ate, they realized they had forgotten to peel the potatoes like Charley's grandmother always did, but they also discovered they liked how it tasted and felt.

Night came, and the boys slept the best they had while on the trail.

Day Twenty

Waking with the sun again, the boys knew this day would be the most challenging since they left Winter Park. The shop owner had told them that the road to Rabbit Ears Pass would be the steepest since Hot Sulphur Springs, and he was right! Charley was showing signs of fatigue from his injuries, especially his lacerated foot, arm, and ribs. He wasn't able to keep his foot as clean as he should have, so the cut was tender, and both pairs of his socks were blood-stained, even though he washed them every time they came to a stream. His ribs hurt from the pack, and his arm ached because he kept trying to use it like normal when it very definitely wasn't. The boys had run out of anti-inflammatory medicine but were fortunate enough that the shop owner had given them a bottle, and Tommy bought another one when they were in his store. Happily, most of Charley's other scrapes and cuts were healing well, and he was starting to look more like himself. Tommy noticed Charley was also laughing more and seemed to be a more willing and helpful trekking partner since he had shared what happened to him. Tommy thought the whole ordeal must have been weighing on him as he worked through his prior choices.

The boys made it to the top of the long, flat Rabbit Ears Pass, occasionally catching glimpses of what they guessed was Rabbit Ears Peak, though they were unsure since it appeared to be just two uneven towers of rock atop a larger formation. They were slowed by the steepness of their hike that day and by Charley's injuries. Charley lightened the mood by singing the Camp Wallace Creek camp song, with

Tommy joining in during the choruses. Their evening was much the same as the night before, but without the stew. They ate jerky, cheese, and crushed homemade bread for dinner. They shared a can of peaches for dessert and went to bed, dead tired, without making a fire.

Day Twenty-One

This was the day Tommy hoped to reach Steamboat Springs. It was going to be a shorter walk, and Tommy looked forward to entering a larger town and possibly getting some supplies to replace things that were worn out or forgotten. His biggest wish was to be able to get a hotel room to escape the weather and sleep on a real mattress. He knew he was too young; he had heard rumors that you needed to be twenty-one to book a hotel room, but his father always told him that the answer is no unless you ask.

Based on what the shop owner told the boys and what the views looked like while they hiked, they expected the day to be all downhill. After the previous day, which was all uphill, they were looking forward to the change. Their packs were lighter because they had eaten almost everything they carried, but they still had some jerky, a sleeve of crackers, some cheese, an apple, and one energy bar—that was it.

The day was easier, but the cut on Charley's foot was aggravated by the constant downhill in a different way than by the constant uphill. Since they were descending in elevation, the breathing became easier too. During the day's hike, they talked about the abandoned RVs and campers along the road, speculating about what might be inside them. Charley shared what the gang saw when they broke into some of them on their way out of Denver. They saw the wide valley where Steamboat Springs lay nestled among the trees. There was a lake on the right, well below them, sparkling in the light. When they came across a runaway truck ramp, they clambered onto it to investigate and found the ground covered with loose rocks. Finally, they entered the far outskirts of Steamboat Springs, where condos and other homes began to occasionally line the road.

The boys were tired as the hike leveled off when they saw a wagon and a team of horses at an intersection, along with a couple of other guys in their twenties, as well as a neatly dressed man and woman. The man wore a clean collared shirt with equally clean overalls, and the woman was in a clean and pressed peach calico dress. The man waved to the boys and encouraged them to come over.

"Would you boys like some cold tea?" she asked, offering them tea from a big glass cooler draped with wet canvas.

"That sounds amazing," said Charley, hobbling over to the wagon.

"We also have some cookies," the lady said, presenting them on a nice plate of china with a handkerchief draped over it to keep the flies away.

"Thank you."

Tommy was still wary of the crowd around the wagon when a man walked over and asked where they were from.

"We're walking from Denver to Steamboat and maybe further," Tommy responded, still cautious.

"That's a long walk."

"It has been, but we've gotten into shape."

"Your friend looks worse for wear."

"He had some trouble several days ago."

"Is he okay?"

"Yes."

"You seem to be cautious. Our tea is delicious, and the cookies are energizing!" There was an awkward pause. "Can we offer you a ride? It will save you a few miles of walking," Sarah Jane suggested.

"That sounds tempting," said Tommy, thinking of Charley's injuries.

"We're about to load up. Isn't that right, Sarah Jane?"

"Yes, sir. Do these boys need a ride too, Edgar?"

"Yes, ma'am. Let's help them get their packs into the wagon."

The four travelers loaded their packs into the wagon, and Edgar helped Charley climb aboard. Edgar sat on the buckboard up front with

Sarah Jane, and after they got going, she offered the travelers a free dinner of roast chicken, mashed potatoes, salad, and homemade rolls, along with dessert of cobbler and clean beds for the night. The two young men and Charley eagerly accepted the offer, while Tommy decided to remain silent, going along for Charley's sake.

Edgar gently drove the horses to a turnoff leading to a dirt road. The six passengers on the wagon rode on for at least an hour between farms and ranches until they saw a large log cabin with a spacious board-and-batten barn and several other board-and-batten buildings scattered around a small, stream-fed lake.

"Here we are, gentlemen!" proclaimed Edgar.

"Welcome to our little slice of heaven!"

As the wagon moved further into the compound, Tommy noticed unusual boxes with slats on their sides. While he was trying to get a closer look, he was distracted by several people coming out of the side buildings, waving and enthusiastically greeting the newcomers. It seemed each new arrival had one or two people to help them carry their bags. Tommy's helper was waved away by Edgar and Sarah Jane, who assisted him and guided him to what was apparently the dining area in the large log cabin. While Edgar and Sarah Jane were talking to Tommy, expressing their happiness at finding him, Tommy was trying to listen to what the others were being told, especially Charley. He heard several mentions of how excited they were for the newcomers to meet the founders.

"Who are the founders?" Tommy asked Edgar and then Sarah Jane, as Edgar continued to rave about how good the food was.

"Oh, they're very special people. I'm sorry for not mentioning them to you before."

"That doesn't tell me anything. Who are the founders, and where are we?"

"The founders are a couple who started the Heavenly Ranch and Farm, and that's where we are."

Tommy decided not to press his luck and stayed quiet. The new arrivals and their guides (that's what Tommy decided to call them) all sat down at a large table. Tommy noticed that no newcomer sat next to another; each newcomer had a guide on both sides. The whole thing felt too orchestrated to be coincidental. He also noticed there was an empty chair at each end of the table with place settings.

All the guides stood up and encouraged their newcomers to stand as well. The guides politely and quietly clapped while looking up at a balcony leading to stairs. Tommy followed their adoring gazes. Above them stood a neatly dressed gentleman with a clean-shaven face and salt-and-pepper hair, holding hands with a woman with graying blonde hair in a white dress similar to the women guides. They subtly acknowledged the welcome and descended the split-log stairs. As they got closer, Tommy noticed both of them had striking blue eyes, accentuated by their healthy tanned skin.

"Welcome to our humble ranch and farm," said the gentleman, quietly yet firmly.

"Yes, welcome to our special home," said the lady sweetly and even more softly. So quietly that Tommy had to put his hand to his ear to hear her properly.

"Let us give thanks. We thank thee, oh Maker and co-worker of this land. To our nourishment and your praise, we eat," intoned the man. The lady and the guides all joined him in his short prayer.

Everyone sat down to dinner, which included roast chicken, mashed potatoes, corn, salad, and homemade rolls. The salad featured fresh tomatoes, the first Tommy had seen since the earliest days of the event.

"Where did you get tomatoes?"

"We have a greenhouse we use for special fruits and vegetables. Aren't they wonderful?" said Sarah Jane.

Tommy enjoyed the meal with the tea he was offered. He tried to keep to himself as Edgar and Mary Jane engaged him in casual conversation. They asked him about the weather, how his walk was, and sought his opinion on the "lovely" homestead. As Tommy attempted to listen to other conversations, he kept hearing about a "new opportunity" and "special family." He also barely noticed the neatly dressed gentleman raise an eyebrow while looking at Edgar, who very slightly nodded while maintaining eye contact with the gentleman.

As the dishes from the main meal were cleared, bowls were distributed, and a couple of cast iron Dutch ovens were brought out from what must have been the kitchen. The Dutch ovens were steaming with the aroma of peaches and cinnamon. Just behind them came a metal cylinder with a plastic lid. Tommy then realized it resembled the container his grandfather used when making homemade ice cream. Tommy couldn't believe his eyes. Ice cream without electricity? How did they accomplish that? He thought that without electricity, you wouldn't have ice to make the ice cream. His grandfather always used an electric ice cream maker, but his friends talked about their grandparents making them crank the maker for their ice cream on hot summer holidays, so he knew that part could be done without electricity. But what about ice?

Edgar leaned over and said, "You're amazed by the ice cream. I can tell. You're wondering how we did it. We hand-cranked it, of course, but our founders, in their wisdom, built an ice cave into the basement of their special house, where they keep ice cut from the pure water of the small lake out front."

Tommy looked at Edgar, who wore a smug, superior grin on his face.

After dessert, it was still quite early in the evening; the sun was still above the horizon, and the guides took the newcomers on a tour of the grounds around the main cabin. The guides kept the new arrivals away from the weird slatted boxes but showed them all the board and batten buildings, which turned out to be sleeping quarters for the ranch and farm hands, as the guides called them. Tommy thought the layout looked more like military barracks he'd seen in movies. The biggest of the board and batten buildings turned out to be a two-story farmhouse holding some straw and hay, with stalls for horses and cows. The cow stalls were set up for milking. There were two smaller work buildings: one was a workshop with a room for woodworking and another room for mechanical and metal work, while the other small building held pigs and small farm animals. Nearby was a chicken coop and a rabbit hutch. The guides told the newcomers about the ranching and farming that was nearby but out of sight. This time, when Tommy tried to listen in on other conversations, all he heard was the same thing being told to each of the four of them.

The tours ended, and each newcomer was taken to a different bunkhouse. Tommy was guided by Edgar and Sarah Jane to a small cottage he had missed before. Sarah Jane showed him to a bedroom with a washbasin and pitcher on a chest of drawers, a twin bed with a quilt and blanket, and finally, a bedside table. His backpack was waiting in the room. Edgar took Tommy to a separate small building that turned out to be a shower with wood-stove-heated water. Edgar told him the warm water didn't last long but encouraged him to enjoy cleaning up.

The shower felt luxurious, more so than anything he remembered. He lathered up and rinsed off, taking his time with the rinsing, letting the warm water run over his head, relaxing in a way he had never felt before. When he stepped out of the shower, he found a fresh set of pajamas. He returned to the small cottage and his room. Even though it was early, he lay down in bed and immediately fell asleep.

Day Twenty-Two

His habit since the event was to wake up with the rising sun. He heard roosters crowing by the chicken coop and lingered in bed. He felt guilty about his suspicions regarding the hospitality shown to him at the Heavenly Ranch and Farm. Still, everything felt too artificial and purposeful for a group just wanting to help wanderers in the aftermath of the event. It was undeniable how good the food was and how nice it was to shower and sleep in a real bed with clean sheets. Still skeptical, he slipped out of bed and repacked his most important items into a small collapsible day pack he carried: his letter from his dad and his father's mentor, Richard; his wallet with a picture of his parents and his brother; his pocket survival kit; his favorite pocket knife; a lighter he picked up in Hot Sulphur Springs; and a few other things, just in case. He peeked out of his bedroom and saw no one, so he snuck through the cottage and then out the door leading to the shower. He looked around and saw a small hinged door in the foundation of the house, where he placed his stuff sack. He snuck back into his room just as he heard the front door open.

"Hello?" he called.

"Oh, it's just me," said Sarah Jane's sweet voice.

Tommy went to the door and opened it.

"You're up. Good. We'll be serving breakfast for the four of you in half an hour."

Tommy found that his clothes had all been taken away and replaced with two sets of garments similar to what Edgar and the other men were wearing. He shrugged and got dressed; his shoes were still there, and he put on his socks and shoes.

When he joined the others, accompanied by Sarah Jane to the log cabin, he noticed that they were all dressed in the same clothes as he was. He looked at Charley and caught his eye.

Charley smiled and gave Tommy the thumbs-up sign with his good hand. Tommy noticed that all of Charley's bandages had been replaced, and his injured arm was re-splinted much better, with a proper sling. The other two newcomers, whom Tommy didn't really know, were similarly in much better shape. Charley and the other two looked cleaner and better rested than when Tommy had seen them last.

Breakfast consisted of scrambled eggs with bacon, biscuits and gravy, toasted homemade bread, and raspberry preserves on the side. When the kitchen staff came out, they offered each newcomer a choice of coffee, hot cocoa, or milk. The guides were given water. The founders came down the stairs to a quieter reception this morning, but still received the adoring gazes of the guides. The lady apologized with a shrug and a smile for the lack of orange juice, saying they had run out the previous week and didn't expect to get any soon. The guides quietly laughed, and everyone resumed eating. The dining table was much quieter this morning. The founders excused themselves, thanking everyone for a lovely breakfast and expressing their gratitude for the food at the end of the meal this time.

The other newcomers were being led to the door when Edgar gently took Tommy's elbow and said, "Tommy, Carl Albert wants to talk to you. Please, let me take you to him."

Looking around, Tommy was taken aback and confused but agreed to follow Edgar.

Edgar guided Tommy up the stairs and down a short, quiet carpeted hallway to a set of twin pine doors and lightly knocked.

"Come in," replied the strong voice of the gentleman founder, Carl Albert.

Edgar opened the door and led Tommy into a large office. The pine log walls were lined with heavily filled bookshelves and enormous floor-to-ceiling windows. A small fire burned in the fireplace set in the middle of the window behind Carl Albert, who sat at the desk working with some papers. In front of the desk, two couches faced each other, and a coffee table made of logs was arranged on an ornate maroon rug.

"Tommy, please take a seat," said Carl Albert, pointing to one of the couches.

Tommy sat down, still confused but fascinated by the room and the man who inhabited it.

"Thank you, Edgar. I will bring Tommy to the dining room when we are done."

Edgar nodded and left the room, closing the door behind him.

Coming around the desk, Carl Albert took a seat diagonally from Tommy. Settling his piercing blue eyes on Tommy, he said, "You're intrigued and suspicious. You have every right to be. This is a strange place in a strange time. We are very comfortable. You've never told any of us your name, but we've all known it. We also know Charley's name. The other two we just found on the road. How do we know your name and Charley's, you're now wondering? I have a lot of friends in these mountains, and we heard about you from some in Winter Park. You and your friend are very conspicuous, if you were unaware. In this time, or any time really, two teen boys walking along highways – one of them clearly hurt – are bound to raise an eyebrow or two. Other friends along your route wrote to tell me how you led your friend and yourself very ably, and my wife and I needed to keep our eyes out for you.

"You look startled. There are powerful people in these mountains maintaining an informal communications network primarily of horseback riders in a modified tradition of the old Pony Express. We are making a few extra dollars, just enough, mind you, by carrying letters for regular people between our mountain towns. But when the event happened, I saw a need and sent a small group of my followers out on horseback with letters to other powerful people, and we agreed to establish this new network for our own purposes and safety."

"Anyway, you two were seen, and you were recognized as a strong, young leader. As the time approached, I sent Edgar and Sarah Jane to a point on the road where we knew you were going to pass. The other two just happened to be walking along ahead of you. We will have a use for them here at the Ranch and Farm.

Tommy was taken aback at Carl Albert's disclosures. He never thought about anyone having such a spider's web of information. The fact he was one of the subjects of this web was disconcerting. For his and Charley's safety he decided to continue listening instead of running, like every fiber of his being was shouting.

Carl Albert was still talking, "Let me tell you the story of Heavenly Ranch and Farm. My father was very successful. He worked his way up from the mail room to lead a large, privately held financial concern and wanted a place where he was still able to do business, but also escape the day to day of New York, Chicago, and Los Angeles. He bought this land and built this cabin and some of the buildings you saw yesterday. The cottage Edgar and Sarah Jane are living in was the caretakers' cottage. I am my parent's only child, they had me late in life and I was schooled in the best private, residential schools in the world. My father passed away when I was only thirty and I inherited this place. I was already on track to take over my father's position in the firm but was cut out by others. Distraught, I retreated to our family's hideout in the mountains. That was quite some time ago. Our son and daughter have received the same education as I did, and I hope my daughter is on her way here from New York. I worry about our son since he was in London when the event occurred. My children have used the connections made in a life like mine to create their own success, but we always return to Heavenly Ranch. After I was forced out, in my retreat, I bought additional land adjoining the land my father bought, and I inherited.

"By nature, I have always been preparing for catastrophe. That nature was only fertilized by my removal from places I felt entitled to having, keeping, and using. As I implied, I had many wealthy and powerful friends, and I reached out to them and invited them to our Ranch and Farm. At the time we weren't yet farming but changed soon after my friends started visiting. While they were here I offered them the opportunity to create a safe haven if everything were to fall apart. There are many bunkers built in these mountains with deceptively designed small cabins built over their entrances. We never expected 'falling apart' to mean what it has come to mean, we expected world war or societal collapse, not total loss of electricity. But we were prepared. The lack of electricity has caught us off guard, but only a little. We have improvised using existing stocks of kerosene and lamps. Everything here has been built to withstand multiple failure points.

"Only a small number of my friends have made it to our hideaway. I hope to see many of them as time passes and they are able to make it here. Most of the people you have met so far are either believers in me and my wife as visionaries or are employees of the Farm and Ranch who have come to appreciate our foresight. The employees are now working alongside the believers enjoying a new life few since the event are enjoying. We are now preparing for a new world, changed by this massive event.

"My friends have contacted me via our informal network to tell me of the chaos occurring in big cities. Mass deaths caused by the lack of electricity, riots of the dispossessed, and gang rule. I've heard reports of a few cities maintaining some rule of law. Denver is one of the few. In most cases the cities maintaining rule of law have a presence of the full-time military and commanders who maintained close communication with the civilian authorities. These friends of mine are wealthy and powerful, but they aren't scientists or technicians, they employ them. They tell me they are told by their brightest minds no one has any idea what happened and have no idea if things are ever going to change. I will use that to my advantage.

"Why have I told you all this? You, this boy who I have never met. It is because people I see greatness in you, and I need a backup plan if my children never make it back to me. You have the bearing of a leader. Don't get me wrong, if my children make it here they will have precedence over you, but you will be well placed to take over or help them as a closely trusted aide. I want to train you to be a great man, Tommy. What do you think?

Tommy was more overwhelmed. He didn't know such hidden things still existed in this day and age. Of course he read about stuff like what Carl Albert described in books, but he thought those were relegated to the past or were the entertaining imagings of authors. He never thought he might be confronted with the reality of such a thing.

"I don't know what to say...."

"Would you like a drink? I have water or soda? Yes, I have soda, I said I was prepared for anything, didn't I? I realize what I have told you and asked of you is big, bigger than you have probably ever imagined, and you may need some time."

Carl Albert brought out a silver tray with crystal pitcher, matching glasses and a bottle of cola with a silver insulated ice bucket with tongs for the ice on a tray. He poured himself a glass of water and placed two chunks of ice in it and sliced a lime that came from some unseen place.

"Thanks, I, uh, I'll take a glass of cola, I guess."

Carl Albert served him, then walked over to the giant window.

"It is beautiful isn't it?"

Tommy barely even saw the room, much less the view from the window. His mind was reeling. Trying to mentally grab on to something remotely within his previous world he wondered what happened to Charley and where he was.

"What happened to Charley?" he asked meekly.

"Charley? Oh, I told my staff to take him to the wood shop. He isn't healed enough to work the farm or the ranch part of the operation so I thought we might see if he was able to help there."

"Was all this for me?"

"All what? Oh, you mean the dinner and the breakfast? Yes, mostly. When we recruit people, refugees, off the road, we usually feed them and clothe them, but not so lavishly. You see this is a much nicer version of our usual recruitment of our people. That's what we call the men and women who work the ranch and farm. Our People.

"We educate the new arrivals about our vision for the future, and some come to it easily, others need a fuller picture. It really is wonderful this new reality of fewer but healthier people draining the resources of the land. My wife, Emmy, and I really want you to join us in our vision for the future."

His mind still trying to fathom what he has just heard, Tommy asked, "Do you mind if I can have some time to take it all in? What you've told me is an awful lot to process."

"Certainly, I respect that you want to think about our offer. Keep in mind this is a special opportunity for you. Where would you like to think?"

"Do you mind if I go for a walk around the lake?"

"Not at all, let me take you there."

Carl Albert guided Tommy out of his office. He asked for a moment at the top of the stairs and walked over to the other side of the balcony and disappeared behind another double door and came out with his wife, Emmy. The three walked down the stairs and out of a door Tommy had not seen.

"What do you think of this special opportunity Tommy?" asked Emmy.

"It's a lot to take in. The only reason I'm here, near Steamboat, is because I am trying to get home to my family."

"Family is important. We miss both of our children. Hopefully our daughter will make it here soon. But we're trying to be realistic about her chances. It's a long way from New York and even longer from London where our son was when the event occurred."

"Do you know how far it is to New York?"

"I didn't before the event. Carl Albert brought out his maps and using string and rulers we think it is about two thousand miles. He thinks it will take her about three months to get here if she started right away, I think it will take her longer. No matter what, she will be delayed if she runs into any problems, but if there's anyone who can overcome challenges, it's her. She's incredibly strong."

"I know someone like that...."

"Oh, really? Can you tell me more about her?"

"I met her in Denver. She volunteered immediately to work the first aid station in the airport. When we finally left I saw her get attacked, but she fought back and managed to escape. After a good night's sleep, she was able to shake it off and keep going."

"She got attacked? I hope our daughter doesn't get attacked, but I'm sure she would be just as tough. Do you miss this girl?"

"I do. She's from where I'm from, and I hope she makes it back safely."

"Was it just the two of you?"

"Oh, no, her parents were with us the whole time. I left them in Denver. They're staying with old friends."

"What's Denver like now? I've heard rumors but haven't actually talked to anyone who's been there. We expect some of our friends any time now, but we haven't seen any. We have a couple of families here, but they were on vacation when everything happened," said Emmy.

"Denver is doing okay, I guess. I've only ever been to Denver for connecting flights or driving through it to go skiing. At the intersection of the interstates, there's a big market that has just kind of emerged. There are gangs, of course, but Carl Albert tells me Denver is doing better than most big cities. That makes sense to me. We did see some police; I don't know."

"Here's the lake. It's not really a lake, more like a big pond, but we call it a lake. Carl Albert mentioned you wanted to walk around it and think."

"Carl Albert?" Looking at the man walking ahead of them, Tommy continued, "Why is he called that? Is it his full name?"

"No, it isn't his full name. It's his first name and middle name. His mother always called him that, and it stuck. Even his friends in school took to calling him Carl Albert after they heard his mother. I look forward to hearing your thoughts about what we've proposed. See you soon, Tommy."

Tommy nodded and awkwardly said goodbye to the older couple who were now standing together holding hands. He watched them turn around and return to the cabin. Then Tommy turned around and took in the view of the lake before starting to walk around it.

~~~

The offer blindsided Tommy, and he was unable to shake the sense of unease he felt from the moment he saw Edgar and Sarah Jane on the side of the road. He really just wanted to get home and see his parents. He knew the life he had left at the beginning of the summer was gone, but he also knew his mother, father, brother, and all of his friends were back in Sacramento. Heavenly Ranch and Farm was very nice, and the founders treated him with more respect than he had ever received from anyone except his family and the Browns. But was it enough to stay? Hearing what they thought he was capable of was very flattering—so flattering it made him suspicious. It felt creepy, and he wasn't falling for it. He always thought of himself as a capable kid, but he tried to be realistic. He was nothing super special, just above average, or so he liked to tell himself. Tommy smiled at that.

What was he suspicious of? Why did he not trust what he was seeing, aside from the flattery? He was just unable to put his finger on it. Maybe it was the overly nice atmosphere? Everyone he saw who was part of the Ranch and Farm was nicely dressed in clean work clothes, and the food was marvelous. He understood it was especially complimentary to try to recruit him (was that a red flag?). Outside of the log cabin, everything was simple but well-made.

Tommy hadn't seen Charley since breakfast and wondered how he was getting along in the shop. Thinking of Charley, what about those other two? Carl Albert indicated they just kind of benefited from being in the right place at the right time (or was it the right place at the wrong time?), but he also said they recruited others to be a part of this place. Carl Albert didn't tell him what they were doing.

Tommy remembered hearing about cults. He'd watched old videos of people being deprogrammed and other newscasts of lots of people lying outdoors, dead. He wondered if this place was a cult or if he was just making things up to support his feelings.

Looking up, he saw he was almost back at the spot where the founders had left him. He wondered if he had only made one lap around the lake. He looked back. Tommy thought to himself that he'd give it a try for a day or two and then decide. At least it would give Charley more time to heal; after all, it had only been a week since he found him broken, lying between two train tracks. In the meantime, he'd keep his stuff sack hidden. Besides, he wanted to talk to Charley.

~~~

Tommy didn't have to wait long. He heard the ringing of a bell. He looked up at the cabin and saw Carl Albert waving to him, beckoning him to come back. When Tommy got closer, Carl Albert told him it was lunch.

Tommy was escorted to the dining room by Carl Albert and Emmy. Charley was there with his guide, and Edgar and Sarah Jane were also present; however, there was no sign of the other two newcomers. Charley and his guide were talking with Edgar and Sarah Jane, and they all had smiles on their faces. Charley saw Tommy and, without thinking, waved with his injured hand. He winced, pulled his arm back down, and waved at Tommy again with his good hand. Tommy, Carl Albert, and Emmy joined the other four at the smaller table. The more intimate space allowed conversation to flow among everyone; yet, the founders still kept to themselves, occasionally leaning over to mention something to Tommy. Tommy was still separated from Charley, and it frustrated him.

After lunch, Tommy was guided to the horses, and Edgar asked if he'd ever ridden one. He replied that he had only ever ridden the horses at summer camp, and those had all been in a line, nose-to-tail. Edgar said that was enough experience to get started. Edgar helped Tommy mount a sorrel horse and then got on a gray one himself. With some assistance from Edgar, Tommy was riding the horse behind him and a little to the side. The purpose of the ride was to familiarize Tommy with some of the operations of Heavenly Ranch and Farm. The farm operations were mostly run in the broad valley behind the housing area. Closest to the buildings were fruit and vegetable crops tended mostly by women and a handful of men. They were in the early harvest season, and Tommy noticed many of the farmhands were carrying baskets. Edgar explained that the fruit and vegetables were usually eaten on the property, with a large amount of extra produce sold at area farmers' markets and to local restaurants. Due to the event, the decision was made to process them on-site using the most appropriate methods, like canning or cool storage. Some of the men were reassigned to build root cellars for this purpose. The orchards came next, featuring apples, cherries, pears, and peaches. Edgar handed Tommy one of the peaches, and it was the best peach he had ever eaten in his life. Edgar smiled and told him they were descended from the famous Palisade peaches grown near Grand Junction. He mentioned that the most recent crop had been cultivated to match the preferred taste of the founders. Finally, they came to the grain crops of wheat, oats, and corn. When Tommy expressed his confusion about growing corn in both the vegetable area and the grain area, Edgar clarified that the two corns were different types: sweet corn for eating, like on the cob, and dent corn for making cornmeal. He also explained that there were some other varieties for special purposes, like popcorn. Tommy didn't know anything about agriculture and said he was amazed that the place had such a carefully designed setup. Edgar then pointed out that they tried to be very space-efficient, locating compatible crops together and planting fruit and nut trees along areas needing shade or that were otherwise not used for anything else.

The ranch operation was potentially everywhere else without farming or the special residents. Edgar mentioned that there were several hunters among the special residents, and they worked to manage the rangelands to encourage elk, deer, and small game. The livestock they managed consisted mostly of cattle, but also included some sheep for wool. The farm animals they kept were pigs, dairy cows, and goats. Every animal was managed to utilize as much as possible—from milk to meat to skin to wool.

"Our founder likes to use the quote, 'everything but the oink,' to describe our ranch operation."

"You've certainly thought of everything. When I met you, I didn't realize you were so important to such a large operation."

"We all do our part, and that's always been part of our founder's goal. His father, whom I didn't have the fortune to meet, just liked to come here to recover from his hard work. Mr. Carl Albert and Mrs. Emmy are true visionaries. If any of the others had any doubts before, they were all erased when the event happened."

The tour was an important experience for Tommy. While this ride wasn't exhilarating, it was exciting because it felt like real horse riding. Above all, he appreciated the scope of what Carl Albert and Emmy were doing. He wanted to visit some of the special homes and maybe meet some of their residents.

At dinner, Carl Albert asked Tommy what he thought and if he had decided yet. Tommy told him he was impressed with what they were doing and realized how much there was to do. He also explained that he still missed his family, but he understood better what a great experience and opportunity he was being offered. Tommy asked for another day or two to make up his mind. Carl Albert said he understood and hoped Tommy would join him the following day to get a taste of what running the Heavenly Ranch and Farm was like.

When Tommy got back to his room in Edgar and Sarah Jane's cottage, he took his first opportunity to sneak his father's letter from his pack. He missed his family so much and wasn't sure if saying yes to Carl Albert was the right choice. The letter had been with him all this time, and he still hadn't read it; he hoped reading it would give him some guidance or peace.

Dear Tommy,

This summer has been a big summer for you. When I went to Camp Wallace Creek when I was fourteen it was the summer that was the most important for me. Like you I was finally among the older boys. It felt like the world opened up. As a part of the senior boys cabin we got to do real adventures. You've been talking non-stop about the backpacking trip the older boys get to take and let me tell you it was the adventure of my life up to that point and I hope it was for you too.

But it's not all about adventure, there's a lot of learning I hope you got to do this summer. These are your first steps at becoming a man, an adult. You're not there yet, but you soon will be, sooner than your mother and I want, and, I imagine, not soon enough for you. You will be given independence and responsibility this summer. When I was at Wallace Creek we older boys were put in charge of making sure the younger boys cleaned their tables after meals and the counselors no longer cleaned the bathrooms for us, we did it ourselves. The counselors also expected us to keep our bunk and the bunkhouse clean. We didn't get away with unmade beds and clothes on the floor like we had in the past.

You'll see these next four years in high school will be the same. Your mother and I will have higher expectations of you. We know you are ready, and we hope these expectations will help mold you into a great man, husband, and father. Adulthood is hard work, but there are rewards you cannot yet comprehend. Fatherhood is among those rewards, and it is so rewarding and heartwarming to see you move into the senior boys cabin, the same cabin where I was a senior boy so long ago.

Love,

Dad

Tears spattered on the page as Tommy finished the last paragraph of the letter in his father's neat script. He wiped them away. His yearning for home only increased as he heard his father's voice in the letter he wrote. He leaned back against the pillows of his bed and thought of home. His mother making dinner, he and his brother playing one sort of a game or another or doing homework at the kitchen table, and his father coming in and filling the room with his warm presence. Dinner time was filled with everyone catching up with each other or excitement for some upcoming event. Both boys were always hungry, and their mother always had an exasperated smile and laugh with their father at how much milk two boys drank.

His reminiscence over, Tommy decided he needed to get home and help Charley get to his home, however different it was from his. Now he needed to figure out how to tell Carl Albert and Emmy, he figured that he would wait a day or two to let Charley heal a little more.

Day Twenty-Three

Tommy didn't like awkward conversations, and he knew the one he had to have with Carl Albert was going to be uncomfortable. When he got to the dining room, he realized Charley wasn't there. In fact, he didn't remember seeing Charley at dinner the previous night. When Carl Albert and Emmy joined the smaller gathering, which now included just Tommy, Edgar, and Sarah Jane, he asked the older man about Charley.

"Oh, he has joined the rest of our People at their dining facility. It's now time to integrate you two into your proper roles."

"Really?" Tommy's mind was racing. Carl Albert already assumed the two of them were going to stay. How was he going to tell him they were leaving now? "What is Charley going to do?

"The wood-shop master tells me Charley is a natural, and since we have so many people joining us, he needs the extra help. We decided he will apprentice with him."

After breakfast, Carl Albert and Emmy led Tommy back up to Carl Albert's office.

"We thought it would be a good idea for you to see what a regular day looks like," said Emmy, looking adoringly at her husband.

"Yes, it is important to understand what this is really about before you make your decision. It has certainly changed in the weeks since the event. You see on the desk my phone, which no longer works. Hopefully, in the near future, normal mail service will return, but until then, I am communicating with my peers via the improvised messenger network. As the day goes on, I want you by my side as I make decisions, solve problems, and uncover opportunities. You will see me doing these things with the help of Edgar and the advice of Emmy. I am only one man and cannot achieve success without the help of great people like them."

Emmy left the room with a cheerful wave and said she would be in her room if Carl Albert needed anything. Carl Albert showed Tommy a foot-activated mechanical ringer he used to call Edgar when he needed assistance. As the day went on, he saw Edgar come and go several times, sometimes to deliver messages and other times to address issues for Carl Albert. Many tasks were crossing his desk: how many root cellars to build, when to expect any special residents and which ones, what preparations needed to be made for the soon-to-arrive special residents, and other operational challenges like how to get supplies to repair broken wagons. He also needed to find out if the United States Bureau of Land Management was going to hold the Sand Wash Basin Herd Management Area adoption event to acquire more horses, as they needed as many as possible for the foreseeable future. The last challenge saw Carl Albert summon Edgar to get a messenger. The messenger arrived dressed in worn blue jeans with chaps featuring little ornamentation, only tooling indicating that the rider was from Heavenly Ranch and Farm, a rugged-looking shirt, a cowboy hat with a chin strap, and sunglasses. Carl Albert told him where he needed to go and handed him an envelope. The rider brusquely took the envelope in his gloved hand and carefully put it in a discreet pocket in his chaps. The messenger curtly asked if there was anything else, and Carl Albert said he wanted him to return from Craig, Colorado, through Pagoda and Toponas, and drop by Kremmling to check on any urgent messages. After the messenger left, Tommy asked Carl Albert how long the ride was expected to take. Carl Albert told him that if everything went well, he should make it to Craig and the Sand Wash Basin headquarters that evening, wait for a response the next day, and then the rest of the circuit should take three or four more days. Carl Albert didn't expect to leave right away, and he mentioned that they usually don't conduct the adoptions at the headquarters, but he asked if that was going to change because of the event. He wanted to know as soon as possible so he could arrange his schedule and anyone else he needed to bring with him.

In between all of these activities, Carl Albert was reviewing reports printed before the event and filling out blank accounting sheets he kept "just in case." Twice he told Edgar to call Sarah Jane to take dictation. She took her notes and typed them out in duplicate using carbon paper (Carl Albert explained that carbon paper was a special sheet that transferred what was typed on one page to the one behind it). The second copy was for Carl Albert's files, and he had this done regularly before placing the original into an outgoing basket for messengers. Occasionally, he needed advice from Emmy, and he told Tommy he wanted her thoughts and opinions to help prevent him from making an error due to being too involved in the situation.

By the end of the day, Tommy's mind was spinning. Carl Albert informed Tommy that the next day was their weekly Day of Darkening and that Edgar and Sarah Jane would have his Darkening clothes ready in the morning. Baffled but too mentally exhausted to inquire further, Tommy made his way to his bed. He happened to see Charley long enough to wave and noticed that he seemed to be unhappy about something, scowling as he waved abruptly.

Day Twenty-Four

Darkening Day was one Tommy would not forget. The day started with Tommy finding a plain white floor-length gown laid out for him, accompanied by thin-soled white shoes. Uncertainly, he put on the gown and shoes and went outside, where he found Edgar and Sarah Jane dressed identically. He started to say something, but they both quickly put their forefingers to their lips. They waved for him to follow, and they made their way to the lake, facing the distant mountains. All the others—more than he realized were there—flowed in from the different buildings, wordlessly forming neat lines like an auditorium with a center aisle, but standing. In the first aisle, Tommy heard a light gong and turned around to see what the source was. He was blinded by the sunrise but just barely made out the figures of Carl Albert and Emmy, dressed in the same white gowns, but draped over both were wide purple scarves, and they wore purple slippers.

The couple walked slowly down the center aisle while everyone kept their eyes on them until they reached the front of the gathered people. They turned around and let their eyes roam over the crowd, finally coming to rest on Tommy.

"Thank you for your silence. We ask for your silence today for a special purpose. Darkening Day is our weekly pause to remember what we lost and, more importantly, who we lost on the day of the event. By participating in the silence, we deepen our remembrance.

"Many of you have come to us with tears in your eyes after receiving a letter, sharing your very personal stories of loss—of a family member or close friend who could not receive treatment due to the lack of electricity. Some of you have shared different stories of losing someone on the day of the event because they were in a car or a plane that lost control. We pause to remember them and your loss. We also pause to reflect on what life was like before we lost so much else.

"But we also pause to celebrate what we have gained! We have gained so much by slowing down. We have more time to appreciate our work and our handcrafting, whether it involves wood, husbandry, farming, or helping others. Because of the changes since the event, we have more opportunities to connect with one another in our special place here at Heavenly Ranch and Farm. Those of you who were here when this great change occurred have witnessed our deepening connection to one another, and we have had opportunities to welcome others into our special community.

"Let us pause now and intone our special words: We Love and We Share, We Love and We Share...." The gathered crowd began to chant along, swaying forward and back instead of the natural side-to-side motion. Initially, it felt awkward to Tommy as he sensed Sarah Jane's hand on one side and Edgar's on the other, taking his hands and connecting with others in the unusual swaying. The chanting and swaying lasted much longer than Tommy felt was appropriate. He grew unsettled, and nausea began to build.

Finally, Emmy raised her hands and spoke, "As you know, our special group has gained several new members this week. We want to welcome one of them in particular today. Tommy, please join us up here."

Embarrassed but acutely aware of everyone looking at him, Tommy walked toward Emmy and Carl Albert, who each took a hand. He wanted to wrench his sweating hands away from theirs but felt paralyzed by the strangeness of the moment. This was Tommy's first opportunity to look back at the large group now that the ceremony had started, and when he gazed into the crowd's eyes, he saw expressions of worshipful adoration, including those of the two others who had joined Charley and him on the wagon ride from the road. Charley's eyes, however, were clearly fixed on Tommy with guarded curiosity.

"Tommy joins us after a long walk from Denver. He is a special boy, and you will see him around the Ranch and Farm. Treat him with the same respect you show any of us, especially the respect you show to Edgar or Carl Albert." Emmy paused and placed a lighter-colored purple scarf around his neck. "As we move into this new era, we want to ensure we are well positioned for the future."

Carl Albert then concluded the gathering with, "Thank you, and please respect the silence of this day as we remember the first day of darkening. Our own light shall be a beacon for others in this new era."

As the gathering dispersed, the large group sang some unintelligible song together while Emmy and Carl Albert continued to lightly but firmly grip Tommy's hands. Charley looked around at the entire strange scene, shook his head, and followed the others. After everyone left, including Edgar and Sarah Jane, the couple reached out to one another, joining hands so that the three of them formed a triangle, looking at one another. Tommy felt very weird and awkward, while his nausea persisted. The older couple's faces were filled with an eerie peace, their eyes glazed and jaws slack. The entire time, he sensed extreme pressure to go along with the people led by Carl Albert and Emmy, but he was unable to shake his discomfort with the community.

"So special," said Emmy.

"Yes, what a great new beginning," agreed Carl Albert.

"Thank you?" said Tommy uncertainly.

Carl Albert said, almost in a whisper, "Tommy, thank you for being here on your first Darkness Day. Go contemplate, and come back to us and share your wonderful decision."

The older couple let go of Tommy's hands and turned around, still holding each other's hands as they walked off to circle the lake. Baffled and shaking his clammy hands, Tommy set off to find Charley.

After an hour, Tommy was still searching everywhere he thought Charley might be, including less obvious places. He started by going to where Charley was bunked but only found an empty building filled with identical cots, all made up. There was no way to know which cot belonged to Charley. On his way to the wood shop to check for Charley, he noticed that everyone he saw was still in their odd white gowns, either sitting and staring off into the distance or aimlessly wandering with unfocused eyes. There were no sounds of voices, only the wind and birds. He peeked into the shop and saw no one. He then went to the group dining shelter and found more people engaged in the same disconcerting, meditative behavior. Eventually, giving up his search in despair, Tommy went to a large flat boulder behind Edgar and Sarah Jane's cottage and sat down, trying to figure out what to do.

Tommy thought it was a bad idea to go get his book from its hiding place in the pack beneath the cottage, so he decided to retrace the events of the last several days. Hopelessness filled his mind as he lay back on the warming granite and tried to let his thoughts drift. It was hard to shake the feeling that something was wrong about the way everyone acted around one another. In some cases, the people interacting with each other appeared to work in a trance-like state, their eyes unfocused on anything unless there was a complication. No one looked directly at Carl Albert or Emmy except for Edgar and Sarah Jane, who seemed more like intermediaries acting as translators or message bearers for the founders. The only time they looked directly at Carl Albert or Emmy was this morning at the ceremony, and their adulation felt very creepy. No one ever challenged Carl Albert or Emmy; no one. Another odd thing was that Edgar and Sarah Jane seemed to be empty vessels, with practically no personality—almost like robots. Now that he thought about it, the only member of the Founders' People who seemed to have any personality was the rude horseback messenger, and even then it was very abrupt and businesslike.

As a matter of fact, Tommy sat up with the realization that he still never saw the special residents, not even at the Darkening Day ceremony, as far as he could tell. His intuition told him they existed but were kept away from everyone except Carl Albert and Emmy. Nothing about the whole place felt right to Tommy. He kept thinking and never came up with any sense of normality, only the undeniable false beauty and uneasy serenity of the place.

Finally, Tommy felt like the contingency plan if Carl Albert and Emmy's children didn't make it home. It felt strange to be told he was being asked to be someone's "just-in-case." He didn't want to be someone's "just-in-case."

Eventually, Tommy dozed off on the sun-warmed boulder. After some time, the cooling of the day caused him to wake up. He rose with a decision unequivocally made. He was going to go home, hopefully with Charley, but he was going home.

Even though he didn't trust them, he thought it was the right thing to do to tell Carl Albert and Emmy as soon as he decided. Tommy walked over to the large log cabin, feeling lighter than he had in quite some time, certain in his decision. He knocked quietly on the double doors to Carl Albert's office. Carl Albert invited him in. When Tommy entered the office, he saw Edgar, and they both blandly smiled at him.

"Welcome, Tommy. We were just sharing our enthusiasm for your future here," said Carl Albert.

"That's what I wanted to talk to you about."

"Go ahead, Tommy. Go ahead."

In an effort to appease the couple, Tommy said, "Carl Albert, you have been incredibly generous to me and Charley. The opportunity you are offering me is absolutely incredible, but I feel an undeniable pull to go home to my family. The right choice is for me to continue my journey home. I hope Charley will join me, but it is his decision if he wants to stay. I also hope you understand my choice."

"I see," responded Carl Albert. He waved Edgar over and whispered something in his ear. Edgar nodded and left the office.

"Well, that certainly changes things. You are old enough to make your own decisions. Let's see if there's anything we need to do."

Tommy was pleased by Carl Albert's response. Carl Albert stood up and escorted Tommy out of his office. When they opened one of the doors, Tommy saw Emmy, still dressed in her ceremonial gown like her husband, standing at the top of the stairs with tears streaming down her face. He guessed Edgar told her and didn't expect that reaction, but his decision was firm. She still held onto the hope of her children coming back. In fact, the lack of faith in their successful return was something he hadn't realized until that moment. The three of them walked down the stairs, but instead of going out the main door, Carl Albert steered Tommy toward the doors set in the middle of the giant windows that looked out on the lake. When Tommy looked out, he saw all the Founders' People, still dressed in their white gowns, gathered there again.

Carl Albert walked out to the edge of the patio at the top step and said to the gathering, "We have just received some disappointing news. Tommy just shared with me that he doesn't think very highly of the opportunity we have offered him here."

Tommy looked around, confused. That was not what he said!

Carl Albert continued, "He has told me he wants to leave us! Us!"

There were shocked gasps among the gathered crowd. Tommy noticed several people had tears streaming down their faces.

"We know what that means!"

Tommy felt two sets of strong hands grab him by the upper arms. He looked and saw two large men holding him with grim determination in their eyes. He struggled against them, but he was nowhere near strong enough to resist.

"We are a special retreat from this corrupted world! We are the core of a new era in the human story! We are not yet ready for the news of our unique society to be spread by someone who does not appreciate who we are! We can only hope to educate Tommy!"

Now Carl Albert led Tommy and his captors away from the patio and the lake toward the odd latticed boxes he had seen when they first arrived. Emmy, Edgar, Sarah Jane, and all the gathered people followed silently. Tommy didn't see Charley in the crowd. The two large men took Tommy to the nearest box and forced him to lie on it, chest down. Tommy fruitlessly struggled again until he heard Carl Albert.

"It is time to educate Tommy," he said with great solemnity.

Carl Albert extended his right hand, and Edgar placed a thick black hose in it. Tommy looked on in horror, realizing what he meant by "education." Carl Albert walked over to Tommy, who was trying to shrink away from him. Carl Albert raised his hands, holding the thick black hose.

He said, "We love."

The gathered crowd murmured, "We love."

Then he struck Tommy's back with great force, knocking the breath out of him.

"We share."

He struck him again.

"We share." The gathered people joined his intonation this time.

Another strike.

"We love." Everyone continued.

After those four, there were more, so many that Tommy lost count. Eventually, he passed out from the pain.

Day Twenty-Five

When Tommy woke up, still in his robes, he was shivering and his legs were cramping. All he felt was cold and pain—pain in his cramped legs and across his back. He didn't know how long he had been unconscious, but it was now dark, and the moon was a sliver on the lake. He tried to turn over and stretch his legs but realized he was crammed into the latticed box. He panicked and tried to move. Tommy was curled up in a child-like position, face down in the dirt on his knees in the box just big enough to keep him stuck in that position. When he struggled, his back hit the top of the box, and the bruises made him call out in pain. He panicked again and passed out.

When he woke up again in his very restricted space, he evaluated his situation. He remembered everything up to passing out on top of the box and waking in the box the first time. He didn't understand what had happened, but he did remember it. He looked around in the faint moonlight and saw that the box was locked shut with a padlock. What he had thought were wooden boxes he now saw were metal with the opening at the top. He guessed that after he had passed out, they must have crammed him into the box and left him. He panicked again, straining against the pain, the lattice, and the top of the box. He screamed in frustration. It was no use.

As he lay in the box, struggling to find a comfortable position, Tommy heard a whispered, "Hey!"

"Who is it?"

"It's me, Charley," he whispered. "Keep quiet! There's a guard leaning against that box over there, asleep."

Tommy looked around and didn't see anything.

"You can't see him; you're facing the wrong way. I'm going to get you out."

"How?" he said, panicked and breathless.

"I've got my tricks. Close your eyes and cover your face."

Tommy did as Charley directed. He then heard the sound of metal on metal above him. Next, he heard a sharp sound like a sledgehammer hitting a tent stake, followed by the sound of metal breaking. He opened his eyes and saw the top opening up, then it abruptly fell down with a bang! Tommy saw legs scuffling and heard the sound of metal hitting skin and bone, then he saw a large set of legs fall over. It was one of the big guys who had held him earlier. The top opened up again, and Tommy saw Charley's face offering him a hand to help him up.

As Tommy tried to stand, pushing up out of the box, his cramped legs gave out. Charley caught him and helped him over the side of the box. He felt excruciating pain across his back, a reminder of the beating with the black hose.

"Let's go, we've got to get out of here," whispered Charley.

"Wait, I've got to get my backpack."

"You've still got it?"

"No, not the whole thing. They took everything, but before they did, I hid some of my things in a stuff sack."

"Okay, go get it, and I'll meet you at that last tree, the big aspen, before the road opens up."

"I think so. I'll see you there."

Tommy went as fast as his cramped legs and bruise-covered back would allow. As he started moving, his muscles loosened enough for him to painfully jog to the cottage. As quietly as he could, he opened the hideaway spot. The door scraped and squealed as he opened it. He paused, afraid that he'd wake up Edgar or Sarah Jane. He didn't hear anything from inside the cottage. He quickly and carefully grabbed his stashed bag and proceeded to meet Charley.

Charley was waiting at the tree with two beat-up mountain bikes. He bent over and handed Tommy some overalls and a shirt. Tommy quickly changed. He was still in the lightweight white shoes, but they'd have to do.

"Okay, let's go."

The two boys got on their bikes. The chains on both bikes were stiff from lack of use, and each had a flat tire. Neither was able to move very effectively. They rode their bikes as quickly as the long-unused bikes would allow until they could no longer see any of the buildings.

"What do we do? We can't keep going like this," said Tommy to Charley.

"I've got an idea."

Charley got off his bike, grabbed the sidewall of the dried-up tire, and, with some difficulty, wrenched it off the rim of the wheel. Then he grabbed handfuls of coarse grass growing on the side of the road and started stuffing it into the tire. Tommy saw what he was doing and tried to do the same. As exhausted as he was, his muscles weren't cooperating. Charley noticed Tommy struggling and helped him remove one side of the tire. Tommy then started to fill his tire with grass. Both boys were wrestling with the frame of each bike since they weren't able to take the wheel off to make the makeshift repair in the dim light of the night.

After the boys filled their tires with as much grass as they could, they twisted the tires back onto the wheel rims. They got back on their bikes and started riding. It was still rough, but much better. It seemed like a good compromise.

The boys rode and rode, the dirt road never feeling like it would end. After a couple of hours, still in the darkness, they made it to the pavement. They got off their bikes, and Charley took a couple of bottles out of a bag tied to the rack on his bike. They each took a long drink of water.

"Thank you."

"We're not safe yet. Let's get to Steamboat first."

After the ride down the dirt road, the grass in the tires had compacted quite a lot, so the boys refilled their tires. This time it was easier since they had done it before, and the tires had loosened up with use. So had the chains, and the bikes were riding more smoothly. It didn't matter; it was better than walking. Every rotation of the pedal took them farther and farther away from what rapidly became a nightmare.

During the uncomfortable ride to Steamboat Springs, the boys started off on a paved road they only vaguely remembered before eventually getting to the main highway, not caring how conspicuous they were. At one of their occasional stops, Tommy noticed that Charley wasn't wearing his sling. He asked him about it.

"Yeah, I'm supposed to – and bumps definitely hurt, but I just want to get away from that place. We thought it was going to be a great chance to rest, but we were wrong."

"Yeah, every time I saw you, you looked less happy."

"When we first got there, it was great. We were eating delicious meals in the main cabin, and they let me rest a little bit. The sleeping barracks were strange, though. If we weren't in bed, everything, and I mean everything, had to be put away. They got angry with me about leaving something out—I don't even remember what it was—and warned me that once I was healed, I wouldn't like the consequences. I saw a guy who had been there longer than us receive a "consequence," and it was a lighter version of what they did to you. They weren't angry like that Carl Albert guy; they just whipped him a couple of times and moved on. When I asked about it, the answer was, 'It is as it ought to be. We love, we share.' I got over those words quickly. When they started chanting it yesterday morning, I was ready to run, but I stayed because I couldn't just leave you—we hadn't even talked."

"I wanted to talk to you, too. They sure found a lot of ways to keep me from talking to anybody, especially you."

"Yeah, after the first day, you became off-limits."

"What happened to me? Did you see what was going on? I didn't see you."

"I was trying to keep out of everybody's sight, but I was there, all right. It was shocking. When they held you down on that ugly box and hit you with the hose, I just wanted to rush them. I don't know what I wanted to do, but it felt violent. Two weeks ago, I wouldn't have stopped, but after everything I've been through and all our talks, I held back. I don't know if it was the right choice because after they were done stuffing you into that box, two different thugs walked up behind me, dragged me to my bunk, and tied me to it. I got out though; like I said, I have my tricks.

Then I snuck out and found the sledgehammer and a piece of angle iron to break the lock." Charley paused. "We got away, though, didn't we?"

"Yeah, we did. We'd better keep riding so we can get to the safety of Steamboat."

They continued through the remainder of the night, and the boys finally made it to Steamboat Springs. By then, it was morning, but there wasn't much activity. It seemed like the most normal town they had seen since the event, even without electricity. They spotted a few folks whom they guessed were ranchers, as they were riding horses or were in horse-drawn wagons. After receiving a few odd looks, they waved one down. They asked if he knew of any place where they could get breakfast, and he directed them to a nearby spot. On their way to the restaurant, Tommy asked how they were going to pay, and Charley told him he had stashed some money before all his stuff was taken. As they rode to the restaurant, they saw a couple of bike shops and decided to check if they could get some inner tubes after they ate.

At the restaurant, they were given handwritten menus, and the waitress apologized for the limited selection. The boys both ordered biscuits and gravy with coffee. Tommy hadn't liked coffee in the past but decided to drink some after the all-night bike ride to wake up.

The waitress brought them their food and said, "You two are pretty young… and dressed oddly."

"Yeah, we're just hungry, and your place is open," Charley replied a little defensively. Then she asked, "You boys aren't from around here, are you?"

"No, we're just trying to get home," Tommy replied.

"Oh, okay. I thought you might be from the freaky cult up in the mountains."

"That cult?"

"Yeah, they showed up a few years ago. The owners used to come here for breakfast. He drove a really fancy SUV, and she always seemed to be wearing really expensive clothes. Then they came in one time dressed like you two in your white pajamas. They acted super strange, but still really elitist, like they were better than everybody else."

"We spent a couple of nights there," said Charley.

"Do you know anything else about them? We don't know much," asked Tommy.

The waitress asked them to wait a minute while she served some other tables. She brought a fresh pot of coffee for the boys and sat down with them after she waved to the cook.

"I've only heard the rumors floating around town."

"Those rumors are more than we know. We freaked out and escaped last night," said Tommy.

"Okay, so here's the deal…"

The waitress went on to tell the boys that the rumor was the cult leader was stealing and drugging people, then putting them to work. She said that after the event, she didn't see the older couple anymore, and no one saw anyone else from the place except for one other couple who came into town to pick up supplies and messages. She guessed they were a wealthy couple who had moved in from out of town and owned a big fake ranch, and then just snapped. She mentioned that before the event, her brother saw some other very expensively dressed people fly in and get picked up by the couple or by the other couple in the same fancy SUV, but it didn't happen very often. Tommy asked when they seemed to suddenly change. The waitress replied it was about a year and a half ago; her brother heard their son and daughter had died in a car wreck in New York. He saw them once more, and they were acting very strangely. The older couple started wearing simple clothes, not acknowledging anyone but their staff, and walking very stiffly, while the other couple began treating them reverentially and no longer made eye contact with the cult leader or his wife.

Tommy let out a long whistle and said, "Whoa! That explains a lot!"

The waitress stood up, poured them some more coffee, and, raising an eyebrow, told them, "What do you mean? Never mind, I need to get back to work—anytime, boys."

Charley looked at Tommy and asked, "What was that whistle about?"

"Carl Albert and Emmy asked me to learn how to run the place in case their kids couldn't make it back," said Tommy, looking stunned, with a searching look in his eyes as he leaned back in his chair.

"What? No way – you were being recruited to be their new son!? That's even creepier than I thought!"

"Yeah, super weird! The whole thing spooked me, and that was why I wanted to talk to you to see if you had the same feeling. What was it like for you?"

"The wood shop was okay, but mealtime, once I stopped eating with you, was strange. At every meal, there was this blue liquid everybody was required to drink. I took a tiny sip of it, and it tasted like blue raspberry with a lot—and I mean a lot—of chemicals in it. So I wouldn't get beat like somebody else when they refused to drink it, I carefully poured it out on the ground. After everybody drank it, they got even more spaced out, staring off into the distance, and when they were bumped into, they slowly looked at you and then said, 'Founder's blessings upon you…' for an hour or two. I felt nervous, so I faked it. But after I saw the drinks and the beatings, I wanted out of there so badly; I was just waiting for you. You seemed to be the only guest who wasn't spaced out of your mind. Even those two guys we showed up with ended up spaced out."

Tommy looked at his coffee suspiciously, picked it up and sniffed it, then took a cautious sip followed by a regular drink.

Tommy said, "Yikes! I didn't know about all that. They just kept trying to make it sound like a dream come true. I just didn't want to imagine not going home."

"Me too. I didn't trust them from the beginning."

"Yeah. When I told Carl Albert I wasn't going to accept their offer, I didn't expect what they did afterward… He just calmly walked me out…"

"Oh, we were told there was some tragic news and to gather at the cabin patio."

"I wondered how everyone got there. You saw what happened after that."

"Yeah, I don't want to remember it. I'm glad we got out of there."

The two boys finished their breakfasts and settled up, leaving the waitress a very generous tip. They retraced their steps and found only one bike shop open. Inside, they received the same strange look they had gotten from everyone else in town because of their cult clothing, but they each bought a couple of inner tubes, a patch kit, and a tire pump to share. They inquired about oil for their chains, and the guy assisting them laughed, saying he had something better, and sold them a special bottle of liquid he claimed was perfect for the mountains.

~~~

While the boys were fixing their bikes on the side of the building, they saw a horse-drawn wagon slowly moving forward, with Edgar and the four big guys who had rough-handled them the night before carefully scanning each side of the street, straining their eyes into each shop. The one that Charley had whacked with the piece of angle iron wore a bloody bandage on his head. Charley saw them first and yanked Tommy, pulling him back into the shop. The boys hid behind clothing racks and display bikes while keeping their eyes on the men in the wagon.

Looking down at their clothes, the boys realized how conspicuous they must have looked. They asked the guy who helped them in the shop where they might find a second-hand store, and he told them there was one just a couple of miles away. The boys thanked him and got on their bikes. To avoid the wagon and hopefully outrun it, the boys rode down side streets as far as they could. They realized they had passed it when they saw the tail end of the wagon one street over on the highway. They reached the end of the side street and needed to get onto the main highway. They got on the highway and rode as fast as they could to the thrift store, hiding their bikes behind some bushes. As they shopped for regular clothes, two of the big guys entered the shop. The boys crouched down behind a clothing rack and sneaked over to the dressing rooms. Each boy slipped into a separate stall and changed into what they had found. They waited until they thought they heard the men leave. When they approached the counter to pay, the cute cashier asked them if the big, scary men were looking for them, and they said, "Yes."

"Guys, take those clothes on the house. Those cult people used to come in here, and they're creepy and mean. If you're running from them, go get sleeping bags too; you'll need them." She took the clothes the boys were wearing and threw them in the trash can beside her.

The boys thanked the cashier and went to find a couple of sleeping bags. In the camping section, Tommy found a tarp and insisted on paying for it. Back at their bikes, they secured their gear and took off, staying alert for the wagon or any of the men who were with it.

Charley asked Tommy where they were going next, and he replied he wasn't sure. They pulled over, and Tommy looked through his pack and realized he had forgotten to put the maps in it when he packed his day pack back at the cult. While rifling through the pack, he saw the letter from his father's mentor and was struck with an idea.

"When we were flying back from San Antonio, an old guy sat next to me and said he was my dad's mentor, and he gave me a letter. He's from Glenwood Springs. That's a lot closer to us right now than Salt Lake City or Sacramento."

"How do we get there, though?"

"We're close to the restaurant; why don't we go ask the waitress?"

The two of them did just that. They groaned when they realized they had to go back in the direction of Heavenly Ranch and Farm.

"We can do it; we just need to be careful," said Charley.

"I know we can, but I don't want to."

"We've got this."

"Okay."

The boys refilled their small water bottles that Charley had brought. The waitress told them to wait for a minute and went back to the kitchen. When she emerged, she quietly handed them a couple more water bottles and a couple of sandwiches each, wishing them the best of luck. The boys got on their bikes and cautiously rode back the way they had come. They never saw the wagon again. As they approached the intersection where the road to the ranch began, they pulled off the road to see if anyone was watching for them. They spotted a small group of people at the highway, looking in both directions, and someone was even watching the road to the ranch. The boys sneaked back a few hundred yards, crossed the highway, and found a set of train tracks to walk behind. The tracks were built up on a ridge of ballast, and if they crouched slightly while walking beside their bikes, they were invisible to the watchers. They walked for about three miles, carefully watching in all directions. When they came to a lightly used dirt road leading back to the highway—so lightly used that grass was growing across it—they walked their bikes up to the road and got back on them. Hunger gnawed at the boys since it was lunchtime, but they chose to keep riding to put more distance between themselves and the cult members and their creepy ranch.

Taking a back road led them along a lightly farmed valley and past a large reservoir with a state park. They emerged back onto the main road, and just a few miles further down, they passed through a town with many train tracks side by side and saw people working around them.

Later in the afternoon, the boys stopped to eat the sandwiches the waitress had given them. They finished all the water they had brought from Steamboat, but fortunately, they were able to get water from roadside ponds and streams. While they were eating lunch, it dawned on them that they had no other food. They kept riding and found a storefront with the word "Groceries" on the front. When they went in, they discovered there was a little bit of everything. They put together a small pile of items to buy but realized they didn't have enough money. The boys asked if there was anything they could do in trade for their supplies. The man behind the counter told them they could help catch up on cleaning and organizing. Charley swept while Tommy helped the man move several full boxes into the store and a bunch of broken-down boxes into a storage shed behind the shop. The heavy lifting was very challenging for Tommy—every time he exerted himself, he felt the beating from the night before, his muscles aching from the bruises. The boys ended up working for a couple of hours. Like before in Hot Sulphur Springs, the man was so appreciative of their hard work that he gave them a couple of sandwiches as a thank-you.

The boys got back on their bikes and soon rode past a tower-shaped rock. After an hour without trees, they made it almost two-fifths of the way to Glenwood Springs before they became too tired to continue. They found a gully where they set up an inconspicuous camp, ate their sandwiches from the grocery store, and finally fell into a deep sleep after an incredibly long day.

Day Twenty-Six

Tommy woke up first the next morning. While he was lying in his sleeping bag thinking about the day ahead he realized he never read the letter that Richard gave him a million years ago.

Dear Tommy,

We've never met, but I feel like you are one of my nephews. Your father tells me about you and your little brother all the time. I feel like I have watched you grow up through your father's descriptions. When your father found out we were going to be able to share a flight from San Antonio to Denver he asked me to check up on you and to give you his letter. I am taking the advantage of sharing my own with you.

I first met your father when I was in college working as a senior counselor at Camp Wallace Creek when he was a first year. We hit it off and began a friendship that matured into a mentorship when I had the opportunity to hire him right after he graduated from college. He watched me raise my son and daughter and I've gotten to share hard earned knowledge about business and raising a family with him. He was there for me when I lost my wife and the mother to my children and was an incredibly strong shoulder to lean on.

You are on the cusp of so many things. You will experience hardship and its rewards. You will find the strength to carry on when it seems like there is nothing left. The experiences you have and the relationships you build at Camp Wallace Creek will help you through those rough times and they will help you celebrate the good times.

There may be other young men there you don't like, even ones that are your nemesis right now that may become your closest ally in the future. You will all look back at those formative experiences at Camp Wallace Creek with great fondness, even the times that seem difficult right now.

Whenever you are in Glenwood Springs look me up, make sure to bring your father with you so we can catch up, too. You will find me at home or at the college campus. Since I retired from business I've gotten the great pleasure to teach some courses there and have an office. We might even be able to grab a bite to eat. I know how hungry a teen-aged boy can be.

Sincerely,

Richard

Tommy noticed a business card in the envelope when he folded the letter and put it away. The business card had Richard's phone number and campus address. As he was putting the envelope in his backpack, he heard Charley stirring. He thought to himself, "Richard was right about your nemesis becoming your closest ally. I never suspected Charley would turn out to be such a good friend."

The two young men ate their breakfast and struck their camp. They rode into the wide, flat valley near Toponas and then climbed back into the trees, enjoying the welcomed shade over the little highway. As the boys coasted, they saw giant piles of rocks and, all of a sudden, a tree farm. Just after their first hour and a half, Tommy felt a jerk and heard a "pop!" Abruptly, his pedals spun without resistance. He had just crested a hill and was going downhill, gaining speed. He put all his hand strength into gripping the brake levers to stop himself. Even then, the bike went sideways, and Tommy had to put a foot down, skidding to a stop. Charley stopped a couple of hundred feet ahead, looked back at a panting Tommy, and asked what the problem was. Wild-eyed, Tommy shrugged uncertainly and looked down. His chain was gone! Still out of breath, he hurried back the way he had come and found the broken chain on the road. Charley rode back to him, and the two of them examined the chain. One of the links had broken right at a rivet. They didn't have a spare chain; they hadn't thought to get one at the bike shop back in Steamboat.

They sat down on the side of the road and pondered the tedious prospect of walking again after riding so quickly on their mountain bikes.

"Hey! Don't you have some sort of survival kit with you? The one I teased you about back at Camp Wallace Creek?" said Charley.

"Yeah," then, "Yeah! I do!"

Tommy rummaged through his backpack and found a small plastic container made of two curved pieces that slid into one another. He opened it up and, after a moment, let out a yelp.

"I think I've got something! Thanks, Charley."

Tommy pulled out a piece of wire intended for making a snare for small game, but he thought he might be able to fix the chain with it. He got his multi-tool and secured the chain in place on the sprockets. He told Charley he would probably be unable to shift gears until they got to a bike shop, but both young men were happy to get back on the road – on their bikes. As they continued toward the highway, a river ran alongside them for most of the ride. Charley imagined aloud how much better floating on a raft would have been. They also saw a train track heading west and wondered if they could ride their bikes on it. Eventually, they decided to stay on the road since Tommy's chain was broken. The repair worked out better than either of the young men expected, and by the time they reached the interstate after crossing the Eagle River, their confidence was much higher. Tommy and Charley decided to stay off the actual interstate so they could be closer to the river for water.

As Tommy and Charley approached the town of Eagle, they noticed a small group of sentries stationed on the road into town, similar to what they had experienced in Fraser. They slowed down and cautiously approached the blockade.

Tommy said to Charley, "Were you able to keep your wallet? These guys look a lot more serious than we've seen before."

"Yeah, didn't you see me pull it out in Steamboat?"

"Oh, yeah. I forgot."

This time, the barricade was a bit more formal, featuring a swinging gate arm. They stopped at the gate, and a man with a shotgun asked them for their identification and reason for coming to Eagle. They handed the guard the identification they had used for their flights and told him they were traveling through to get to Glenwood Springs.

The guard looked at their cards and said to them both, "You're a long way from home, boys."

"We got stuck in Denver when we were flying home," said Charley. "How else do you think we'd get home?"

Tommy cringed at Charley's back talk.

"You could take a train."

"There aren't any trains running."

"You two must be out of touch. Trains started coming through a few days ago."

"Excuse me," said Tommy as politely as he could, "How are the trains working? Is the electricity back on?"

"They're using old steam trains. I don't know how they got them working, but somebody did."

"Really? That will save us a lot of time if we can get on one!"

"I think they're only allowing work trains so far, though they may be getting ready for regular service. You can go through. Be careful. If you need to shop or eat, try to stick to the main road."

The young men got on their bikes, a little baffled but excited to see a train actually moving. They kept riding through Eagle and other towns, encountering the same setup every time. As they traveled, they learned that the road guards started soon after the event because of gangs (Tommy gave Charley a hard time after they found out) and individual outlaws. After the town of Dostero, the ride became wild with four long tunnels on a curvy road suspended above the Colorado River in Glenwood Canyon, which was so steeply walled that it was shaded in the afternoon. When they arrived in Glenwood Springs in the late afternoon, both of them were saddle-sore after riding for almost two days straight. Charley's arm was very sore and tender, and Tommy's back was aching and stiff.

As they were getting their identification checked at the gate to enter the city, they asked the guard how to get to the college campus. He gave them directions, and they found their way across a bridge high over the Colorado River to the modern red brick building. The doors were locked, and they were at a loss for what to do to find Richard. Across the street, they saw a grocery store and thought they'd try their luck to see if they had any ideas.

The store was guarded, but less so than the grocery stores Tommy had seen in Denver. Charley offered to watch the bikes while Tommy went inside through the open doors. Without air conditioning, most shops kept all the doors they could safely open. He found a cashier who pointed him to the customer service desk. The clerk pulled out a phone book for Tommy. This was the first time Tommy had ever used a phone book, but it was pretty self-explanatory. He found Richard's name in the white pages and wrote down the address on a torn piece of paper. He asked for directions, and the clerk pulled out a map and showed Tommy the route.

Tommy and Charley made their way to Richard's house. It wasn't far, and it was down a cool, tree-lined street. Tommy double-checked what he'd written down, and they found the address. The house was well-kept and modest, with an older SUV parked in the driveway that clearly hadn't been driven in weeks, like every other vehicle the boys had seen. Nervously, Tommy approached the door and pressed the doorbell. After hearing nothing and realizing his mistake, he knocked on the door.

"Tommy? Tommy! What are you doing? How did you make it here?" said a flabbergasted Richard.

"Hi Richard, that's a long story."

"Come in, come in! It looks like you brought a friend. Bring him in too!"

Tommy waved Charley in. Charley and Tommy took the bikes and hid them behind the SUV before entering Richard's house.

Tommy introduced Richard to Charley.

"Oh, the boy who gave you so much trouble at camp?" Richard said, raising his eyebrow.

Charley looked sheepish at Richard's friendly comment.

"He kept giving me trouble after we landed, but that's behind us now."

The house was homey and filled with love-worn furniture. Richard took the young men through the house and to the backyard where the three of them sat around a tree-shaded patio table in comfortable chairs. The exhausted boys let out big sighs as they settled in.

"Tell me about your journey!" implored Richard.

Tommy recounted their journey and experiences as they made their way to Glenwood. Charley interjected animatedly whenever he thought there were important details Tommy missed. Richard was fascinated, alternately laughing and grimacing as the story unfolded. He was genuinely concerned and asked quite a few questions about Carl Albert and Emma.

"That's quite an adventure, even for an old guy like me. I think I might know that Carl Albert guy – indirectly. Maybe we can go to a coffee shop later and I'll ask some of my friends. We meet there every day or so to catch up and trade news about what's going on."

"How did *you* get home?"

"Oh, that was an adventure in itself, not as adventurous as you two, but for me, it was the experience of a lifetime.

"After I left the plane the three of us were on, I hurried out to the parking shuttle. We had just left the terminal when our shuttle came to a strange, rolling stop. The driver tried to restart it, and when he was unable, he attempted to radio his shop but got no response. Then he pulled out his phone, and it was dead. All six of us, if I remember correctly, pulled out our phones, and they were all dead. Looking around, I noticed that all the vehicles were dead too. We all got out of the shuttle, and everyone in their cars was doing the same. It wasn't long before we saw the first plane crash in the distance. That got everyone's attention. I gathered with a couple of the other bus riders, and we decided to get to our cars to try to figure things out. By the time we reached our cars, we still didn't know what was going on, and nobody knew anything except that nothing electric-powered was working. I was able to use my keys to get into my car, so I left my big suitcase in the trunk and grabbed my easy-to-carry items to walk to the nearest hotel, as did the others from the bus. We found the nearest hotel and convinced the front desk clerk to rent each of us a room. I prepaid with cash like the others, and I never saw the other riders again. It was a struggle to get into the room, but the onsite repairman helped me in. I locked the door with the locks inside the room and managed to get a good night's sleep, even though it felt surreal with no lights or television. I was able to crack the window open. It was so quiet, and there were no city lights. I got up early and confirmed that nothing had changed, so I went to the front desk, checked out, and grabbed a couple of water bottles and some snacks. As I began my trip home, I saw many people sleeping in their cars, and many had left their cars in the road. At my car, I changed from a suit into a t-shirt and shorts and put on my running shoes, expecting to walk. So, I just started walking west to get home. I didn't know what to expect.

"By the middle of the morning, one of the first horse-drawn wagons from the airport with hospital patients came by, and I talked them into letting me ride along. That helped a lot."

"I wish we had thought of that," interrupted Tommy.

Smiling, Richard continued, "There was still a lot of confusion everywhere, and it took me a couple of days to get across Denver. By the time I reached the west side of Denver, someone had set up a stagecoach; I think it must have been from one of those Wild West steak dinner places for tourists on that side of town. I paid way too much for a ticket on one headed to Grand Junction. There were six of us crammed into the stagecoach. It was a miserable experience. The horses and coachmen seemed unprepared for such a long journey. The horses kept getting slower and slower during the trip. It took us two days to get to Glenwood; we stopped about halfway to Grand Junction in Eagle and stayed in one of the hotels there. They swapped the horses there too. Home was so close, but I didn't want to walk the last thirty miles home. Sometimes we were going slow enough that we could walk beside the coach just to stretch our legs and avoid smelling each other's breath. The seats were incredibly uncomfortable after only an hour on them. The seat backs were upright, and the cushion pressed into the wood below it, causing our bones to bang against the wood. Everybody's backs and legs were cramping by the third hour. The highway was a mess; we were forced to weave in and out of abandoned cars. There were still a few people who refused to leave them, worried about vandalism and looting. We saw a handful of looted shops from the highway, mostly big chain stores. Almost every grocery store was already guarded by groups of locals, though. Some young idiot tried to hold us up, but the driver had a bodyguard with a coach gun, and he got out of there pretty quick.

"They fed us alright, just some sandwiches and bottled water until we had dinner in Eagle. But that's how I got home. Never in a million years did I imagine riding in a stagecoach to actually get somewhere, but I did. Since then, I've heard about several running between towns about a day apart. It sounds like they are making a lot of money. Now they are only accepting silver, gold, or other valuables since no one knows what is going to happen with the government."

"What have you heard about that? About the police and the army?" asked Charley.

"As far as law enforcement goes, most small towns around here figured it out pretty quickly. The other news I've heard is just rumors from the coffee shop. Salt Lake City and Denver are supposed to be rough, but not as bad as cities on the West Coast or south of here. We've heard Albuquerque is completely out of control, just like San Francisco, Los Angeles, and Las Vegas. No one around here has really heard anything about Chicago, New York, or Washington D.C., not to mention Texas or any of the big cities in the South. There are some rumors that the military is starting to really get their act together, but those are just rumors. No one actually knows what that means."

"How are you getting food and water?" asked Tommy.

"That's a good question," said Richard, looking at his glass of water. "For water, some folks walk down to the Roaring Fork or Colorado Rivers and haul it back to their homes in whatever they can use to carry it —buckets, jugs, pitchers... Others, like me, pay someone to bring water in horse-drawn wagons to fill whatever containers we have. I have a big blue fifty-five-gallon drum that I have them fill. Food is getting scarcer every day. The grocery store is being restocked by a couple of large horse-drawn wagons from their warehouse in Denver. The restocks only include non-perishable foods and items like paper towels. Fresh food is gone unless you get it at the farmers' markets or grow your own. I've always grown a small garden, but since I got home, I've made it a lot bigger. I hope to harvest a crop before it freezes this winter. I'm making a cold frame to try to extend my growing season as much as possible. I've never tried it before, but I'm giving it a shot."

"What's a cold frame?"

"It's like a mini-greenhouse built around the garden itself. I don't have any glass, but I am using sheets of clear plastic. It's supposed to soak up warmth from the sun and help keep it in the ground. A neighbor told me that when it gets below freezing at night, I need to cover it with blankets and then take them off in the mornings. We'll see if it works; I hope so. I've never needed to rely on my garden before; it's always just supplemented what we got at the grocery store with fresh tomatoes and other things like that."

"Let's get you boys cleaned up before we go get some coffee."

Richard went over to his barbecue grill and started a small fire. He asked the boys to bring him a couple of large pots filled with water, which he placed on the fire to heat up. The boys then half-filled the bathtub, and when the pots were hot enough, they dumped the hot water in for their baths.

When Tommy got in the bath, he thought he'd never felt anything so good in his life. Dirt just slid off him as he soaped up and rinsed off with the cup and washcloth Richard gave him. He quickly noticed his back was still sensitive and painful from the beating he received from Carl Albert. He'd disliked baths for a long time and preferred showering, but now he didn't care. It had been since the cult ranch that he'd gotten clean, and it felt incredibly good.

Each young man got fresh water. Richard insisted, and Charley didn't complain since he was second in line for a bath. Tommy and Charley put on the clean clothes Richard offered them. In appreciation, the boys volunteered to clean the bathtub. The bathtub was more disgusting than they expected, so they flipped a coin to see who had to clean it. Charley won and reluctantly cleaned the bathtub, and then they all headed over to the coffee shop.

~~~

The Hot Springs Coffee Shop was just a few blocks from Richard's house in an old brick building. Outside, a few folks enjoyed the early autumn afternoon sun on black, steel mesh patio chairs around tables with green umbrellas. The snippets of conversations were all about how they were doing, giving one another advice about the new day-to-day, or sharing rumors about various occurrences. Ever since the event, it seemed the only thing people talked about was that event.

As they walked into the welcoming atmosphere of the shop, Richard saw his friends, two older gentlemen, in the back. Richard waved to them and led the two young men to their table. The table was too small for all five of them, so Charley grabbed an extra chair from a neighboring table. A leather-covered notebook lay open on the table, its pages fluttering in the breeze from an open window. The pages were filled with small, neat, printed writing.

"How are you doing, Hank? Jim?"

"We're doing fine, or at least Jim told me he was fine; I know I am," said the man Tommy guessed was Hank.

"Who are these young men you've brought into our little *sanctum sanctorum*?" said Jim with a raised eyebrow and a knowing grin.

"Well, this is one of my best protégé's sons."

"I'm Tom," said Tommy, reaching out his hand to shake both men's hands.

Charley gave Tommy a questioning look and then introduced himself, "I'm Tom's friend, Charles."

Hank, with his faded red hair and sun-wrinkled face, stroked his mustache and said to Richard, "You've got a lively pair there. You said Tom is the son of one of your protégés?"

"Yes, I never got a chance to meet Tom until we were both on the plane back from San Antonio. He attended the summer camp where I met his father eons ago when we were young."

The two young men and their guide ordered their coffee. Tom felt a greater sense of civilization at that moment than he had since his Boysenberry shake in the airport, just before the event. As he stood at the counter waiting, he watched the baristas making drinks with old-style coffee percolators and French presses on camping stoves. He saw how they were preparing espresso-like drinks with a pressure pot he heard his mother call a moka pot. Tom was very excited about getting a drink like this.

He asked, "Where are they getting the milk?"

"They get it from a local farmer who is milking some of the cows he was fattening up for sale but saw the town needed milk from a local source," said Jim.

"This sure is a different world than it was a few weeks ago," offered Charles.

"There are many ways things are the same," said Richard. He then asked, "What's the latest you two have heard?"

Jim, who looked older than either of the other two men but was more neatly dressed than either, was the first to respond, "I've finally gotten a couple of responses to some of the letters I've sent to friends around the country."

The other two older gentlemen expressed their pleasant surprise.

"Apparently, the state governments around here have gotten together with the federal government, as they are operating, and started asking the railroads and the historic railroads to try to get some coal-fired steam engines running. The idea came from some hobbyists who used their trains to help the governor of Pennsylvania get to Washington, D.C."

While Jim was talking, Richard leaned over and whispered to Tom, "Jim is a retired railroad executive, and Hank is a lobbyist who travels between Salt Lake, Denver, and Washington, D.C. all the time."

"That's big news!" said Hank.

Looking around and quietly speaking to the others, Jim said, "There's supposed to be a troop train coming through here headed to the West Coast in a couple of days. Right now, all train traffic will be for government and emergency use only. But it's the first sign of a national response."

Richard encouraged Tom to tell the other two men what he heard from Jason Brown and about their time at the airport. As he shared what he knew, Hank blew a quiet whistle through his bushy mustache, and Jim rubbed his clean-shaven chin thoughtfully.

"The fact they have no idea what happened, at least last time you heard, sure matches the rumors I've gathered from my people," said Hank.

"I don't know how Denver has managed to keep it all together, but I'm glad they have. Maybe we're lucky being so far away from other major cities out here in the western mountains," said Richard.

Their server approached with the new drinks for Richard, Tom, and Charles and asked if the other men needed a refill. She poured them their drinks.

Looking at Charles and Tom, Jim asked, "Where are you two from originally, and what are you doing here?"

"I'm from Salt Lake City, and I went to the same camp as Tom. We were on a layover at the Denver airport when the event happened," said Charles.

"I'm from Sacramento, and we decided to walk home. It's been quite an adventure so far."

"Tell them your story, Tom. I'm sure they'll learn a lot from it," said Richard.

Tom told their story again, with Charles adding new details as the two young men remembered more in the second telling. Hank and Jim asked questions that deepened the narrative. They teased out Charles' time in the gang and how he had started the summer off on the wrong foot at Camp Wallace Creek.

"It sounds like the two of you have done a lot of growing up in the last few weeks," said Jim.

"I know I have," offered Tom.

"I thought being tough was the best way for me to show I was a good leader when I first came to Camp Wallace Creek," said Charles. "I missed my dad and my old camp, so maybe I was more insecure than I realized. I think the gangs were able to recruit me because of that.

It was fun at first, and I felt really grown-up. After I got beat up, and Tommy, I mean Tom, helped me, we had all the time to walk and talk. Watching him deal with people made me realize how I was making poor choices. After the weird cult ranch and helping Tom escape, I'm unable to even recognize who I was."

"That's some serious self-reflection, young man. It takes a lot of maturity to say something like that," said Hank with serious eyes.

"Are you two still planning on walking home?" asked Jim.

The two young men looked at each other, and Tom turned to the older man and said, "Yeah. We'll go to Salt Lake City first, and then I'll head home. We've got our bikes now, and that makes the trip a lot faster. It'll be more pleasant to get through Utah and Nevada that way."

"What if I told you I might be able to get you on a train?"

"What?!" both boys exclaimed at the same time.

"Now hold your horses. I didn't say definitely, but I have some connections, and maybe I could try to get you on that troop train. You might have to earn your keep, but I'll see if I can work some magic."

After getting back to Richard's house, both young men were so excited they were chattering like birds until Richard told them to calm down. No one knew when the train might be arriving or if it even existed.

But he advised them to clean all their gear and do an inventory so they would be prepared for either outcome. He also encouraged them to try to fix the bikes in case they needed them.

Sobered by Richard's words, the young men remained hopeful and went to work cleaning their clothes and laying out their meager gear. The Heavenly Ranch and Farm had significantly reduced the amount of gear Tom had carefully collected. Of course, he still had the personally important items and the small amount of useful things he hid away in his day pack. Charles had even less—just what he had in his pockets and a few other things he grabbed while rushing out the door to get the bikes and rescue Tom.

Tom looked at everything he had left laid out on the bed Richard was letting him use for the next few days. He had his pocket knife, his summer camp survival kit, his *Watership Down* book, a good water bottle, a map of Colorado and a compass, his personal first aid kit that Bethany had helped improve, a lighter, and some matches in a medicine bottle. He'd forgotten to get any extra clothes or a hat. Fortunately, he had his sleeping bag and the tarp from the second-hand shop. He still had the letters from his father and Richard, in addition to his wallet. That was about it. In the next room, Charles had his stuff laid out too. Like Tom, he had a sleeping bag and his own wallet, but he also had a pocket knife and a multi-tool. Charles actually had a hat and jacket he had grabbed from the cult ranch, and he also had a lighter. When the two were on their bike ride, they were glad Charles had also grabbed a bunch of mason's string from the wood shop.

After looking at their inventory, they asked Richard if he knew of any second-hand shop that might have some gear to fill in their kit. Richard asked what they needed, and Charles said they needed a backpack and something to cook in. Tom added that it might be nice to have a jacket, and both of them needed extra socks. He asked them to wait a minute and left the room. When he came back in, he was carrying a backpacking cook set and an old internal-frame backpack.

"Okay, there's some stuff I won't be using anymore, anyway. Let's go check out the downtown thrift shop."

The three of them went to a nearby thrift shop and found a jacket for Tom. Then they went to another shop to find a couple of new pairs of socks each. During their shopping, Tom was amazed at how ordinary it felt, except for the lack of electricity and the changes local shops made to cope with it, like written receipts and all the open windows. He heard this was not what most places were experiencing and was grateful that many of the small towns he and Charles went through had figured out a way to keep going in an almost normal way. He hoped they would continue to experience the resilience these towns had shown so far.

Day Twenty-Seven

The next morning, after a very restful sleep without the presence of a weird cult, both young men woke up later than usual since Tom had found Charles on the ground outside of Moffat Tunnel. Like those days at the tunnel, it was raining hard, and the two young men were thankful they were in a house this time. The rain was accompanied by a strong cold front, and as they ate the breakfast of bacon, eggs, and biscuits that Richard made for them, they discussed getting pants and sweaters or sweatshirts at the thrift shop since they hadn't thought about them the day before. After they went to the thrift shop, the three of them dropped by the coffee shop again to check for any updates. Charles and Tom met a couple more of Richard's friends and were disappointed that Jim wasn't there. Just as they were about to leave, Jim came in, grinning ear to ear.

"Is it good news?" asked Tom.

"Very good! I went down to the train station, and my friend told me a troop train was coming through early in the morning the day after tomorrow. The stationmaster mentioned that he thought he could sneak you two on board. Like me, he thinks you'll have to earn your way. No one really knows what to expect, though. Steam engines stopped running around here shortly after World War Two. He was told to expect to see a couple of helper pusher-type engines come through today or tomorrow ahead of the main steam train. He told me he actually helped a work train on its way through last night. They're pre-positioning pusher engines where the train historians say they were in the past. There's one in Utah and one in Nevada that these guys know about. He thinks the Nevada team will use a pusher from somewhere in California.

"I can't imagine the engines and railcars they're bringing out of storage—maybe display and tourist trains—to get a nationwide network working again. The stationmaster told me they may need me to 'un-retire' to help with all the logistics that need to be done by hand."

Jim looked excited for Charles and Tom, but he also considered the challenge for himself. Richard's other friends congratulated the boys. Their story spread among his friends and was starting to circulate around the area. The staff at the coffee shop even brought them each a piece of cake, telling them how amazing their adventure must have been. Richard and the young men then sat down and enjoyed the good mood and warm atmosphere of the shop on the cool day.

Richard, Tom, and Charles walked back to his house in the continuing rain. Tom still thought it might be prudent for them to repair the bikes in case they were allowed to bring them along on the train. They spent the rest of the day working on their bikes, chasing down a new chain from a local bike shop. The shop was an experience in itself. It seemed busier than ever, as people were fixing bikes that had been in sheds and backyards for years. One lady was yelling irrationally at the counter clerk after he told her they were out of inner tubes when Charles and Tom left.

Day Twenty-Eight

The next day was much the same as the day before. Jim confirmed his news to the two travelers. Charles offered to split wood for Richard in appreciation for everything he had done for them, since a cord of un-split wood had just been delivered to heat his house for the winter. He told them that woodcutters were so busy bucking logs by hand and delivering wood with horses and wagons that everyone needed to split their own. He happily accepted Charles's offer, and the two young men alternated splitting and stacking wood in the afternoon, working through the pain of the last couple of weeks. In the evening, the three of them speculated about what the train ride might bring. Richard found his old wind-up travel clock so they wouldn't miss the train. Tom kept the clock next to him for their three o'clock alarm. Each of the three struggled to fall asleep in anticipation of their next adventure early the following morning.

Day Twenty-Nine

Richard didn't tell Tom or Charles he had a regular wind-up alarm of his own. When the young men woke up, they found Richard in the kerosene lantern light of his kitchen, having made them breakfast and with coffee waiting. Richard's own bike was ready to join their ride to the train station.

When the three of them arrived at the station, there was a small send-off party of Richard's friends and a couple of the coffee shop staff who had become friends with the two young adventurers. Jim discovered his watch wasn't correct because everyone had forgotten the train didn't have electric lighting, so it was only traveling during daylight. They sneaked their starting time to leave stations at morning twilight, allowing them to travel as much as thirteen hours a day.

The train didn't actually arrive until a little before noon. The send-off party shrank as people had other obligations. The station master had the group hide behind the red stone walls of the station since he was supposed to keep Tom and Charles boarding the train very quiet. Their story was what helped them obtain the ride, and the powerful people making the trains run didn't want anyone to start getting crazy ideas about passenger travel until they got the rule of law in place again and established important freight before anything else.

Neither Charles nor Tom had ever ridden a train or even been close to one, so they were unprepared for the overwhelming experience of seeing, hearing, feeling, and smelling a giant steam train built for hauling freight and passengers over and through the mountains. The engine was huge, almost two stories high. It was mostly painted black, with a front so silver it was almost white and red and orange striping on the sides. Behind the engine and coal and water tender was a motley collection of passenger and freight cars, with a caboose at the end.

The conductor and engineer of the train, both older men, had the look of experienced hobbyists training the younger men who accompanied them. Tom and Charles later learned that the younger men were by no means inexperienced; they just had never run steam engines before. The four of them talked to the station manager, who pointed over to Tom, Charles, Richard, and Jim. The experienced engineer waved them over. He shook hands with Jim first, and they seemed to know one another, not as former colleagues, but as fellow train enthusiasts. There were then introductions all around.

The steam engineer told the boys they would be helping with communications between the engine and the rest of the train, acting as runners as long as they were onboard. Confirming the rumors, he said the train was full of civilian leaders, scientists, and military members. The train was taking the scientists to the University of California, Davis campus, where there was going to be a meeting of experts from across the Western United States to try to figure out what was happening. They were told something similar was occurring in Washington D.C.

"Why U.C. Davis?" asked Richard.

"It's a good place to meet—broadly accessible to the west of the Rockies and suitable for train travel," replied the younger engineer.

The freight trains were filled with supplies to be transferred to Salt Lake City and Sacramento, where the stops might be longer than the other limited short stops. They said the train was being operated as a modified express train.

Everyone said their goodbyes, and Tom promised Richard he'd write as soon as he got home; he would also have his father write. Charles told Richard he'd write him as well. After everyone got on board, the older engineer told the young men to hold their ears and let the whistle blow its two long blasts, signaling that the brakes were being released and they were heading out. He informed them that their next stop would be in Grand Junction in about an hour and a half. The old engineer smiled, and with a twinkle in his eye, said he didn't know the exact times because it had been so long since anyone used steam trains for work; all they had to rely on were old train schedules. He looked at the younger conductor and asked him to give Tom and Charles a tour, providing them with a better idea of what to expect in order to earn their keep.

The conductor told the young men that steam trains usually communicated with whistles and lights, but since this was new to most people, they were backing everything up with a runner. Before the event, the only whistle signals they used were the grade-crossing warning of two long, one short, and one long blast; two or three short blasts to indicate that the engineer had received a signal to start the train forward or backward; and one long blast when a train was approaching a station on a track next to a platform. He was very happy that Tom and Charles were taking over that duty since he had been doing most of it since Chicago.

Since this was its first trip, the train was made up of only four passenger cars, four freight cars, a dining car, and a caboose. The caboose was a special kind that allowed for a helper or pusher engine to assist the train up significant grades, such as out of Denver on the way to the Moffat Tunnel. When Tom and Charles heard that, they told the conductor the story of how Charles was found on the western side of the tunnel. Tom asked why they weren't using modern cars, and the conductor told them that for the first runs, they were using caution since there weren't very many of the old engines that ran.

"Are they doing anything about the shortage?" asked Tom.

The conductor replied, "They're currently trying to locate all the working steam engines. Next, they'll look for display engines and determine which ones can be brought back into service. I think after that, they'll decide which engines to use where. Of course, if the electricity comes back, all of this won't matter, but right now, it matters a lot."

As they went through the passenger cars, they noticed one had roomettes for senior military officers, older scientists, and public officials, while the other cars were just coach cars with seats. The passengers in the coach cars separated themselves into a military car, a scientist car, and a public official car, with some soldiers spilling into the public official car since they outnumbered everyone else. In each car, the travelers overheard discussions speculating about the event and plans to respond to it. It amazed Tom that there was still so much to figure out so long after the event occurred. They made their way to the dining car, which was filled with men and women snacking and drinking coffee or tea, engaged in similar animated conversations. After a thrilling walk up and over the moving freight cars, they finally reached the caboose and met the rest of the crew. The two of them decided they would work shifts of four hours each unless they both needed to assist, allowing them to stay rested throughout the day.

During their tour, as they ran messages back and forth, they looked out the windows and saw the ruby-red earth change to limestone, with small communities interspersed among fields where people struggled with harvesting after a lifetime of using tractors and machinery. The canyon widened and then tightened again. The number of abandoned vehicles on the highway was still astounding. Some work had obviously been done to clear the roads so wagons could travel from town to town, but none of the vehicles had been pulled completely off the roads. As the train approached Grand Junction, they saw people waving and schoolchildren cheering for the train. It must have been incredible for the people to see a machine working after so many weeks without them.

After a short stop at the Grand Junction station, where several people got out to stretch their legs or smoke, they picked up a renowned, retired physicist and continued on to Helper, Utah, where they picked up one of those helper cars they had heard about when they first boarded the train. This was when the two runners worked hardest, running confirmations and instructions between the main engine and the pusher engine. The scenery was also changing from mountains and farmland to high desert. They were surrounded by gravelly hills and book cliffs. The pusher engine demonstrated its value as the train moved slowly up the curves to Soldier Summit.

Another quick stop in Provo, and the train kept moving on. They coursed their way across bridges and overpasses. Everywhere they went, they were met with waving and cheering people. The whole time, the train was making its chuffing sounds, and the self-made winds were lightly filled with soot and ashes. The vibrations and rocking were so constant that a person quickly adopted a sort of sea legs for the train, swaying with the motion instead of fighting it. Tom and Charles soon learned how soothing the train was for sleep back in the caboose. The rail workers explained they needed the caboose for better communication with the helper engine and as a place to rest, like the two of them. The steam engine was more demanding for everyone since each of them was applying the knowledge they had previously learned with modern diesel engines and cars to this new—old technology.

As they pulled into Salt Lake City, it showed the signs of a bigger city without the tight-knit community of the small towns the two young men had experienced for so long together. There was more evidence of lawlessness that must have occurred in the first few days after the event. But, as they had heard, Salt Lake seemed to be back under some rule of law. The people there were happy to see them and came out of their homes and places of work to wave and cheer, too. There were burned-out cars and evidence of recently burned buildings, but they all looked days, if not weeks, old.

This station had a more industrial feel than the charming newer station in Provo, resembling a larger, functional station like Helper, with many metal buildings and modern industrial architecture spruced up in various corners. Charles realized he was in his hometown and looked stunned. Tom encouraged him to pick up his bag to disembark. The two of them got off the train, knowing they had an hour or two to kill before the train resumed its western journey, as it was adding a passenger car to accommodate the additional people headed to U.C. Davis. The engineers met with the scientists, and they decided to keep moving through the night if they could find a powerful enough gas lamp.

Looking Tom in the eye and shaking his hand, Charles said, "Thank you. You saved my life. It has been an amazing experience, Mommy's Boy. I hope we can see each other again."

"You would have done it for me."

"Not at that time I wouldn't have. Your help changed me. Our long walk and the cult..." Charles's eyes misted over.

"Don't do that. Remember, you're tough."

"I guess I'm not as tough as I thought."

"Maybe not, but you're also tougher than you ever expected. You know you saved my life, too. I don't think whatever was going to happen at that cult would have ended well."

The two young men walked over to a coffee shop and reminisced about their journey. They promised to write to each other. Charles said he needed to work on his relationship with both of his parents, but that he'd head to his grandparents' house to start. He looked hopeful and healed. He hadn't worn his sling since their bike ride to Glenwood and hadn't worn his splint since his first bath at Richard's place. The two walked back to the train station.

"Hey! I forgot my bike," said Charles.

After they pulled it out of the train, Charles turned to Tom.

"When you see Bethany again, give her this," he said, handing Tom Bethany's teddy bear.

Stunned, Tom looked at Charles. "Where did you get this?"

"It was in her suitcase. I don't know why I grabbed it, but I did. I've kept it safe ever since."

"I mean, wow! I don't know what to say. I'm sure she thought it was gone forever."

"It's a little beat up, but not any rougher than when I got it. She must have loved it. I guess the better part of me didn't want to see it damaged or burned in one of our bonfires."

"There was some good in you, even in your darkest days. Thank you."

"Apologize to her and her parents for me. If I ever meet them, I will too. Thanks again. Hey! The conductor is calling; you've got to get on the train!"

"Good luck! Charles, thanks for everything!" Uncharacteristically, Tom hugged Charles. Surprised, Charles hugged him back just as awkwardly.

~~~

Bethany came back to Tom's mind after the train pulled out of the station with its additional passenger car, no longer pushed by the helper engine. He assisted with delivering messages back and forth as the train resumed its route. Now that it had quieted down, he wondered what she was doing and whether she and her parents were still with the Muellers. With this first full train making its way to Sacramento, he figured it wouldn't be long before they might open up passenger train travel. He hoped they hadn't tried to book a trip on the stagecoaches and were waiting for the trains. But no matter what, he missed her.

His mind also wandered to the mail. He hadn't thought about how it might work after the event, even though he had promised the Browns, Richard, and now Charles that he would write to them. He guessed that with the steam engine, official mail service might actually resume.

He looked out the window at the dimming light and the salt flats west of Salt Lake reflecting the remaining light of the day in a strange semi-daylight. He talked with the engineers and conductors, and they thought it best for Tom to find an out-of-the-way spot in the engineer's room to wait for messages, while the younger conductor would wait in the dining car with another junior rail worker in the caboose. The engineer was joined by another worker, and they both kept their eyes ahead on the track, trying to avoid any collisions. Fortunately, the pusher helper engines had traveled through the area the day before, so any vehicles or large obstructions had been cleared.

Tom settled into a folding chair he found in one of the passenger cars, putting a sweater between his head and a corner, and dozed off. He woke occasionally, looking up and blearily checking to see what was going on.

Day Thirty

By this point in the trip, the engineers and their helpers were more comfortable with their duties. They stopped to reload coal and fill with water at stations using makeshift setups, manually shoveling coal into the coal cars instead of using a coal bin. However, those stops were usually short, and they quickly walked the length of the train, checking bogies and oiling all the necessary components. Around five in the morning, Tom was unable to sleep any longer, so he looked out the windows. The view was different from what he expected; his family never drove much past Reno when they traveled into Nevada. As they approached the Sierra Nevada mountains, the terrain was much more varied than he had anticipated. He caught glimpses of the Humboldt River to the west until they reached Lovelock and turned south. He heard the engineers talking to one another; they decided to stay in the engine together until Reno, planning for the next pusher engine to join them in Fernley, Nevada. They called Tom over and confirmed he knew what he would need to do. During the journey on the train, Tom discovered he was most useful during the two sections with the helper engine providing extra power to climb the steeper grades. This time, they were going to ascend to Donner Pass.

When they arrived in Fernley, they reloaded their coal and water and went through the refill process. This time, he watched them hook the pusher engine to the caboose. Because they knew he was out there, he just ran back and forth on the ground. They found this actually worked better and faster, and later said they were going to make a permanent change. Even though Tom wasn't often used in his messenger role, the engineers and conductors said they would want messengers on all trips for the foreseeable future because everyone, even the old-timer enthusiasts, were really novices when it came to cross-country train travel.

The trip up and over Donner Pass was beautiful; the terrain and plant life gradually changed, but it felt quick compared to riding a bike or walking, as they were moving at steam train speeds of 60 miles per hour uphill. The Truckee River flowed alongside them to the south, and the terrain gradually became hillier. It was so steep that the train had to use a long switchback. Next to the river were small communities of red brick buildings and occasional patches of green fields interrupted by aspens and conifers. As they pulled into Reno, Tom began to feel like he was getting close to home when he saw familiar landmarks in the distance. The train station was a long stucco-covered building with large arched doors and windows. It was a welcome sight for many of the passengers and crew. When the train stopped, almost everyone got out to loosen tight muscles and escape the ever-present sounds of the train while walking around the beautiful station. The station master opened the doors, and the passengers wandered in and out, some gazing numbly at the empty fountain inside the building.

After the usual refilling routine and the decoupling of the helper engine, they were ready to go. The conductors and Tom ran around the station to get everyone to re-board the train when the boarding whistle went unacknowledged by many of the travel-weary passengers. Tom got back on the train, unable to believe that in just a few short hours he would be able to get off the train and ride his bike through familiar streets to his home.

Even though the train ride only took about three hours, it felt like forever. The cute town of Colfax, California, was just a quick drive from his house in Sacramento, but it seemed like there was no end to the distance between. Tom saw the expansive grass valley leading to his hometown and kept noticing more and more familiar buildings as the train chuffed its way into the city. There was no more welcome sight on his trip from Denver than the building he had only seen while driving around town and had never been in—the red brick Sacramento Valley train station.

He hurriedly thanked all of the train crew he saw, grabbed his bike and bag, and almost jumped off the train onto the platform. He didn't notice the large mural in the vaulted waiting room as he rushed through the station and jumped on his bike to ride the four miles to his home. A few passengers disembarked again to smoke or walk around, this time for a shorter stop since it was only a refill stop, each of them unaware of the drama unfolding for a fourteen-year-old young man trying to get home after almost a month.

The bike wasn't fast enough for young Tom; he kept trying to pedal faster and faster, changing the gears to keep up with his legs and the bike. He rode past businesses and buildings he had seen a million times before, their passing barely registering. The tree-lined streets were only vague in his sight; so much of the route he was taking he knew by heart. The light in the sky was the kind you see in the very early autumn, the autumn of still-hot football games and friends reacquainting themselves as they returned to school and the habits of the classroom and hallway. Tom didn't see that either. His only thoughts were of his parents and his brother, and the doorway to his lifelong home, the sound of the screen door slamming as he came inside to hear the stories of his family's day. He rode even harder under the overpass leading the way home.

He was almost there. Tom was riding down the middle of the street, now filled with homes on either side; the road was never deserted enough to ride right down the center. These streets were better cleared than many of the ones he had seen in other large cities on his long journey across Colorado, Utah, Nevada, and finally California, but he never got very far into the neighborhoods of those cities; he didn't live in those places.

He turned down more and more familiar streets until he saw it! It was just a hundred yards away! He couldn't believe it; he was almost home! He raced past houses where people he knew lived, past trees in whose shade he had played all his life, and then he was there. He almost crashed his bike in his excitement when he stopped. He tumbled up the steps and didn't even hear the neighbors saying to each other in disbelief, "Is that Tommy?" It was; he had done it! He traveled almost twelve hundred miles, and he was home!

He ran to the side door like he always did, opened it, and yelled, "Mom! Dad! I'm home!"

Acknowledgments

First books are tenuous things that need much feeding and care, not just from the author but from many of those around him. For me, the first and greatest helper and cheerleader has been my wife, without whom I would not have been able to finish this book. My proofreader and first editor, Niki Richardson, made my writing more precise and effective, giving me gentle and not-so-gentle guidance. My son, daughter, and son-in-law were great sounding boards and helped provide "younger eyes" to see through some things I thought were cool but were clearly past their sell-by date.

mikeritterhouse.com

www.ingramcontent.com/pod-product-compliance
Lightning Source LLC
Chambersburg PA
CBHW051107030726
47504CB00006B/1824